Wings of Grace

Tania Roberts

Format: Paperback Large Print

ISBN   978-1-99-117463-5

Cover Design: Kura Carpenter Design, kuracarpenter.com

Cover Image: Arcangel Images Limited

Back Cover Image: Alamy

Chapter One

"Ladies! Ladies! Your attention please."

Grace and Betsy held hands, nervous, yet excited by the adventure they'd agreed to embark on. Grace wasn't at all intimidated by the short solid woman on the stage, whose booming voice echoed around the Christchurch Town Hall like cannon fire. She reminded Grace of her mother, who was of similar stature and always seemed to be yelling over the raucous noise made by Grace's four older brothers. They, having all gone off to war, were part of her inspiration for being here today.

Her other reason was Betsy. Grace gave Betsy's hand a gentle squeeze of encouragement. She knew Betsy's heart wasn't with the Women's Land Corp and she was reluctantly signing up at Grace's insistence that she knew what was best for her friend. Betsy's fiancé, Roland, had enlisted and already left for the Middle East. Betsy had received weekly letters when he was in training camp, but nothing since his regiment had left New Zealand several months ago. Roland had been granted forty-eight hours leave before his departure. Where the couple had disappeared to for those two days, Grace hadn't yet been able to discover.

Every time it was mentioned, Betsy coloured from head to toe, fondled the new small gold band that adorned her finger and went mysteriously quiet. Grace thought her friend was in love, but already she could see the worry caused by the waiting, was impacting on Betsy's health. Dark shadows had appeared beneath her normally sparkly-brown eyes. Betsy needed a distraction, she needed the fresh air of the countryside and the physicality of farming instead of the tedium of the typing pool, where they had worked eight hours a day in the confines of a stuffy office.

The buzz of conversation abated slightly but continued to fill the hall. The woman on the stage checked the hem of her khaki jacket was straight and adjusted the brow of her Women's War Service

Auxiliary felt hat to the correct angle. She frowned, scanned the large group of young women volunteering for the Women's Land Corps, and banged the gavel on the wooden lectern. Finally, heads turned her way and the chatter hushed.

"Thank you, ladies. Now that I have your attention, I would first like to commend you for taking action to assist in New Zealand's war effort. What you have agreed to do, will not be easy. The work will be arduous, the hours long, the conditions not as pleasant as you have most likely been accustomed."

Grace and Betsy smiled at one another while the woman's address continued.

"We have, I'm pleased to announce, been successful in obtaining overalls and gumboots for you. These will be distributed today. One pair each. You must take care, maintain and preserve your allocation. We cannot guarantee, in these times when all must make sacrifices, that there will be funds to provide you with anymore."

Signing up for the land girls wasn't a sacrifice for Grace. She revelled in the outdoors. Compared to what her brothers and all the other soldiers had to do; this would be a walk in the park.

"I will soon read the list of placements." The woman raised her clipboard to indicate the list and banged it down on the lectern again to silence the murmuring running through the group. "I assure you that the Placement Officer, with your best interests in mind, has only selected farms offering good conditions and prepared to pay the minimum wage of thirty-five shillings per week for dairy farms and thirty shillings per week for other farms. The government is paying the farm owners a subsidy and in return you will be provided with full board and lodgings. You are not expected to do housework beyond caring for your own quarters."

"When I call your name," she continued, "you will, in the correct order, approach the desk to your left. You will be given an envelope with the necessary details of where you have been assigned. Proceed from there to collect your overalls and gumboots. There are limited numbers in various sizes, ensure you obtain the correct size. After that you are excused to make your arrangements to report to the advised farm by Friday."

Betsy gasped. Grace felt her stiffen beside her.

"What's wrong?" Grace nudged Betsy.

"What if we get assigned to different farms?"

Grace swallowed. They hadn't considered that outcome. "Don't worry, it will be fine."

"Miss Alice Clark," came the first name.

Eager to see who the volunteers were, Grace looked back over the gathering, but nobody stood.

"Miss Alice Clark!" The recruitment officer repeated the name louder, her frown deepening.

At the very end of the very last row, a diminutive woman quietly stood, put her shoulders back and straightened her spine.

"That must be Alice. She's tiny," Grace whispered. "She must only be five foot four, if that. I don't know how she's going to handle farming."

Grace watched the woman walk past. Her petite frame, mousy brown hair, and muted clothes-to-match reminded Grace of a sparrow. Her eyes flitted nervously about the hall like a bird needing to be rescued. Grace had spent the better part of her childhood saving birds snared in makeshift box traps constructed by her brothers. Her instinct to save this woman was on high alert.

"Miss Grace Ford."

Grace's mouth fell open. She gripped Betsy's hand even tighter and gave her friend a quick hug. Now was the start of the rest of her life. Grace stepped out from the row and glanced back at Betsy who looked despairingly at the empty space beside her, twisting her hands together. Betsy looked up; her eyes glassy.

"Everything will be alright," Grace mouthed

At the desk, Grace stood beside Alice as the proffered envelopes were ripped open and their contents digested.

"Whipsnade Farm at Orari." Grace stared at Alice. She hadn't heard of Orari, and by the look on Alice's face, neither had she.

"Miss Moira Harvey," was the next name broadcast from the stage.

Grace clenched her jaw and sucked in a breath. It wasn't Betsy's name but curiosity had her scanning the crowd to see who the next recruit was. A red-haired woman clapped her hands together and squealed with delight. There was a collective gasp of admiration from the group as the woman emerged from the rows and walked to the front of the hall. Her red lipstick matched red leather toe-peepers with a flamboyant bow on the top. As she walked, her hips sashayed to the beat of the heels of her shoes on the wooden floor, like a drum roll announcing her arrival.

Grace chuckled. If the woman was trying to shock, she had. The recruiting officer stood wide-eyed and mouth agape. When Moira reached the desk to accept her envelope, Grace looked down at the toe-peepers. Moira's toenails were painted in matching red nail polish. It all seemed a little inappropriate for the occasion, but if unflattering, baggy brown overalls, and black gumboots were going to be their uniform from now on, then she couldn't blame Moira for having a final show.

Moira tore at the flap of her envelope.

"Where on earth is Orari?"

"It's by Geraldine," the woman at the desk replied. "Captain Boyle has offered his farm as a training facility. He's been recalled to the navy so his farm manager Mr McKnight will be training you."

"I hope they have electricity."

"I know they've recently got power in Geraldine so we should be alright," said Grace.

"So, you're going to Orari too?" Moira asked.

"Yes, and Alice too." Grace looked at Betsy, her eyes were closed, her hands palms-together and she faced skyward as if praying to the heavens. Grace too closed her eyes and whispered, "Let it be Betsy next. Please."

"Miss Betsy Nolan."

Grace sighed with relief. In her head she said thank you to whichever power answered her plea. Betsy quickly joined

Grace and the other women at the desk, retrieved her envelope and ripped it open.

"Orari?" Grace asked.

"Yes!"

The pair hugged and jiggled up and down on the spot. It didn't matter who else was going to Orari, they were.

All four were ushered into a side room. Overalls were unfolded and held up against one another. There were only three sizes – small, medium, and large. Small was still too big for Alice. She looked disappointed.

"Don't worry, love," Grace said. "I'll be sure to bring my sewing gear and take them up for you."

Grace barely heard Alice's thank you. She wondered if being so timid came with being so tiny, or there was something else in Alice's past that made her so.

They moved on to the gumboot table.

"I like your shoes," Grace said to Moira as they removed their footwear to try on the gumboots.

"They're the last pair I've been able to buy before the shoe shop where I was working was shut," she replied. "Bloody war has requisitioned the leather supplies to make shoes I wouldn't want to wear. No leather, no shoes, no job."

"No wonder you've got them on today then," Betsy said.

"I like the way they make me feel." Moira pointed to her red toenails. "Besides, this might be the last pedicure I get for a while."

Nobody else had been assigned to Orari, so with gumboots and overalls in hand they exited the hall. As soon as they reached the footpath, Moira pulled a packet of cigarettes from her skirt pocket and lit up.

"Aren't they rationed?" Betsy asked.

"Yeah, I know I should give up." Moira blew a puff of smoke into the air above the group. "But it's one of life's many luxuries, I enjoy."

Grace wondered how suited Moira was going to be to farm life.

"How come you've signed up to go farming?" she asked. "There's unlikely to be many luxuries where we're going."

"Well, look around." Moira waved her arms. "There aren't any single men around here. None worth having, anyway."

"I don't think there are going to be many in the country either," Grace said.

"Essential services." Moira smiled and tapped her nose with her finger. "Farmers are excused from enlisting. If they are in the countryside, then that is where I need to be."

Grace, Betsy, and Alice all stared at Moira. Her brazen attitude stunned them into silence.

"If I have to leave my shoes behind and do some farm work, then so be it." Moira took a deep drag on her cigarette. "I'm not afraid to get my hands dirty. Well, I'd hate to break a nail, but a little dirt I can probably cope with."

"Right, then, I guess we will see you again at the train station on Friday."

The next few days were busy, and Friday arrived all too quickly. Inside the second train carriage, Grace, Betsy, Moira, and Alice found their allotted seats and stowed their suitcases on the overhead mesh racks.

"Did you manage to get everything in your suitcase?" Grace said half-jokingly to Moira. "Yours is bigger than our three put together."

"Those damn gumboots took up a bit of room," replied Moira. "I could only fit half a dozen dresses and a couple of pairs of shoes in."

"Will we need dresses where we're going?" Alice bit her lip. "I haven't packed one."

"They have dances in the country, don't they?" Moira took a seat by the window. "They'd better."

Grace had thought it best to be prepared for all possibilities and had packed a couple of dresses.

"Why didn't you bring a dress?" she asked, judging that the white blouse and calf-length brown skirt Alice was wearing weren't dance attire.

"I don't go to dances." Alice spoke quietly, her head lowered.

Unsure whether Alice was shy and just needed some encouragement, Grace continued.

"What did you do for a job?"

"Something that didn't require a dress, I'm guessing," Moira said.

"We had a uniform."

These days a uniform signified war. Grace couldn't imagine how the tiny Alice would have been accepted into anything military related.

"Were you a nurse?" she asked.

"No." Alice coloured, her cheeks almost as bright as Moira's red toe peepers. "It was just a department store."

"Oh, did you work in Ballantynes?" Moira asked. "That's my favourite store. They have a wonderful shoe department. I don't remember ever seeing you there."

"I was in children's wear."

Moira laughed. "You won't find me in children's wear. The little blighters aren't on my agenda."

A shrill whistle interrupted their conversation to signal the final call for boarding passengers. Only a few people remained on the platform, nobody Grace recognised.

"No hero's farewell for us," Grace said. She'd made the trip out to Lyttleton to see her brothers off, standing amongst the crowds waving off their loved ones.

"Well," Betsy said, taking the opposite window seat. "We're only going farming, not to war."

As the train left Christchurch and travelled south, the colour palette changed from the greys and browns of the city to the greens of the countryside. The flat terrain was dissected by post and wire fences and hedges of boxthorn and houses were fewer and farther between.

"Look! Look! Look!" Moira waved her hand vigorously.

Rows of uniformed men, rifles over their shoulders and packs on their backs marched on a field adjacent to the train track. Beyond the field, lines of tents had been erected, the autumn breeze flapping their canvas sides.

"That will be Burnham Army camp," Grace said. "Doesn't look like you can get their attention, Moira. They must be well trained."

"Great," Moira said. "That means they'll soon thrash the Germans and be home for Christmas."

"A pity Roland isn't still there, Betsy." Grace saw the wistful look in her friend's eyes. "You could have visited him."

"Roland?" Moira's eyes narrowed. "Whose Roland?"

"My fiancé," Betsy replied.
"Her childhood sweetheart who she ran away to marry before he went off to war," Grace added.

Betsy's cheeks went scarlet. "We didn't get married. We just got engaged."

"Mmm," Grace smiled a knowing smile. "I think you had the honeymoon though."

"Good for you, Betsy," Moira said. "Life is too short not to make the most of every opportunity."

The soldiers were soon left behind, replaced by paddocks of sheep oblivious to the train's clickety-clack, clickety-clack as it built up speed heading south. A uniformed ticket officer entered the carriage, checked, and punched their tickets to ensure they couldn't be re-used, as if they'd ever consider that an option.

The train rattled its way over the bridge spanning the muddied waters of the Rakaia River.

"Is this a river or the ocean?" Betsy stared at the water, her hands framing her eyes and the view through the window. "It goes on forever."

"Just a river," Grace replied. "We're going south not overseas."

Another river and another town; the train slowed as it passed through Ashburton. In the distance, the Southern Alps rose, dissecting the South Island, separating east from west along a crooked fault line. Mother Nature had sprinkled a light dusting of snow on the highest of the peaks, a gentle warning that the cooler months were on their way.

"Are we there already?" Moira fidgeted impatiently.

"No," Grace answered. "We just passed Ashburton train station."

"I've had to leave behind so much." Moira turned back to Alice and grumbled.

"Did you have a beau?" Alice asked.

"Well, there was someone. I met him at the weekly dances at the local hall when he got leave from training. We had fun dancing. He wasn't the best of kissers though so no great loss." Moira shrugged.

"We might have to dance with each other if all the men have signed up." Grace laughed and nudged Betsy. "It'll be just like when we were kids and danced about in your mother's clothes."

"Oh, surely not." Moira looked aghast.

The carriage was filled with the noise of the train clattering along the tracks and the squeals of children playing in the seats at the rear. Alice rubbed her arms and gazed down the aisle.

"Are you cold, love?" Moira asked, laughing. "We'll have to find a man to keep you warm too."

Alice shook her head.

The further south they travelled, the more bridges they crossed, and the darker the skies became until ominous black clouds signalled the foul weather they were headed into. By the time the train reached Orari, the unseasonal storm was making its presence felt; large raindrops splattered on the windows, the Southern Alps had disappeared in a thick fog and the waters of the Orari

River had risen to within a foot of the bridge.

"Look at the river!" Betsy closed her eyes and held her breath.

The train was now midway across the bridge and the rushing, flooded river looked as if it would wash them all away.

"We're safe," Grace announced when the train reached the other side. "You can open your eyes again, Betsy. Look! We're here. There's the station."

"But where's Orari?" Moira asked.

"We'd better get our bags and go find out," Grace said.

With suitcases in hand, the land girls disembarked and huddled together on the platform, taking shelter under the veranda.

"Our instructions said someone was going to meet us," Moira said. "I hope they remember."

"Are you worried about your shoes getting wet, Moira?" Grace looked down at Moira's black leather pumps. With a low heel, they looked practical enough for travelling, but Grace was unsure how they'd handle the puddles in the carpark.

Grace scanned the platform, there had only been a few men onboard and she noted there were very few here now, mainly older men greeting their wives off the train. There were several doors into the wooden station building, all painted the standard brown. The middle door, labelled 'ticket office' opened and two men emerged. The pair had similar features, one a younger and taller version of the other, with the same neatly-trimmed head of hair in a darker shade of brown.

Grace watched with amusement as Moira grabbed her compact from her purse and checked her red lipstick and hair in the tiny mirror. Her amusement turned to disbelief when she saw Moira's subtle kick. A kick which knocked her suitcase over into the path of the younger man.

He had no choice but to stop. He picked the suitcase up and came face to face with Moira.

"Thank you," Moira purred, resting her hand on his, a moment too long, before he released the suitcase into her grip.

"My pleasure, miss." The young man scanned the passengers gathered on the platform. "Are you the recruits from the Women's Land Corps?"

"Oh, yes," Moira said. "Are you Mr McKnight? Are you going to train me?"

"Not me." He smiled at the obvious flirtation. "I'm William McKnight. My father, Duncan McKnight is, though. Dad, here are your new farmworkers."

Moira went quiet.

"Mr McKnight?" Grace asked. It wasn't the 'done' thing, but she held out her hand to shake Duncan's.

Duncan McKnight nodded, looked down at Grace's hand then back at her face before finally engulfing her hand in his. Grace felt the vice-like grip of the large, rough farmer's hand but didn't falter, if she wanted to be bold and shake hands, then she now knew what to expect. She introduced herself and the other women by name.

"Right," Duncan said after he'd nodded an acknowledgement to each of them. "Gather your bags, we'd best get back to the farm. There is work to be done."

The party left the shelter of the platform, hurrying to where the truck was parked.

"Sorry," William apologised as he held a canvas over the tray of the truck. "It's the only transport we've got. Two of you can hop in front if you want."

Grace saw Moira open her mouth to speak and interrupted. "No, thank you, we'll be alright together on the back."

William helped the four women climb aboard and handed up their luggage, before draping the canvas down over them.

"What did you do that for?" Moira asked. "Two of us could have been in the nice dry cab."

"Yes," Grace replied. "But which two? I think we'd better stick together over the next three months. Look out for one another. Mr McKnight didn't look like he is going to do us any favours."

"I'm sure Mr McKnight junior could help me with a few favours." Moira laughed.

The splatter of rain drops on the canvas stifled any further conversation. Grace shivered against the cold and wet and wondered what on earth they'd signed up for.

Chapter Two

The rain had eased by the time Duncan parked the truck outside Captain Boyle's residence, the main house at Whipsnade Farm. William jumped out of the cab and lifted the canvas off the women.

"Right then, this is where you'll sleep. You'll have your meals with us. That's our house over there." Duncan pointed to a smaller single storey house over to the left. "I'll need two of you to do the afternoon milking. Do any of you have any experience?"

"We don't," Grace replied. "Sorry. Betsy and I have been in a typing pool, but we are quick learners."

"I worked in a shoe store," Moira offered.

"I worked in a department store," Alice added.

Duncan rubbed his forehead with his fingers as if their answers had given him a headache.

"Mrs Terrill, our neighbour, will be inside to show you to your rooms. She's been employed by Captain Boyle to take care of the homestead while he is away," Duncan said as William helped unload the suitcases and gave the women a hand down off the tray. "The cowshed is down beyond our house. We'll meet you there at three."

He turned to leave, then hesitated. "You'll need to get changed. You do have farm clothes, don't you?"

Grace and Betsy both nodded and replied 'yes' in unison.

"Then everyone can meet me at the cowshed at three o'clock and we'll assign the jobs to be done. Come on, William, let's go. I need a cup of tea."

The noise of the truck's engine muffled Moira's wolf whistle to all except Grace who was standing closest to her.

"Would you look at that." Moira laughed and spread her arms to take in the view of the house in front of her. "Is that not every woman's dream? A beautiful home in the country with a white picket fence and flowers in the garden. I might have to find a way to stay longer."

Grace wondered if Moira ever thought of anything other than men. She picked up her suitcase and led the way up the concrete path to the front door to ring the doorbell mounted between stained-glass panels.

"Welcome. Come in ladies." A tall slender woman with short greying hair opened the door and ushered the land girls into the house. "I'm Mrs Terrill, one of the neighbours. Captain Boyle has employed me to look after the house and you ladies."

Moira's face lit up at the reminder that the house was owned by a 'captain.' Grace glanced around the expansive foyer and breathed a sigh of relief at the sight of the light switches. They wouldn't be reliant on candlelight and gas lamps after all.

"I'll do your laundry and clean the house. Your meals will be with the McKnights. Nel, I mean Mrs McKnight is a fine cook. You won't go hungry."

"Will Captain Boyle be joining us?" Moira asked.

"No, no, he's been called back to the Navy," Mrs Terrill replied.

"Bugger," Moira cursed under her breath.

Again, Grace who was standing closest, heard the muttering. Shocked at Moira's audacity, Grace elbowed her in the ribs. Moira just glared at her.

"The bedrooms are up this way." Mrs Terrill headed up the central wooden staircase. At the top of the landing, she stopped and waited for the women to catch up. "This is Captain Boyle's room. I've given it a spring clean and shut it up until his return."

"He'll be back soon, will he?" Moira asked.

"Depends on how long this dreadful war lasts." Mrs Terrill sighed. "Hopefully by Christmas."

It was March, the land girls were only here for three months so would be long gone before Christmas.

"There are only three other rooms so two of you will have to share." Mrs Terrill continued down the passage.

Grace and Betsy smiled at one another, silently communicating that they were happy to room together and keep each other company. Two single beds in the first bedroom were quickly claimed by them.

"This is me." Moira licked her lips as soon as she eyed a large double bed in the next room.

"That leaves this one at the end for you dear," Mrs Terrill said to Alice as she opened the door to the room at the end of the hallway. "It's quite small but very comfortable."

Alice walked into the tiny room, stood on the faded rag rug in the centre and slowly turned around. A single wrought iron bed sat along the outside wall where lace curtains hung in a dormer window. On the opposite wall a chest of drawers had a vase of fresh pansies on top, whose painted faces appeared to be smiling. Alice smiled back.

"So, you'll be alright in here then?" Mrs Terrill asked from the doorway.

"Oh yes. Thank you," Alice replied.

"The bathroom and toilet are downstairs beside the kitchen. I'll leave you to settle in then. I'll be back on Monday," Mrs Terrill said in farewell.

Grace heard the delight in Alice's voice and came in to check her room.

"Is the view good?" Grace asked Alice who'd knelt on the bed and pulled back the lace curtain to reveal the flower garden below.

When Alice turned back to look at Grace, her eyes were glassy, and tears threatened.

"A week ago, I didn't have a job or a home and now ... now I have my own little room with a view and a job to boot. I'm going to do everything I can to hang on to them."

"No job? No home? What happened?" Grace asked.

Alice went quiet and turned back to look out the window. Grace wasn't going to get an answer today.

The land girls made sure they were at the cowshed by three o'clock. A deep cough signalled Duncan's and William's approach. The women stood in a line as if reporting for duty, the creases on their brand-new overalls were as upright as them. Together with their black rubber boots they provided a uniform.

At least it would have been a uniform if Moira hadn't cinched her waist in with a thin, black belt, tucked the legs of her overall pants into her gumboots and folded the tops of the boots down to create a contrasting cuff. Grace wondered why the redhead seemed determined to stand out from the crowd. Grace had always been the tallest at primary school and was glad when she her friends finally started to catch up and she no longer stood out.

Alice had folded her gumboots down too, not as a fashion statement but because they were too big and hard to walk with the tops covering her knees. She'd also had to tie knots in the straps of her overalls to stop the crutch from hanging below her knees. Even a small size was too big for Alice. Grace would have to do some alterations for her.

"Does anyone know how to ride a horse?" Duncan asked.

"I do." Alice's face lit up. "When I was a child. There was a horse. It was my job to feed and exercise it."

"Well, son." Duncan rubbed his forehead again, exhaled loudly and looked at William. "Jess is probably bigger than a childhood pony, but she's your horse. Are you okay with that?"

William nodded and smiled at Alice. "You're a lightweight. Jess won't have any problems with you. She's pretty gentle, so you shouldn't have any problems with her either. She's in the small paddock beside the house, the cows are in the paddock on the right at the end of the race. All you have to do is get them from the paddock back to here."

"Go, Alice!" Moira cheered, fidgeting with the cigarette packet in her pocket.

"Okay, Alice?" Duncan asked.

"Yes." Alice turned to go find the horse.

"Alice." Duncan called to her back. "There should be thirty cows."

Alice nodded.

"Alice." Duncan shook his head and pointed to the back of the machine room door. "You'll probably want Jess's bridle."

Moira giggled until Duncan's glare silenced her.

"And one last thing," Duncan added. "Take Patch with you and he'll round up any stragglers."

Alice nodded. She had to stand on tip toe to lift the leather bridle and reins from its hook. The metal bit hit the ground with a clang. She hurried to hoist the bridle onto her shoulder before darting out the door.

"William," Duncan said. "I suggest you tag along, make sure she gets all the cows and doesn't take all day doing it."

Duncan began the next lesson to the remaining three students.

"We collect the milk in these milk cans. You need to put the gauze over the can while it's filling to catch any sediment. You'll need to keep checking the cans and change the gauze and the pipe to the next can when they are full. Be sure to put the lids on the full cans tight, we don't want any insects getting into the milk." Duncan scanned the faces of his audience obviously trying to judge the level of comprehension.

"How many cows does it usually take to fill a can?" Betsy asked.

Grace saw a little smile creep onto Duncan's face; it was good to see he wasn't grumpy all the time.

"A good question," he acknowledged. "These milk cans hold thirty gallons each. At this time of year, when the cows are nearly ready to be dried off for winter, they probably produce about five gallons a day."

"So, about six cows per can," Betsy promptly replied.

"Yes!" Duncan was visibly impressed. "But remembering we milk them twice a day so it will be about half at each milking."

He led them from the machine room to the cow shed.

"The cows will come into the yard from here. Make sure you shut the gate after them or some of them will disappear back to the paddock. We don't want to take any chances with Captain Boyle's prizewinning Friesians.

You'll need to wash their teats before you put the cups on. Make sure you've got all the shit off." Duncan paused momentarily to check whether his words had caused offence, before he continued. "We don't want any contamination." He ushered the group over to the two bails. "This chain here," he demonstrated, "needs to be hooked up behind the cow so it doesn't back out of the bale. The cows are pretty friendly but there are ropes here beside each bale if you need to tie their legs up. We don't want anyone getting kicked."

Grace wondered how long Moira's manicured fingernails—now painted in baby pink coloured polish—would last. Moira appeared to be paying more attention to them than to Duncan.

"Hold the cups in one hand, like this," Duncan explained as he demonstrated.

"Fold the rubbers over to cut off the air and then unfold them one by one as you put them on the teats. When they've finished being milked, bend the rubber to break the suction and remove the cups. Pull this lever to release the cows back into the race to head to the next paddock."

"How will we know when they are finished?" Betsy asked.

"They'll start getting fidgety. You'll get to know. You can remove the cups and strip the last of the milk out by hand. Just put it in these buckets and we'll have it for house milk."

The bellowing of cows drew the group's attention towards the race. There were thirty cows plodding happily to the shed, chewing their cud. Alice was beaming from ear to ear, despite the drizzle soaked into her clothes, as she and Jess ushered the herd along; William and Patch walked along behind.

"Right, here they come." Duncan breathed a sigh of relief. "I only need two of you for this job."

"Betsy and Grace, you can go first," offered Moira.

"Right, Betsy and Grace it is. You'll find aprons hanging up behind the machine room door. Best you put them on, and I'll help you with the first few cows."
The first cows were milked and released from the bail without incident.

"We'll leave you to it then," Duncan said. "William, you can take these two and go and feed the pigs. I'll go and check on the sheep, then come back here to make sure everything is on track."

The rhythm of the milking machines lulled the cows into their usual routine. They were content to stand in the yard, chewing their cud, awaiting their turn in the bails. Just as well, Grace thought. It seemed to be taking her and Betsy a while to milk each one.

"I'd better check the milk can." Grace released another cow from the bail. "We'd don't want any spillage on our first day."

"Good idea. We want to prove to Mr McKnight that we can do this." Betsy stripped the last of the milk from a cow's udder into the house bucket as instructed.

"Have you got all the milk?" Grace asked.

"I think so." Betsy ran her palm down the cow's udder. "I haven't quite worked out how to tell. Her bag isn't as tight, and the milk flow seems to be getting less."

Grace made it to the machine room just in time. The first dribble of milk was escaping over the brim of the milk can. Not one to panic, she calmly shut off the milk pipe. An empty milk can was required but the full one had to be moved first and the lid wouldn't go on when it was so full. Grace swapped the gauze filter over to the new can and found a small billy to transfer some of the milk.

She discovered a full milk can was heavy. There was no way she would be able to lift it. She made sure the lid was on tight, wrenched it over to an angle and prayed her legs would support the weight as she rolled it towards the other cans. Steel grated on concrete, then steel against steel clanged as she settled the can into the row for delivery to the milk factory.

Grace returned to the shed just as Betsy's cow raised its tail. Green sloppy effluent poured from the cow's behind and hit the concrete floor with a plop, splattering Betsy's gumboots. And just to make sure that Betsy's full attention was on milking, the cow flicked its long tail from side to side, the dirty tassel of coarse hair whipped Betsy about the face, painting khaki stripes across her cheeks.

"That's a good look, Betsy," Grace joked.

Startled, Betsy clambered awkwardly to her feet, her leg kicked out to the side and sent the bucket of house milk flying.

"Blast!" With a curse, Betsy scrambled to set the bucket upright to rescue the remaining milk as the rest meandered its way across the concrete, merging with the cow dung.

Grace stopped laughing when she saw Betsy's tears. "No need for tears, Betsy."

"I've spilled the blasted milk." Betsy raised her hands to wipe her face, looked at their filth and decided against it. "I've made a mess of things."

"You've made a mess of yourself, but if you remove those cups, you can replace the milk in the bucket, and nobody will be any the wiser."

"I should have just stayed in town." Betsy sniffed as she washed her hands and face in a bucket of cold water. "I should have kept working at the typing pool."

"It's only our first day, you can't expect everything to go right straight away."

Betsy's smile was feeble. She removed the cups and pulled the house bucket into place under the cow's udder. Resting her head on the cow's belly, she stripped the remainder of the milk from the cow's teats.

"So, what is really the matter?" Grace sat down on her milking stool in the next bail. "You weren't really crying over spilt milk, were you?"

"Roland," Betsy replied as if that one word said everything.

"What has Roland done?"

"Nothing ... everything ..." Betsy sobbed. "That's the problem, I just don't know."

"You still haven't heard from him?"

"No!" Betsy howled, tears rolled freely down her cheeks as she rocked backwards and forwards on the small stool.

"Oh Betsy." Grace wanted to get up and hug her friend, but the cow in front of her demanded her attention. "It'll just be the mail taking its time. You'll see. A whole bundle of letters will arrive any day now."

"But how? He won't know that I've moved."

"Your mother will send the mail on. She knows where you are."

"Perhaps," Betsy said. "I should ask the McKnights if I can phone her. Ask her if she has received anything. It'll be a toll call, but they can take the cost out of my wages."

"Then you can write back to him and discuss your plans for the future." Grace didn't have any plans of her own, not yet, but she knew Betsy had always wanted a big family.

"Sometimes it feels just like a dream," Betsy replied. "Like I've imagined it all."

"You've got the ring to prove it."

"But what if he's already been injured, or worse still, killed?"

Grace wanted to reassure Betsy that that wouldn't happen, but nobody could give that guarantee. Every day the newspapers carried the names of those who would never return. "Then you will be notified as the next of kin."

"I won't be. His parents will be. I don't even think they know what we did."

"They know you've been friends since childhood," Grace said. "I'm sure they would be in contact with any news."

"I hope so."

"The only thing we do know." Grace tried to distract Betsy and bring her back to the task at hand, "is we have to finish the milking first."

Chapter Three

Duncan opened the kitchen door at the farmhouse. "Nel, the land girls are here." He rolled his eyes, and placed the billy of milk on the bench. "Not as much as usual, there was a bit of a mishap. Girls, meet my wife."

"Sorry," Betsy apologised as she greeted Nel. "I'm so sorry."

"It's alright. These things happen." Nel wiped her hands on her apron. "As long as there is enough for tomorrow's porridge, I can collect more in the morning. Oh, dear, your eyes. You've not been crying over spilt milk, have you?"

"Betsy's a little bit distracted," Grace explained. "Her fiancé Roland has gone to war, and it's been a while since she's had a letter."

"Oh, Betsy, love." Nel held out her arms to embrace Betsy. "That must be awful for you. I'm so fortunate William is still here. Just you wait and see. There'll be a letter in the post any day now. Now sit down at the table, dear. You ladies must be hungry after all of your hard work. I've cooked a lovely roast to celebrate your arrival."

"A roast?" Duncan cocked his eyebrow. "We only have those on special occasions."

"Duncan!" Nel looked askance at her husband. "This is a special occasion."

"It smells delicious." Grace felt uncomfortable and glanced around the room. Duncan cursed under his breath. If she wasn't mistaken, he'd uttered 'damn women.'

The small kitchen was plain and functional, nothing as grand as the one at Captain Boyle's house. It was humble and clean. The extra effort Mrs McKnight had gone to, clearly evident. The table was set with a white linen cloth and silver cutlery, all arranged just as Grace had been taught t the , her mother had sent her to in the hope that one day she'd

A small posy of flowers from the garden, arranged haphazardly in a crystal vase, sat in the centre.

"Where are the others, Duncan?" Nel asked. "Did you not check on them?"

Duncan was about to take his seat at the head of the table but hesitated at Nel's question. It was answered by the noise of the back door opening.

"Hellooooo! Anybody home?" Moira chimed from the wash house.

"Come in, come in. Welcome." Nel rushed to open the door and greet her guests. "Oh, look at you, you do look lovely, dear."

Moira's cologne filled the room before she did. Alice was dressed in the white blouse and brown skirt she'd travelled in, but Moira had selected one of the dresses she'd packed. The dress's low-cut bodice and belted waist moulded her hourglass figure. The cream fabric was covered in tiny polka dots, the same colour as Moira's hazel eyes.

"Oh darn." Betsy looked down at her dirty overalls. "Sorry, we should have changed."

"Nonsense, you'll be fine," Nel said. "You don't have to dress for dinner around here."

"Well, I wasn't going anywhere looking or smelling like a pigsty."

"And I thought you loved the pigs," William joked as he came through the passage door. "Well, until you broke a fingernail."

"Those blasted buckets." Moira held her hand up for all to see. "Ripped a chunk clean off my fingernail."

The small chip from Moira's ring fingernail was barely visible to Grace whose own nails were always kept short. It was easier to type when the tips of your fingers, not your fingernails, hit the keys.

Nobody was certain how to react to Moira. The clock's ticktock was the only noise to be heard as they stood around awkwardly.

"Have a seat then," Nel said to break the silence. "It's been a long time since we've had so many for dinner."

Seven people seated at a six-seater table meant Grace, Betsy and Alice had to squeeze along one side. Grace was comfortable sitting next to Duncan; Alice quickly took the middle and that left Betsy on the other end opposite Moira.

"Here's a seat for you, William." Moira patted the chair beside her.

"That's Mum's seat," he replied. "I'll sit on the end here."

Grace watched Moira's hand disappear under the table. Just what she did wasn't visible, but William shifted uncomfortably and coloured from ear to ear. Grace shook her head in disbelief. It appeared Moira had found her first young farmer.

"Can I help you, Mrs McKnight?" Grace offered.

"Call me Nel, dear," Nel replied. "That would be lovely. The peas are in the pot, just put them in that serving dish, and on the table please."

Nel carried the roast on the meat platter and placed it in front of Duncan for carving. She quickly made some gravy in the roasting dish while he cut the meat. The plates, warmed on the rack above the coal range, were passed up the table towards Duncan. On each of the women's plates he placed two slices of mutton, on his and William's he placed three.

"Could you pass the potatoes please, Moira?" William asked.

"Certainly," she purred. "Anything else you would like?"

William coughed. Grace saw him scan the group. When their eyes met, she rolled hers to acknowledge his discomfort. He smiled sheepishly and turned towards Betsy. Grace was unsure whether it was simply to avoid Moira, or that William liked what he saw. Men usually liked what they saw in Betsy; she had the deepest brown eyes shaded by long dark lashes. Her smile could light up a room, but with all her worry about Roland and the war, Grace hadn't seen her friend smile for some time. She hoped that farming and the countryside would change that.

The room chimed with the clinking of serving spoons, the clunking of dishes being passed and a polite thank you as everyone tried to remember their best table manners. When everyone was served, Nel seized the moment of silence.

"Would anyone like to say grace?" she asked. "We don't usually, but if anyone wishes to, please do so."

"Grmmph." Duncan's grunt of obvious disapproval filled the room, and everyone else stayed silent.

"Ooh, gravy." Moira picked up the gravy jug and smothered her meat and vegetables with a generous helping of the smooth brown syrup. A drip of gravy fell from the spout to the tablecloth. Marking the white linen it became a black mark against her name.

"Oops, sorry," she apologised, picking the jug back up and wiping the dribble off with her finger. Moira looked defiantly at Duncan as she put her finger in her mouth and slurped it clean.

Grace saw Duncan's scowl and heard Nel's gasp. She anticipated an unpleasant reaction from their new boss, not a good way to start their three month stay, but he stayed quiet and started eating his dinner.

"Right, clockwise around the table, please let me know all about yourselves," Nel requested.

Alice was seated on Nel's left so that made her first. She shuffled on her seat while the small audience looked at her expectantly.

"I'm Alice. I'm from Christchurch. I used to work in Ballantynes before signing on for the land girls," Alice uttered quickly and indicated to Moira it was her turn.

"And how old are you, dear?" Nel asked. "I saw you in my vegetable garden. I thought you were the neighbour's goat come to eat my prized cabbages again."

"Sorry, ma'am, I just came to get a carrot for the horse. William said Jess would like me if I brought her a carrot."

"It's alright, dear," Nel said. "I saw you had two legs and not four so wasn't going to chase you with my broom. You could have been one of those poor children from the village. I'd never condone theft but I couldn't let a child go hungry either, not when their fathers are away fighting, leaving the mothers struggling to feed the brood. So, how old are you?"

"Twenty-two last birthday, ma'am," Alice replied.

Nel hid her surprise with a slow nodding of her head, and with another question, "And did you leave behind family, Alice?"

"Just my mother, ma'am." Alice glanced around uneasily, a pained look on her face as she bit her lip.

Grace itched to speak up and take over from Alice, to relieve her from whatever was causing her obvious discomfort, but Nel kept prying.

"And has your father been sent away in this awful war?"

Alice froze, inhaled sharply, and looked wide-eyed at the sets of eyes opposite hers.

"No ... no, ma'am," she stammered. She lowered her head, cut a large piece of meat, and stuffed her mouth full to prevent herself having to say anything further.

Grace seized the pause in conversation to introduce herself. "I'm Grace."

"Grace, what a beautiful name." Nel smiled at the blonde woman seated opposite her.

"Not looking so beautiful at the moment." Grace laughed and pushed an errant wave of hair back under the headscarf that was meant to keep it under control. "The cows knew we were beginners and were good at catching us unawares. Weren't they Betsy?" Grace laughed again as she pictured Betsy being swiped about the head with a cow's filthy tail.

"I wasn't paying attention and a cow involved me with its daily ablutions."

Betsy tried to explain with words appropriate for the dinner table. "I will be paying attention from now on, I can assure you."

"See Duncan, I hope you appreciate you've been blessed with lovely, keen trainees."

Duncan finished his mouthful before replying. "We've made it through the first day."

The room went quiet except for the clatter of cutlery on plates. Even that was quieter than Grace was used to. Her brothers had always liked to show their appreciation with a loud belch, frequently resulting in a contest to see who could burp the loudest or longest or even in a tune.

Moira looked around the table.

"I'm Moira." She lifted a languid hand and let the words roll off her tongue then paused, indicating nothing more was required.

"And I'm guessing you're from the city?" Nel queried.

"I'm from Christchurch as well. I used to work in Logie's shoe shop but thanks to this war there's no more leather for the kinds of shoes our customers like to wear."

"Mmm, shoes. Not really a priority around here, I'm afraid. But, please continue, age, family, fiancé?"

"None of either." Moira cleared her throat. "Well, obviously I have an age but it's not polite to insist a lady reveal her age, now, is it?" Moira giggled. "My parents are both dead and I haven't quite found the right man. Yet."

Moira gave William a flirtatious smile. Grace almost choked on her mouthful when she realised the brazen invitation the smile likely carried. She sighed with relief when Nel moved the conversation onto Betsy.

"Are you and your fiancé from Christchurch too, Betsy?" Nel asked.

"Yes. It was all a bit of a rush with the war." Betsy breathed deeply. "We didn't have time to make any plans for the future."

"All those things you have to look forward to when he comes home, dear." Nel smiled and nodded as if agreeing with herself would guarantee their happy future. "What did you do in the city?"

"Grace and I worked in a typing pool," Betsy said. "Grace convinced me to take up farming. I'm not sure it is the greatest of ideas, but we're determined to give it our best efforts."

"Talking about farming," Duncan interrupted, his serious tone matching his demeanour. "Seeing as that is what we are here to do. We'll have to be up at first light, so I suggest you all have an early night."

"It might be difficult for anyone to sleep if that banging doesn't stop," Nel said. "What is that noise?"

"It's gunfire," William replied excitedly. "The army are holding a training exercise. Trying to emulate a live battle so the soldiers know what to expect when they're at the front."

"What?" Nel's jaw dropped. "Are we caught in the middle of a battle?"

"Just a pretend one," William replied. "I wish I was with them, all the same," he said wistfully.

"No. No." Nel shook her head in denial. "No, William don't say that."

"I will be soon."

"Pardon?" Duncan and Nel said in unison, their eyes wide.

William straightened in his seat, with his shoulders back and head held high he proudly announced.

"I've enlisted. I have to be in Christchurch on Sunday."

Nel's anguish escaped her mouth in an agonising howl. She grabbed both corners of her apron and clutched them to her face as she fought back tears.

"It'll be alright, dear." Duncan quietly placed his knife and fork down beside his half-eaten dinner, rested his elbows on the table and lowered his head into his hands.

Grace's heart went out to them. She watched as Duncan took several long, deep breaths, knowing, that just like her own father, he would be digesting the news, processing the announcement that his son was going to be a soldier. Pride that William had chosen to serve his country would be mixed with trepidation that William may be unfortunate like so many others and not return or come back permanently maimed. When he finally lifted his head, Duncan's face reflected the stoicism that the situation required.

"Congratulations, son." He stood, walked down to the other end of the table, gripped William's hand in both of his and shook it. "I'm proud of you."

The land girls watched on in silence, apprehensive at being witness to a private family scene.

"Thank you, Dad. Will you and Mum be alright?" William glanced across at his mother, her distress visible.

Nel smiled weakly. Her obvious but unconvincing attempt to follow her husband's lead was thwarted by a glassy veneer of tears and the uncontrollable trembling of her body.

"Don't worry about us, son. You just keep yourself safe, thrash those bloody Nazis and come home as soon as possible." Duncan returned to his seat, picked up his knife and fork and resumed eating his dinner as if the conversation had never occurred.

William, the land girls and then, after a minute or so when her composure had returned, Nel followed Duncan's lead until there wasn't a morsel or drop of gravy left on anyone's plate. Above the sounds of eating, the clock could be heard, ticking loudly like a time bomb waiting to detonate.

"Isn't Moira a bit of work?" Grace asked Betsy. They were lying in the darkness, warm in their single beds with the bedroom door closed.

"Well, you can't blame her for flirting with William. He's pretty handsome."

Grace pictured William. She hadn't considered whether he was handsome or not. He did have a strong square jaw and a tiny dimple that appeared when he smiled. She compared him to her brothers; he was as tall and as broad as them and she assumed that came from his physical work.

"Betsy Nolan." Grace tutted. "I thought you only had eyes for your childhood sweetheart."

"Don't get me wrong, I love Roland. But ..." Betsy hesitated as if reluctant to share her thoughts. "That's just it, we've known each other since we were children."

"Does that make him less handsome?"

"No. But we've been friends for so long it's difficult to look at him any other way."

"I hate to point out the obvious, but you clearly have. You're wearing his ring."

"Yes, but …"

"Yes, but what?" Grace sat up in her bed. "Are you having second thoughts, Betsy? Have you done something you're going to regret?"

"No. No, I gave Roland something he dearly wanted. I'll never regret doing that."

Grace was trying to decipher Betsy's meaning, to glean what she wasn't saying from what she was.

"Please explain," she requested.

"He's gone away to war, Grace.
I may never see him again. We
pinkie-promised as children we'd save
ourselves for each other. If he'd gone
and we hadn't, then, well, he may never
have got to have that experience."

Grace was aghast. "So, you lost your
virginity because of a pinkie-promise?"

"Oh Grace, don't make it sound so silly."

"I'm sorry. I'm just trying to understand.
What happens if, I mean, when Roland
comes home? Are you going to be
happily married to your friend?"

"I was," replied Betsy.

"Was?" Grace raised her eyebrows in
disbelief, but in the darkness of the
room, only she knew Betsy's revelation

had drained the colour from her face. "That's past tense, Betsy."

"Well, I hadn't met William before, had I?"

A shiver coursed down the length of Grace's spine. She snuggled back down under the covers, unsure whether it was the cold or the thought of Betsy being unfaithful that unsettled her.

"You won't do anything you'll be sorry about, will you?" she asked. "You've only just met William. You can't possibly love him more than Roland."

"It's not a competition, Grace. Something happens inside me, whenever I'm close to William. It's not a feeling I can ignore. It hasn't happened before. Not with Roland."

Grace couldn't relate, any males she'd taken a fancy too had been quickly chased away by her brothers. She'd never got to the point of having feelings she couldn't ignore, other than annoyance at her brothers for interfering.

"But William's enlisting too." Grace hoped he'd be gone before Betsy had the chance to get too close to him.

"He's essential services. They might not take him."

"He said he wants to go, Betsy." Grace sighed. "They're taking anyone and everyone."

"It's only because he thinks it will be exciting. I'll tell him about the hours and hours of marching Roland had to do, dis-assembling and re-assembling his rifle, sleeping in tents. He'll see it's not so much fun."

"Nel will be happier if you do but I don't like your chances."

"I have to try, Grace."

Grace heard the desperation in Betsy's voice. She couldn't understand how the friend she thought she knew could be smitten with a man she'd only just met.

"Just be careful," Grace said. "Be very careful my dear friend."

Chapter Four

Grace and Betsy, under the watchful eyes of Duncan and William, had already started milking the first cows when Moira sauntered into the cowshed savouring every inhalation of her morning nicotine fix.

"You're late." Duncan scowled.

Moira took one last, long drag on her cigarette. With a look of defiance, she dropped the butt and smudged it into the concrete with the sole of her gumboot.

"Can any of you drive?" Duncan asked.

"I can," Grace called out. Her oldest brother, Jed, had a Morris Eight. It was his pride and joy, but Grace had pestered him, as only a little sister could, until he'd agreed to teach her to drive. She was fourteen at the time but already tall for her age so was able to reach the pedals. Jed, wary of damaging his car, insisted they begin on the rugby field down the road from their house. Grace was a natural, even Jed admitted it, and before long she was driving him around the quiet streets of Rangiora. The local constable overlooked any misdemeanour underage driving may have been.

"Right. William, you and Betsy finish the milking. Grace, Moira and I will go and move the sheep."

Grace squeezed her eyes shut and tsked. She'd just caused the very thing she planned to try and prevent – letting William and Betsy spend time together. Grace pulled the lever to release the cow she'd finished milking and moved to look at her friend. Betsy was hand milking a cow. She appeared focused on the task and didn't make eye contact. If she was aware of the implications of Duncan's instructions, she wasn't letting on.

"Right, Grace, let's see how you can drive. Moira, you climb on the back, you can open and shut the gates."

Duncan whistled his dogs and tails wagging excitedly, they leapt, onto the deck. Their keen noses were eager to sniff out the stranger on the back of the truck. Moira growled like a vicious hound and held them at bay.

Her disgust at the apparent punishment dished out by Duncan was evident in the glare she sent his way, but she had no option but to follow his instructions. Duncan climbed in the passenger seat and slid the small window in the rear of the cab open so Moira could hear him and Grace.

"What about Alice?" Moira dared to ask through the window.

"She's fed the pigs and is having breakfast."

In the rear vision mirror, Grace saw Moira's eyebrows arch skywards as she sucked in a breath before her face settled into a sullen look. Grace hoped Moira was wise enough to stay quiet.

"After this, I'll show her how to plough a paddock," Duncan continued. "We need to ready it for a winter crop. There is lots to be done now we've got this patch of fine weather. All going well, we'll get the crop in and the last of the hay harvested as well." Duncan's shoulders slumped with exhaustion. "Before William leaves."

Eager not to add another burden to Duncan's load, Grace concentrated on driving. The truck was bigger and higher off the ground than Jed's car, but Grace recognised the various gauges and switches on the dashboard and the gears were etched into the gearstick knob. Remembering everything Jed had taught her, Grace turned the key in the ignition, found reverse without crunching the gears and slowly edged her way out of the shed.

"Over this way." Duncan pointed to the track. "Second gear would be good. We haven't got all day."

Grace giggled nervously. She knew she could change gears. She'd done it a hundred times in Jed's car. She just had to do it now, in front of Duncan, without crunching gears or a bunny hop. She sucked in a breath, pushed in the clutch and pulled back the gear stick. Grace didn't breathe again until the truck moved ahead in second gear. Yes! She silently congratulated herself.

"Open this gate," Duncan yelled through the window, as Grace stopped the truck in front of a hinged wooden gate. "And close it after we've driven through."

Moira did as she was requested without audible protest. The truck rumbled along the well-worn track. They passed through several paddocks; each time Moira climbed off the deck to open the gate, waited for Grace to drive the truck through, closed the gate and climbed back onto the truck.

While she waited for Moira, Grace got to admire the countryside, undulating green hills rose in the distance before her. She could see the river over to her right, weaving in and out of patches of willow trees and imagined its path from the mountains out toward the sea. A hawk hovered, catching the wind drafts beneath its outstretched wings while it searched for a feast. Overhead, puffy white clouds ambled by, yesterday's rain clouds long gone. In front of the truck, a fantail flitted in and out of the clumps of broom, pecking at the seed pods eager to burst in the warm autumn sun. Memories of Grace's childhood flooded back.

Oooga! Duncan leaned over and blasted on the truck's horn. "What the devil is that woman doing? It doesn't take that long to shut a gate."

Grace, her reverie interrupted, looked in the rear vision mirror to see Moira jump, quickly shut the gate and climb back onto the truck.

It had been a long time since Grace had the opportunity to be in the wide-open plains and listen to the bleating of sheep and the chirping of birds. This time the peaceful sounds of the country were interrupted by the boom of cannon fire, the rat-a-tat of machine guns and the rumble of army tanks.

"It sounds like the army are getting closer," she said.

"The letter I received last week said they could be anywhere around here," Duncan said. "Even dossing down in hay barns and sheds."

Moira grinned from ear to ear. Grace imagined her delight at the thought of soldiers at the farm and hoped she wouldn't do anything to get herself or them into trouble.

The next gate allowed them to enter a large field dotted with sheep. The well-beaten track continued up the centre, and Grace drove slowly along. Duncan inspected the flock as they went. Sheep looked up at the intruders, bleated and lowered their heads to continue eating.

"Open this gate but leave it open," Duncan demanded as they reached the far end of the paddock. "Park the truck off to the left of the gate and switch her off."

Sensing the open gate signalled something was imminent, the closest sheep bleated loudly, a warning to the herd.

"Well-a-go!" Duncan yelled to his dogs, whistling for them to round up the sheep and chase them into the next paddock. "Well-a-go!"

Grace watched with delight as the dogs followed the commands, scooted to the outsides of the paddock, eyed up the sheep, barked and nipped at their heels and headed the flock towards the gate. There were too many to count as the sheep jostled through the narrow exit and into fresh pasture.

"Right, we'll just do a circuit and check for any stragglers." Duncan set off on foot with his shepherd's crook, dogs, and Grace and Moira in tow. "These ewes are in lamb and sometimes they get caste in the sheep ruts, you just need to right them and send them on their way."

Duncan knew the land and knew the areas likely to catch the sheep out. He soon found a sheep, its four legs skywards. The ewe gave a half-hearted bleat, exhausted by the futility of numerous attempts to right itself. Duncan climbed into the rut, wedged his legs in behind the sheep's side, grabbed handfuls of wool as low as he could, and heaved the sheep back up onto its feet. He continued to hold the animal until it regained its equilibrium and was ready to trot off and join the flock.

They were down at the far end of the paddock, when Grace spotted a dirty white mound of wool between clumps of tussock. There were no feet waving about so she approached for a closer look.

"Found one," she called to Duncan when she confirmed it was a sheep.

"Well, turn it over," he replied impatiently.

"It's not looking too good." Grace noticed the sheep's head at an awkward angle, its tongue hanging out and its eyes gazing emptily.

"Bugger!" Duncan moved in front of Grace to inspect the animal. Its nostrils weren't flaring and there was no breathing. "Bugger! It's been caste for too long. It's still warm though. We'll have it for dog tucker."

Duncan grabbed his knife from a leather sheath on his belt, pulled the sheep carcass up against his legs, held the head aloft in one hand so the neck was taut and whipped his knife blade across the sheep's throat with the other.

It all happened before Grace and Moira realised. They had no time to turn away. Grace wasn't shocked, her brothers had killed many a rabbit or possum, skinning and gutting them in front of her. Moira, however, was ashen, all colour drained from her face as if she'd just witnessed her first killing. As blood poured from the sheep's neck, Moira's shoulders lurched, she stumbled out of the rut, doubled over and emptied the contents of her stomach onto the grass.

"When you're ready." Duncan chuckled. "Could you go and get the truck while I gut this."

"Certainly," Grace replied.

"I'll help," Moira added quickly, wiping the back of her hand across her mouth.

Grace didn't need help but figured Moira was keen for any reason to remove herself from the sight of sheep's innards.

They walked back along the track they had earlier driven. The stench of vomit accompanied them, triggering another convulsion of Moira's stomach muscles. She hunched over and retched, again and again until her stomach was empty. Just as Grace's mother had done for her, Grace rubbed Moira's back, in what was meant to be comforting circular motions but, Moira pushed her away.

"I don't think I'll ever be able to eat mutton again," she groaned.

They reached the truck.

"Can I drive?" Moira asked. "It'll help keep my mind off vomit."

"Can you drive?" Grace looked back to where they'd left Duncan. He was bent over the sheep, head down.

"You can teach me." Moira didn't wait for Grace's answer. She climbed in and perched on the edge of the bench seat so her feet could reach the pedals. "I was watching you through the window, it didn't look difficult. If I'm going to get to go to the movies or dances, then I need to learn to drive."

The keys were still in the truck's ignition. Unlike Grace, Moira didn't hesitate to turn the key. When the engine burst into life, she tested the pedals one by one.

"Accelerator?" she asked rhetorically as the loud revving of the motor identified the accelerator. "Brake," she said when a red light appeared on the dash. "Clutch," she addressed the final pedal before pushing it flat to the floor and shoving the gear stick over and up towards the 'one'. Releasing the clutch, and pushing down on the accelerator Moira looked out the windscreen urging the vehicle in the direction she needed to head. The old farm truck lurched forward then stopped abruptly, its engine stalled.

"You forgot the handbrake." Grace pointed to the lever under the dash.

Moira repeated the process and breathed a sigh of relief when the truck headed back down the track towards Duncan. Her knuckles were white as she gripped the steering wheel, trying to hold it on track, but the wheels of the truck seemed to hit every rut possible.

"This isn't as easy as it looks," she conceded.

Duncan had dragged the hollow carcase over to the track.

"I'd better not run him over." Moira came to a halt some five feet before Duncan, yanking the hand brake back on before turning off the engine. "He's glaring at me, but I think I did quite well for a first-time driver."

Grace sensed Duncan's anger and felt responsible. "She wanted to have a go," she said.

"Well, she can have a go at picking up offal." Duncan scowled. "Grab that bucket and shovel off the back of the truck," he instructed Moira. "Put the head and guts in there. We'll chuck it in the offal pit when we get back home. Don't want to leave it here to attract the blowflies."

Moira took one look at the decapitated head, the tongue hanging lifelessly out the side of the mouth, the eyes staring blankly at her. She clutched at her stomach and doubled over to retch yet again.

"Oh, give it here," Duncan grumbled. "Useless woman."

Duncan grabbed the bucket and shovel and finished the job, but he was unable to lift the carcass onto the tray by himself.

"I'll leave the hide on, so the dogs don't devour the meat on the way back. Right, grab a leg each." He indicated for Grace and Moira to grab hold of the woolly back hocks of the sheep.

They looked at Duncan's bloodied hands and then, with horror, down at their own. Reluctantly, they followed his orders.

"Ready?" asked Duncan as the women gingerly placed their hands around the sheep's back legs. "On the count of three... one, two, three, heave!"

The carcass landed with a thud on the wooden tray of the truck.

"Aargh," Duncan yelled. His faced screwed in a painful grimace. "My back."

"What happened?" Grace hurried to Duncan's side. "What's wrong?"

"My bloody back's gone," he groaned, creeping slowly towards the cab of the truck.

Grace held the passenger door open while Duncan gingerly edged himself inside. She closed the door, rushed to the driver's seat and headed the truck towards home. Moira had no choice but to climb onto the tray.

Duncan inhaled sharply each time Grace drove over or into a bump in the track. She sat up taller, looking out for a smoother passage across the paddocks, not wanting to cause him any additional pain. Eventually they arrived back at the cowshed and Grace parked the truck in the same spot she'd left from. She rushed around to open the door for Duncan.

"Aargh," he growled.

Grace couldn't tell if it was from the pain of climbing out of the truck or annoyance at her offer of help as he slammed the door shut.

"You grab that bucket. Dump it in the offal hole. It's over there under that piece of iron. Make sure you replace the iron. We don't want the dogs falling in."

Grace dared to look into the bucket. A vacant black pupil stared up at her from behind short, straight blood encrusted lashes. She felt a choking in her throat. She wasn't going to be sick like Moira so cast her eyes skyward inhaling the fresh air.

Duncan stood beside the tray of the truck waiting for Grace to return. Each time he tried to straighten up, he swore in pain.

"You two will have to do it," he said through gritted teeth.

"Do what?" asked Grace.

"Get this to the cowshed." He pointed at the sheep carcass. "We'll have to hang it and cut the hide away."

Grace and Moira looked at one another and back at the sheep.

"Get a move on." Duncan hobbled off towards the shed. "Before the flies get to it."

Again, they had no option but to grab hold of the sheep's legs. This time, Grace took the front legs and Moira reluctantly took the hind legs. They dragged the carcass to the edge of the tray and absorbed the jolt as the deadweight of its back and belly sagged towards the ground. They lugged it into the cowshed where Duncan waited with rope, gamble and a knife.

"Cut a slit on each leg." He handed the knife to Moira who did as he instructed. "Thread the gamble through ... tie the rope to the gamble ... thread the rope through that pulley. Now pull."

Grace and Moira followed the instructions and watched the sheep rise lifelessly before their eyes, the last traces of blood dripping from its severed neck to the concrete floor. With gritted teeth Duncan tied the other end of the rope securely to a hook on the wall of the shed. He then showed the women how to cut the hide away from the sheep's legs and punch at the pelt to strip it quickly from the corpse.

"You finish," he said to Grace.

Grace had watched her brothers skin possums on many occasions but had never had a go herself. She copied what she'd seen Duncan do, her fist wedging between the pelt and the fat covered meat of the animal. The process required more force than she expected. Her knuckles were red and sore by the time the pelt could be pulled away.

"Hang it on the fence to dry," Duncan told Moira. "In a few days, when its dried, one of you can pluck it. Nel will want the wool to spin and knit into socks."

Moira inhaled deeply before she stepped towards the sheep. She avoided the white fleshy inside of the pelt by grabbing fistfuls of wool and carried the skin outside.

"We'll let this hang–" Duncan said as if the hanging carcass was an everyday occurrence– "while we go have breakfast."

"What have you done now husband?" Nel asked as Duncan hobbled into the kitchen, his clothes bloodstained.

"Had to kill a sheep. Dog tucker." Duncan gingerly sat down at the table and used the back of the chair to brace himself.

"He's hurt his back too." Grace felt obliged to inform Nel.

"It's nothing." Duncan waved Nel away. "No mollycoddling. It's just a pulled muscle."

"Everyone, eat up then," Nel suggested as she dished the last of the bacon onto their plates. "I'll give your back a rub after breakfast, Duncan."

"I haven't got time for that," he growled. "We've got to separate the milk and cream and get the milk to the factory, hitch the plough and get the crop paddock ready for sowing. And Pete's coming with the tractor to cut the hay."

"We'll separate the milk before we take it to the factory." William's face was lit up; his dimple added a comma to his broad grin like a signal there was much more to come.

Grace had hoped Betsy's infatuation was one sided, but it appeared not. She heard the familiarity of the 'we', saw Betsy's flushed appearance and bright glossy eyes, and feared the worst. She may already be too late to stifle any feelings Betsy was developing for William.

"I'm happy to go too," she offered.

"Maybe we can watch the army exercises," William said, excited by the prospect.

"Remember petrol rationing, William," Duncan said, as he broke into the runny yellow yoke of his egg. "Moira can go. Grace and Alice can get the plough ready."

For entirely different reasons, Moira, and Grace both smiled at that news. Grace couldn't see Moira as a chaperone but at least she would be a thorn between the other two, when she wasn't eyeing up soldiers, that is.

"Make sure you get the factory docket, William," Duncan said. "Just put it on the spike on the shelf in the machine room, I'll monitor the production daily from now on." Duncan made eye contact with the land girls, his words and his look issued a challenge. "If milked properly, the cows will still give plenty of milk for another six to eight weeks."

Chapter Five

Duncan was breathless by the time he'd hobbled to the implement shed with Grace and Alice in tow. He hadn't let Nel give his back a rub and now appeared to be paying the price for his stubbornness.

"Bloody back," he groaned, resting against the corrugated iron wall of the shed. "Bloody war, no tractor for ploughing now, requisitioned, melted down to make weapons, I think. Anyway, now we've got to do it with the horse and manual plough. Everything you need: horse collar, harness and plough are in the back of the shed. I'll just rest here while you get it."

Daylight didn't reach the rear of the shed where the collar and harness were gathering dust, hanging from rusty nails long ago hammered into the shed's poles. When Grace's eyes adjusted to the dim-light she soon found the horse collar and turned to pass it to Alice, but Alice's diminutive physique was still silhouetted in the doorway, she hadn't come into the shed. Grace was about to yell out when a movement in the corner stopped her. On the dirt floor was a pile of empty sacks. Grace imagined the movement had just been a rat making a nest among the sacks, but as her pupil's dilated, she could discern that the intruder wasn't a rat but a man. It appeared he wore an army uniform but he was wet, dirty and bedraggled. His face was covered in mud and his short hair stood in erratic spikes. If Grace hadn't seen movement, she would have believed him to be dead. She paused, unsure what to do.

"Have you found it yet?" Duncan yelled. "We haven't got all day."

The soldier's body went rigid, his eyes shot open and stared at Grace. Panic-stricken, he raised a single finger to his lips to silence her. She noticed his soldier's uniform, not in the clean and pressed state that it should be, but with the army insignia ripped from its shirt pocket. Grace guessed the man to be the same age as her youngest brother Frank, a thought that tore at her heart. This could easily be her youngest sibling and he clearly didn't want to be found. She cautiously backed away, slowly nodding her head reassuring him she wouldn't reveal his secret.

Grace had been annoyed that Alice hadn't come into the shed to help but now for the soldier's sake she was glad. Grace didn't know if Alice could keep a secret, she didn't even know if she could either, not one this big.

"Here, take this," she said holding the horse collar out to Alice.

Alice didn't respond. She appeared transfixed, frozen at the doorway, the hairs on her arms stood on end. Grace glanced at Alice and back into the shed.

Had she seen the soldier too? Even if she had, why did she look so terrified?

"Alice," she said, giving the land girl a gentle nudge. "Alice, are you alright?"

Alice shook her head, blinked her eyes rapidly and brought herself back from wherever her mind had gone.

"Sorry … sorry …," she said in a muffled whisper. "Yes, give it to me." She took the horse collar, rushed from the shed, and set it on the ground beside Duncan.

"Right, you seemed to have made friends with Jess," he said. "Fetch the horse and bring her here so we can hitch her up."

Grace was unsure who to be more concerned about, Alice or the soldier, but with Alice away getting the horse,

Grace needed to make sure Duncan didn't discover the man hiding in his shed. She went back in to retrieve the harness. The pile of sacks was now just that, an imprint of a human the only evidence of anyone's presence.

"It's okay," she whispered into the emptiness with more certainty than she felt. "What's your name?"

Grace waited for a reply, knowing that the young man must be here. A noise to her left drew her attention. She thought she heard a sniffle and moved around behind the seeder to find its source. The young man cowered beside a wheel, his entire body trembling.

"Can't …" he croaked with a voice rusty from disuse.

"Well, you're obviously a soldier," Grace said in tones she hoped were inaudible to Duncan. "What's a soldier doing in an implement shed in Orari?"

"Can't," he repeated, his voice quivering. "Can't be a soldier."

Grace heard the fear in his voice, saw the terror shudder through his body. She had watched all four of her brothers go off to war. The first three with gusto and enthusiasm to do their duty for the country, but the fourth only out of obligation, the pressure from peers to sign up and the fear of being labelled a coward. Grace hadn't been able to help her youngest brother, Frankie, but she could help the young lad in front of her.

"Stay here. I'll be back."

It took another half hour before Jess was harnessed and they were on their way to the patchy brown paddock which had previously been cut for hay. Grace was grateful to finally leave the shed and the mystery man safe inside.

"Start at the outside," Duncan instructed. "Go in a clockwise direction around the paddock. Lift the plough at the ends and then lower it back on the other side so we end up with parallel rows heading this way."

Alice stood and nodded as if to affirm she understood the instructions. Grace was only half-listening, her mind pondering what to do about the stranger in the shed.

"If you keep an eye on the fence and try and stay in line you should be right. We need about a foot between each furrow so the wheel will be just to the right of the last furrow."

Alice continued to nod.

"Each furrow should be about four inches deep, so you'll need to apply a bit of pressure to keep the blade about two-thirds in the ground. If you go too deep, you'll dig up too many rocks, the little stones are unavoidable but if you hit a rock you'll come to an abrupt halt. Understand?"

Alice looked from Jess to the paddock and back to Duncan and replied with an unconvincing yes.

"Well, give it a go then," he replied. "I'd show you how, but this blasted back of mine. I'll stay and watch until you've got it sorted."

Alice manoeuvred Jess over to the fence and gave a gentle flick of the reins to get the Clydesdale moving. The two metal handles of the plough were almost at shoulder height on her small stature. Alice had to push them up to make the front of the plough dig into the ground. Slowly but surely the pair set off up the edge of the paddock. The earth was still dark brown with the moisture of the past days' rain. With each step, Alice's gumboots either threatened to stick to the viscous ground or stub her toe into an unearthed stone.

"She's a bit little for a farmer, this one," Duncan said to Grace. "Once she's got the horse sorted you can take over. Jess will do the work; you just have to walk behind."

Duncan made it sound easy. Grace thought it probably was, if you had been farming as long as she imagined Duncan had been. She wondered if this was a test, making Alice plough, a test that Duncan hoped she would fail. She did appear to be struggling. Grace wanted to take over, surely it didn't matter who ploughed the paddock, as long as it was done.

Eventually Alice reached the end of the first row and remembered to lift the blade out of the ground. Duncan hobbled over and inspected her efforts. The tiny figure behind the horse had managed to keep parallel to the fence line and it appeared to be to the required depth. Duncan leaned back on a Totara post and winced.

"Well, I never," he said, surprise peppering his voice. "I don't know if it's good luck or good management, but it seems you've got the knack. I'll leave you two to it."

"Okay Jess, off we go, one row at a time," Alice said to herself as much as the horse.

"Just do one more, Alice and then I'll have a go," said Grace. She stood and watched the tiny woman and the huge horse trudge around the paddock. Whatever had held her in a trance at the shed seemed long gone.

When Alice finished the next round, they swapped and Grace took the reins. The past few days of rain had left the earth stodgy. Grace tried to keep her feet on the solid ground, stepping around the freshly turned earth where she could, but mud clung to the soles of her gumboots and weighed them down. She could feel the black rubber chafing on her heels and dreaded to think what they looked like.

Another few rows and the trio were in a steady rhythm, Alice and Grace swapping over without the need for Jess to stop. They'd been going for a couple of hours when Grace came around again expecting Alice to take over, but instead of waiting by the furrow, she was pacing up and down the fence line.

"What are you doing?" Grace sounded impatient. She wanted to get back to the soldier, not muck around in the paddock.

Alice walked awkwardly over to Grace and shoved her hands between her legs.

"I need to pee," she squeaked as if holding onto her voice as well.

Grace glanced around the paddock. "Nobody here but me and Jess. Just squat in the dirt. It'll drain away."

Alice's mouth fell open, her head shook, voicing the denial that she was unable to utter.

Urinating outside was nothing new to Grace. Her brothers took turns to pee on the lemon tree in the orchard and her mother encouraged it, she said it was good for the tree.

"Whoa, Jess!" Grace pulled on the reins to stop the horse. "That's a girl, just stand still and rest for a minute or two. Alice needs you to hide behind. Go on, off you go, I'll stay here and promise I won't look." Grace chuckled as Alice

disappeared around the other side of Jess.

"I haven't got any toilet paper."

Grace chuckled again. "Oh, you must have been living a life of luxury to have never gone without toilet paper."

"No," Alice protested. "I've had to use strips of old newspaper, but I was a toddler last time I had nothing."

"Well, pretend you're a toddler and jiggle about. We've got to get this horse moving and the paddock finished. There are other things that need my attention."

Jess neighed as well.

"I'm going to have to set up a hospital at this rate," Nel growled. She brought some lunch and a drink over to the paddock when the land girls didn't arrive home for the midday meal. "Stop right this minute."

They hadn't seen or heard Nel approach but certainly heard and obeyed her order to stop. The sun was high in the sky, and they were just over halfway around the paddock.

"Here, have a drink, before you faint with dehydration." Nel passed Alice a glass of water. "Whatever was that husband of mine thinking, leaving you out here without water and sun protection."

Alice's face glowed and Grace imagined hers did too, either from the sun or the exertion required to keep the plough moving in a straight line, it didn't matter, the effect was the same. The burning wasn't confined to her face, her arm muscles ached, large welts covered her palms and blisters had formed, threatening to burst each time she pushed on the plough handles.

"He's hurt his back." Grace doubted her defence of Duncan's actions would be reciprocated when he learnt of their injuries, but she didn't complain, with Alice's size, it must be much harder for her, and she hadn't faltered once.

Grace's mouth was parched, her lips dry and chapped. The sound of Alice gulping down the cool water was torturous. Thankfully, Grace didn't have to wait long until she'd finished, Nel refilled the glass and handed it to her. The cool water provided some relief as Grace gingerly held the glass in her blistered hands.

"Here's a sandwich," Nel said, retrieving two sandwiches wrapped in a checked tea-towel from her basket. "And some apples, one for each of you and one for Jess."

Grace wolfed down the sandwich. She hadn't realised how famished she was. She sat down, perched her bottom on the turned earth, raised her ankle off the ground and rotated it slowly around and around until feeling returned. She daren't take her gumboots off for fear she'd never get them back on.

Alice gave Jess an apple before biting into her own. Juice dribbled down her chin, but she had no energy to wipe it off.

"I think my toes might be broken." Alice slumped down on the dirt next to Grace. "I've kicked so many rocks; I doubt I've got a straight toe left."

"I can't feel mine," Grace replied. She rested her elbows on her knees and her head in her hands.

"Have a quick siesta, lass." Nel patted Grace on the shoulder. "Then you'll be good to get the ploughing finished."

Seagulls circling overhead squawked loudly. The gulls hovered, ready to swoop down to snatch any worms unearthed by the plough. Their piercing shrieks demanded Grace keep moving, reminded her that there was a young man that required her help, and she couldn't help him until she'd finished here.

"No, no," she said shaking her head. "I'll be fine. You rest up Alice while I do the next round. Thank you for the lunch, Nel."

Alice and Jess stopped beside Grace at the end of the last row. The women stood and admired the result of their day's toil.

"We make a pretty good ploughing team, Alice, don't you think?"

"Yes," she replied. "But I hope we don't have to do it again any time soon. I don't think there is any part of me that doesn't ache."

"Me too," Grace agreed. "Let's get this gear back to the shed."

Alice froze. Fear drained the colour from her face. Grace saw her panic, assumed mention of the shed was the pre-emptor but was reluctant to reveal the soldier's presence if he wasn't the cause.

"What is it?" Grace was deliberately vague. "What's scared you?"

Alice looked at Grace, her eyes glassy, her lips quivering, her voice lowered to a whisper.

"I just don't like dark places."

"Oh, Alice." Grace wanted to hug her, both to comfort her and with relief that her own secret was safe. "You take Jess to the paddock, and I'll put the gear away."

Grace made the offer to ensure she was alone at the shed and it worked. She'd follow up on why Alice feared the dark, another time. Back at the implement shed, she made plenty of noise to let the soldier know it was her.

"Are you still here?" she called into the back of the shed.

Slowly, the bedraggled man rose from behind the seeder.

"Are you from the army exercises?" she asked. "What's your name?"

The young man didn't answer, he wouldn't look Grace in the eye, he blinked rapidly and rubbed the back of his neck.

"If you don't want to be a soldier, why don't you go home?"

The man shook his head. "First place they'd look. I'd be shot for desertion or worse still, shipped out to the war to die anyway."

Grace cringed. She didn't want to believe that the army could shoot its own men and she didn't need reminding that her brothers faced death every single day.

"We're short of men to help with farm work around here. I could ask Duncan if you can stay."

"No, no!" The soldier stood, he looked ready to escape. "Don't tell anyone I'm here. Please!"

"You can't stay in the shed forever and not expect to be seen."

"Just a few days. Until the army recruits leave the area. That's all I need. I need to dry out. To get some food. That's all and I'll be out of your way."

Grace looked at the soldier's gaunt face. He did need feeding and to dry his clothing or he'd risk catching pneumonia. She pondered how easy it would be to sneak some leftovers from Nel's kitchen, make an extra sandwich or take some fruit from the trees in the orchard.

She caught a whiff of the soldier. If he didn't have a wash and clean his clothes then his stench would surely give his presence away. Perhaps she could sneak him into the big house, let him have a bath and get his clothes washed and dried. Captain Boyle's room was shut up. No one would know if he slept in there.

"Okay then," Grace agreed. "Just for a few days."

"Thank you, thank you." The young man grinned; his straight white teeth reflected a happiness that reached his eyes.

Grace noticed they were a baby-blue, as pale as hers were dark. She didn't generally study people's eyes but felt his held a vulnerability that drew her in.

"But," she added. "You have to tell me your name."

The smile was gone in an instant, replaced by a blank untrusting stare.

"Just your first name," she said as a compromise. "So, I know what to call you."

He hesitated. His eyes narrowed, and his brow wrinkled.

"I'm Grace," she offered.

He shuffled behind the seeder, looked down at himself and with a look of surrender, mumbled his response.

"Ben,"

"Okay, Ben. Stay here for now," Grace said. "I'll be back."

Chapter Six

The shrill alarm of Grace's clock pierced the silence of the early morning. The clock repeated its ring several times before Grace woke enough to stretch her arm out from beneath the bedclothes and flick the off switch. She quickly replaced her arm back by her side and realised she had been in the same position when she had gone to bed exhausted the night before. Sleep had come easily, every muscle in her body needed time to recuperate.

Deciding she had no option but to start the day, Grace sat up in her bed and pulled back the curtains to see what weather the day had brought. She hadn't heard rain in the night, but then she hadn't heard anything.

The sun was just peaking over the top of the copse of Macrocarpa trees planted at the edge of the garden to provide shelter from the easterlies. The trees stood solid and silent, there was no wind to bend their branches today. The implement shed wasn't visible from this side of the house but Grace pictured the unobtrusive corrugated walls offering protection to the fugitive. The absconder that she had colluded to hide. Would her help render her as guilty as he was? What did the army do to those who aided and abetted escapees?

Would it be a court martial and firing squad for them both? Grace swallowed loudly, the implications of her actions an unknown threat. She needed to confide, to discuss the options with Betsy.

Light filled the room and Betsy had no choice but to open her eyes to the new day.

"Morning, sleepyhead," Grace said. "It's a beautiful day out there."

"It's not going to be a good day at all," Betsy grumbled.

"Why not?" It appeared Grace was not the only one with troubles.

"William leaves today." Betsy swung her legs out and sat on the edge of the bed, her head drooped, supported by her hands.

"I thought you were going to convince him the army wasn't all it was cracked up to be."

"Not a chance." Betsy sighed.

"You've tried then?"

"I've tried everything."

"Everything?" Grace couldn't help but think the worst. "Betsy, I hope you didn't do anything you will regret."

"Grace!" Betsy looked horrified as she realised Grace's implication. "I'm engaged to Roland remember."

"I remember," Grace said. "I was just checking that you remembered."

"I don't think even that would have changed his mind." Betsy retrieved her overalls from the chair at the end of her bed to ready for the morning milking. "He is such a staunch supporter of fighting for King and country. He despises any yellow-bellied cowards who try to shirk their duty."

Grace stifled a cough. Telling Betsy about Ben wasn't an option. Not while William was still around. He'd report Ben for certain. She got herself dressed and decided Ben would remain her secret, for now.

Grace and Betsy finished the morning milking without incident and without the expected inspection by Duncan.

"You go ahead," Grace said to Betsy. "Catch up with William. I'll finish up here and bring the house milk."

As Grace had expected, Betsy didn't hesitate and ran off towards the house. With her gone, Grace turned her attention to food for Ben. It was proving tougher than expected. She'd been able to sneak him some apples from the orchard after dark last night but they wouldn't be enough to build up his strength. She found a small jar on a shelf in the machine room, filled it with milk from the billy and walked back to the house via the implement shed.

"Ben," she whispered. "I got you some milk."

He came out from behind the seeder, snatched the jar from Grace and gulped down the still warm liquid. It was rude, but Grace could see his desperation. Seeing his hunger and knowing the milk wouldn't suffice, Grace knew she'd have to do more.

"I'll try and make some sandwiches for you. I'll be back. Stay out of sight," she said as she left the shed with the billy of house milk.

"Who were you talking to?" Moira sidled up beside Grace. Her and Alice had fed the pigs and were on their way to breakfast.

Grace jumped with fright. Milk spilled from the billy.

"Look what you made me do." Grace deflected the question. "Don't sneak up on people."

"Oh," Moira said. "Touchy. Anyone would think you were hiding something."

Grace felt herself blush, an unavoidable confirmation of her guilt, she turned away and quickened her step to the house. "Just thinking of everything we need to do," she said. Neither the truth nor a lie.

William entered the kitchen with a small bag.

"Are you sure you're taking enough, son?" Nel asked.

"Just underpants and toiletries," he replied. "The army will provide anything else I need."

Nel abandoned the porridge she was stirring on the coal range and presented

William with a small square cake tin with a camel embossed into the lid.

"Thanks, Mum." The aroma of freshly baked Anzac biscuits escaped when William prized open the corner of the tin. He licked his lips and shut the lid tight again to seal in the treat before stuffing the tin into his bag. "I wonder if I'll get to see a real camel."

Grace saw the glassiness in Nel's eyes. It was reminiscent of her own mother's sadness, and she wondered if it was worse with only one son leaving or quadrupled if you had to farewell four off to an uncertain future. She looked across at Betsy. Her eyes held the same pool of tears threatening to overflow.

"And these too, William." Nel handed him a pair of woollen socks she had knitted. "I stayed up late last night to get them finished, I'll knit some more and post them to you."

"Thanks, Mum." William leaned in and gave his mother a hug. "What's for breakfast?"

"Ah! Breakfast! Porridge!" Nel rushed back to the bubbling pot. "Phew! It hasn't stuck. Help yourselves, everyone. I'll just be a moment."

"Where's Dad?" William asked when his mother returned to the kitchen, her composure restored. "Is he still out on the farm?"

"No," replied Nel. "He's laid up in bed. He says his back is giving him what for."

"It's not that bad." Duncan limped into the kitchen and sat at the head of the table. "A man's still got to eat."

Nel dished up a plate full of porridge, stirred through a dollop of cream and placed it in front of her husband. Duncan unfolded the newspaper while he let the porridge cool. The front page was emblazoned with a photograph of the New Zealand troops.

"Our boys have arrived in Greece," he said. "They've even had a parade to welcome them. Now those Nazis better watch out."

Betsy moved so she could see the photo.

"Can you see Roland?" Grace leaned in too but couldn't recognise any of the faces in the blurred black and white image of the back of an army jeep making its way through crowd lined streets. Confirmation that Roland was alive would certainly cheer Betsy up and remind her who she should be thinking about. Grace couldn't tell from William's unperturbed look, whether he was unaware of Betsy's relationship with Roland or not worried.

"No." Betsy's tone carried all the glum she felt. "Just lots of happy women, smiling and waving."

"They're bombing London now, even Buckingham Palace took a hit." Duncan continued to share the news ambivalent to anyone's emotions.

"Were the King and Queen injured?" Nel asked with concern.

"It doesn't say so, they probably escaped to their castle in the country."

"I don't think so," Nel defended the monarchs. "The newspapers said they're subject to restrictions too and have the palace all boarded up."

"Well, you can't believe everything you read in the newspapers." Duncan turned the page, flicking the newsprint to remove a crease. "Well, we'd better believe this story and be on the lookout. Apparently, a soldier was on the northbound express on his way to camp when he jumped from the train. It was going forty miles an hour."

Grace's mouthful of porridge sat like a muzzle she was too afraid to remove. Was the article referring to Ben?

"And why do we have to be on the lookout?" Nel asked.

"Says here, the train was near Orari," Duncan read. "I don't imagine you could get off a train at that speed without getting injured so he's possibly still somewhere close."

Grace recalled the few times she had seen Ben. He was dirty and hungry, but he didn't seem to be injured. Perhaps he wasn't the soldier in the newspaper article. Not that it mattered, he was still a soldier who had deserted his responsibilities. The outcome would be the same if he was recaptured.

"The poor man will be needing our help then," Nel replied.

Grace swallowed. She'd found her ally. Nel would help look after Ben.

"Nel!" Duncan groaned, folded the newspaper, placed it on the table. "Don't you go mollycoddling any escaped soldier."

He blew on a spoonful of porridge and satisfied it had cooled, ate his breakfast.

"I think you should go back to bed," Nel said when he'd finished.

"I am. I am. Stop fussing woman," Duncan growled. "I can still see my son off. William, get the land girls to drive you to the station after they've had breakfast. They can take the milk to the factory at the same time."

Duncan and William eyed one another. The time had come to say goodbye. Father and son shook hands, gripping each other as if their lives depended on it. Their handshake, silently conveying feelings, continued long past what would be customary, both men reluctant to let the moment pass. Eventually, Duncan coughed, released William's hand and stepped back to stand as straight as his back would allow. "Farewell son. Travel safe." He turned and hobbled from the kitchen.

If William was disappointed his father wasn't going to take him to the train, he didn't show it. His eyes were sparkling, and he was looking directly at Betsy.

"You can take me to the station, Betsy." He winked.

Betsy blushed. "I can't drive, William."

"Grace, you can drive, can't you?" William's question may have been for Grace, but Betsy was still the focus of his attention. "You can drive me and Betsy into Orari."

"I can drive too," Moira offered. She ran her tongue over her lips and Grace imagined her wanting a farewell kiss too.

Grace wanted to make sure Betsy didn't make any promises she wouldn't be able to keep. She didn't want Moira to have any opportunities to take advantage of William either. She needed to get food to Ben and to sound Nel out, when no-one was around. She judged that Nel wouldn't want to see a young man sent to war when he clearly didn't want to go. Together, they could take Ben under their wing, feed him up and send him on his way to somewhere safe. Grace pondered who should take priority. In the end she settled on her longest and dearest friend, Betsy.

"You've only driven once, Moira, and that was over the farm. I'll drive," she offered.

"Right, Betsy and Grace, it is then." William swallowed the last of his porridge. "I'll put the milk cans on the truck while you finish eating."

Betsy and Grace waited in the truck while William gave Nel one last hug. When he climbed into the cab, William pulled his handkerchief from his trousers and blew his nose loudly before stuffing all evidence of his emotions back into his pocket.

Grace turned the key in the ignition. When the old truck cranked into action, she shoved the gearstick into first and headed out the driveway. The image of Nel, weeping and forlorn, waving from the back door of the house was etched in the rear-vision mirror.

They travelled in silence. Rain, like tears from heaven, began to fall. The pelting of the raindrops on the cab of the truck sounded like rapid gunfire, an unwanted reminder of the purpose of the trip.

Betsy, snuggled in between Grace and William, reached out to hold his hand. He gladly accepted the offer of comfort. Their hands remained clasped until Grace pulled the truck up in the carpark of the Orari station. The rain had stopped, and the train was already at the platform hissing its readiness, steam billowing from the smokestack.

"We haven't got long." William got out of the truck. "You'd better give me a kiss now, Betsy."

Betsy was unable to look William in the eyes as she coloured from top to toe.

Several young men, all dressed in the same khaki shirt and pants as William wore, arrived at the station. Seeing William with Betsy and Grace, they wolf whistled.

"Woohoo, McKnight!" The group erupted into laughter; their excitement palpable. "Nice leaving party!"

William looked torn. He gave Betsy a quick peck on the cheek and grabbed his bag off the back of the truck.

"I'll write," he said, blew another kiss and ran off to join the men.

William shook the hand of the first man as they slapped each other on the back.

"Are you ready for our big adventure?" the young man asked.

"Sure am, Paul."

"You won't miss your little lady too much?"

"I will." William glanced back at Betsy. "But she's not mine. Yet."

"Aargh! Men!" Betsy slammed the passenger door shut. "If I never see another man, it will be too soon."

"He gave you a kiss. What more did you want?"

"He couldn't wait to be with his mates."

"I guess it's a big, exciting adventure for them. Going overseas. They've probably never left home before." Grace rested her hand on Betsy's shoulder. "And he promised to write."

"So did Roland."

"I'm sure there will be a letter any day now." Unable to think of anything else to say to cheer Betsy up, Grace started the truck. "We'd better get this milk to the factory. Which way do we go?"

"Left," Betsy said. "And then first left again."

Grace followed Betsy's directions and before long, the concrete frontage of the Orari Co-operative Dairy factory came into view. There were several other trucks and horses with carts backed up to the loading bay and Grace concentrated to carefully reverse back in beside them.

"Well, good morning, miss." A young factory worker stood on the platform and greeted Grace when she climbed out of the truck. "Jake's the name, anything you need, I'm your man."

Grace couldn't help but giggle, imagining the reply Moira would have given to that sort of greeting,.

"Hello, Jake," she replied. "We need your help to unload the milk cans, if you don't mind."

"Well, I'll be darned. Will you come over here, Bob?" Jake addressed his work mate. "We've been blessed with two visions of beauty this fine morning."

The other farmers were abandoned, left to unload their own milk cans. Betsy and Grace were the focus of attention.

"We've got to get back," Grace explained knowing that Duncan would be watching the clock and waiting for them, and Ben would be starving. She imagined he'd be gone, thinking she was of no use to him, he'd better move on. "If you could just unload the milk cans, we'll be on our way, thank you."

"We have to know where you're from miss. Names and addresses have got to be recorded against the milk." Bob came to the front of the platform and joined the conversation. "The farmer doesn't get paid if we don't get the paperwork done."

"You got the details yesterday." Betsy's annoyance at men hadn't dissipated. "I was here with William McKnight. We're from Whipsnade Farm."

"Whipsnade Farm," Jake repeated. "Isn't that where land girls are being trained?"

"Yes." Grace thought she'd better reply, before the men undeservingly bore the brunt of Betsy's wrath. "We're land girls."

"So, you're new to the area." Jake's face lit up. "You'll be needing someone to show you the sights then."

Betsy huffed, turned on her heal and climbed back into the cab of the truck, slamming the door.

"We don't really have time for that," Grace replied. "There is a lot of farm work to do."

"All work and no play, that hardly seems fair." Bob untied the rope across the back of the truck and started unloading the milk cans.

"You don't work at night-time, do you?" Jake asked. He rolled a milk can singlehanded to the back of the platform with ease.

"No, not after milking," Grace conceded.

"So, you'd be able to come out after milking?"

"We're usually pretty tired."

"Well, there's a dance coming up at the local hall." Jake persisted, ignoring Grace's excuse. "That would be after milking, wouldn't it?"

Grace nodded. She knew where this was leading and wished Moira was here, not her. She had Ben to be thinking about, not worrying about a dance.

"So, Bob and I could take you two lovely ladies to the dance."

"There's actually four of us so we'll have to decline your kind offer."

Jake looked confused. "Four of you?"

"Two more land girls back at Whipsnade," Grace said.

"Well, we could see you there then ... at the dance ... all four of you.

Knowing that Moira would insist they go to the dance, Grace nodded in agreement.

"But only if you hurry up and unload this milk."

Two men, grinning from ear to ear, quickly removed the full milk cans and replaced them with empty ones.

"Saturday in two weeks' time." Jake kept hold of the factory docket until Grace agreed.

"Okay," she conceded. "In two weeks."

Chapter Seven

Nel was slicing the loaf of bread for lunch time sandwiches when Grace and Betsy's childlike giggles filled the room.

"What's so amusing?" she asked.

"You should have seen Moira. It was hilarious." Betsy wiped the tears from her eyes as she entered the kitchen. "I've laughed so much I've cried."

It was nice to see Betsy's happy tears, but Nel was none the wiser as to their cause.

"Some of the piglets had escaped the paddock," Grace explained.

"We had to catch them." Betsy's face lit up with excitement. "They were so cute, running about, squealing, their tails wiggling crazily."

"Four piglets, one each," Grace said. "We just had to catch them by their back leg, then grab hold of them tight to put them in a pen."

"It was quite easy really," Alice said. "Unless you don't like pigs, hey Moira."

"You lot would've been as reluctant as me if you'd spent more time in the pigsty. I can't get rid of the smell."

"But these ones were outside in the paddock."

"I don't know why you all think it is so funny," Moira said sulkily. "I could've hurt myself.

"Not in that mud hole," Betsy teased, trying to conceal her mirth. "Although you did dive into it with some speed."

Grace, Betsy, and Alice burst into giggles again as they recalled the image of Moira plunging headfirst into a quagmire, the tiny piglet running merrily straight through.

"At least you didn't have to give it the kiss of life like Duncan did the other day." Alice was full of admiration for Duncan's resuscitation of a neglected piglet.

They were still laughing when they sat down at the table to make a sandwich to their liking. With Ben in mind, Grace took an extra two pieces of bread to make a second sandwich.

"Hungry, Grace?" Moira raised an eyebrow.

"Chasing pigs is hard work," Grace joked. "Did you know there is a dance at the Orari Hall in a fortnight?"

"What? How do you know? Who told you?"

"Jake and Bob told us." Grace felt a little smug. She'd managed to change the subject and keep winding Moira up.

"Who are Jake and Bob?"

"They're from the milk factory," Betsy said. "Although why they aren't away at war I don't know."

"Essential services," Nel explained. "Duncan said if they work in certain industries they are excused. I thought that would mean William was excused too but he's chosen to go anyway." Nel sighed with resignation.

"Jake and Bob." Moira redirected the conversation. "Are they young?"

"About your age." Grace had made one sandwich of cold meat, lettuce, boiled egg, and a slice of tomato. She began to make the second.

"Good looking?"

"You'd probably think so." Grace thought Moira believed any young man was good looking enough for what she wanted them for.

"We might be too busy to go to the dance," Alice said.

"I think you will have earned a night off by then." Duncan ran a hand through his dishevelled hair as he hobbled into the room. "Not too late though, there will still be cows to milk in the morning."

"I'm not so good at dancing," Alice said.

"It's not all about dancing, Alice." Moira licked her lips.

Grace cringed. She'd seen Moira flirting. Just what Moira would be doing at the dance, Grace hated to think. This would be the first dance Grace would go to without one or more of her brothers scrutinising every man who dared look her way. Even if one did approach, Grace would be dancing and nothing else.

"It will be an opportunity to meet the locals, Alice," Grace suggested, "and any other land girls in the area."

"Well, it isn't for a fortnight," Duncan said impatiently. "So, you don't need to settle it now. Better eat up first, there is plenty of work to be done between now and then. We need to make the most of this patch of fine weather."

"I'll leave you to do the usual jobs this afternoon. The pigsty needs to be mucked out and the pigs fed. Moira .... Moira." Duncan repeated her name until he was sure he had her attention. "You can show Grace what to do and Betsy, you can show Alice how to milk the cows once she has fetched them in. Do you think you can manage that? I don't like leaving you unsupervised but this damn back of mine. I think another day lying horizontal will fix it."

"We'll be fine," Grace said, with more confidence than she felt.

"I've arranged for Pete, one of the neighbours to come and cut the hay." Grace watched Moira's face light up at the mention of Pete, another man for her to set her sights on.

"The seeding will have to be done tomorrow," Duncan said. "The seeder is still in the shed."

Tomorrow. Seeder. Shed. The words hit Grace like torpedoes. Ben would have to be moved. Today.

The pigsty was a low rectangular building with windows sandwiched between half concrete walls and a rusty iron roof. The windows had been home to generations of spiders and now let in only filtered light.

"Aww, yuck." Moira opened the wooden door at the end of the building and stood back. "The smell doesn't get any less disgusting."

Holding her hand over her nose, she ducked her head and entered the sty. Moira flicked the light switch on, signalling to the sty full of baconers that it was dinner time. An unchoreographed chorus of high-pitched squeals echoed into the iron roof. Those pigs that could, jumped up, rested their trotters on the concrete wall of their pen and angled for a better view.

"Each pen gets one bucket of whey," Moira explained to Grace. "The buckets are here, and the whey is in the tank just outside the door. I'll do that and while they are busy eating, you get in and get all the dirty hay out with the pitchfork and shovel the shit into this channel to be hosed out later."

Grace looked over the wall of the pen where three hairy Tamworth pigs were squealing and jostling for position at the trough. Together they looked up at her in expectation, wiggling the flat end of their round snouts.

Grace imagined that Moira had given her the worst of the two jobs but when she arrived back carrying a bucket of whey, grunting in a non-porcine vocabulary as she strained to lift the weight and tip it into the channel that fed into the trough, Grace was happy to grab the pitchfork and climb into the pen.

The pigs were heads down in the trough and seemingly oblivious to her presence, their tails twirling in happy spirals. As quick as she could manage, she dug the pitchfork under the sodden hay and walked with the load back to the wheelbarrow. Backwards and forwards as fast as she could until the sleeping pen was empty. Then she swapped the pitchfork for a shovel and scraped the excrement towards the drainage channel.

"Can you pass me some fresh hay please?" she asked Moira. The pigs were slurping up the last of the whey and Grace wanted to hurry and finish before they did.

"Sorry, I've got to get the next bucket." Moira disappeared back out of the sty before Grace could protest.

Grace made a mental note not to bother asking Moira for any favours. She ducked out of the pen, grabbed a wedge of hay and slid back through the gate before the pigs had realised. Fluffing out the hay in the sleeping pen made her sneeze. Shaking her head, she turned to see three sets of hazel eyes gazing inquisitively at her. Grace smiled, with pink pointed ears and long ginger eyelashes, the pigs couldn't possibly present a threat. They stood between her and the gate and the middle, slightly larger of the three, came grunting towards her. The pig's torso was against Grace's leg. She braced herself with one hand on the wall of the pen and let her legs become a welcome scratching post.

"You want a scratch, do you?" Grace giggled. Her fingers struggled against the coarse bristly hair of the pig's neck, but it still grunted contentedly and stretched up to welcome more.

"What are you doing?" Moira's face held a glower of disgust. "This isn't funny. It's disgusting, and I don't want to be here forever. Hurry up and get into the next pen."

"Sorry, Mr Pig," Grace said, leaving the pen. "That's all for today."

In the second pen, the baconers sniffed at Grace's gumboots, their slobbery snouts left an appreciative trail of saliva on the new rubber. Grace chuckled when she realised Moira's hair was the same colour as the pigs. She considered pointing out the similarity but thought the better of it and moved onto the next pen.

The women worked their way slowly and methodically through the sty, down one side and back up the other. Grace was oblivious to the odour as she pitchforked hay and shovelled excrement. As each pen was tended to, the cacophony of animal noises slowly abated.

Thoughts of the sandwich stowed in her overalls pocket had Grace's stomach rumbling but knowing that her hunger would be sated by Nel's lovely dinner, she left the sandwich to take to Ben as soon as she'd finished.

"I'll meet you back at the house, Moira." All of the pigs had been fed and their pens cleaned. Grace dumped the last wheelbarrow load of dirty hay on the compost pile. She needed to deliver the sandwich to Ben and encouraged Moira to leave so she was able to go via the implement shed undetected.

"What? Yes. Okay." Moira had already pulled her cigarette packet from her pocket eager to replace the stench of the sty with something more pleasant. She wandered off to enjoy her smoke in peace.

Everything looked untouched at the implement shed, much to Grace's relief. She glanced around, satisfied that she was alone, she whispered into the semi darkness.

"Ben, I've got you a sandwich." It was looking a little worse for wear, having been squashed in her pocket all afternoon, but still edible.

Ben came out from behind the seeder munching on an apple.

"Where'd you get that from?" Grace's tone was more accusatory than what she'd planned.

"The orchard."

"By the house?"

"Yes."

"But you might have been seen." Grace imagined Nel keeping an eagle eye on her garden from the kitchen window.

"I got here without being seen, didn't I?" Ben reached out and took the sandwich. "Thanks."

"We have to move you."

"Why?"

"We've got to do the seeding tomorrow, so you'll be discovered if you're still here in the morning."

"Where to?" Ben took a bite of the sandwich.

Grace watched as he closed his eyes and his cheeks bulged. She imagined the scrunched sandwich was the most substantial food he'd eaten in days.

"Yes, where to, Grace?" Moira approached the shed, blowing the last of her cigarette smoke into the air.

Grace gasped. Her body went rigid as if staying still would make her invisible. She saw the whites of Ben's eyes before he darted back down behind the seeder.

"Moira." Grace tried to stay as casual as she could. "I thought you'd gone back to the house."

"I heard you talking to someone and came to see who it was."

"No-one here," Grace lied. "Just me talking to myself."

"No." Moira peered into the implement shed. "No, I'm certain I heard a man's voice."

A piece of bread caught in Ben's throat; he couldn't suppress his cough. It echoed through the iron shed like a bomb blast.

"There is someone here." Moira scanned the shed looking for the source of the noise, waiting to hear it again.

Grace's secret was no longer hers alone. She'd have to convince Moira that Ben needed their help, or he would be in trouble. The young man with the baby-blue eyes didn't deserve to be in trouble.

"Moira," she said. "I need your help. Ben needs our help."

"Ben?" Moira smiled. "I knew there was a man here. Ben, you'd better come out."

Ben slowly stood behind the seeder. He looked like a frightened, caged animal eyeing up the possible escape routes.

"Well, I never." Moira stubbed out her cigarette on the ground and stood with her hands on her hips.

"We have to move him. Tonight. I was thinking to the big house. In the room that's shut up. No one will find him there. Just for a few days while the army exercise is still going. Ben needs to get cleaned up."

When Grace finally stopped jabbering, she held her breath, waited, waited for Moira's reaction, confirmation that her imploring was successful. Grace watched Moira as she watched Ben, eyeing him up. She imagined Moira seeing through the dirt and crumpled uniform, not to find a frightened soldier needing to escape but picturing a physique that she'd like to get her hands on. It didn't matter as long as she was prepared to help.

Moira looked from Ben to Grace and back to Ben. "We'll have to wait until night-time," she said. "And he'll need a wash or Mrs Terrill will smell him for sure."

"Thank you." Grace and Ben both sighed with relief.

Fortunately, it was a clear night. Grace's path to the shed was illuminated by the moon's light, except when clouds scuttled through and plunged her into momentary darkness.

"Are you there, Ben?" she called quietly into the dark depths of the implement shed. "I've got some more food. Another sandwich. It's all I could get."

"Thanks, Grace. Anything is better than nothing."

It was the first time he had said her name. Grace liked the way it sounded.

"Follow me," she said. "We'll go through the garden so we can hide behind the bushes."

Without any option but to trust her, Ben did as he was told although it seemed difficult for him to keep up with her. He caught up to Grace when she crouched down behind a Camelia bush.

"Got a sore foot," he whispered. "Can't run too fast."

Grace knew then that Ben was the soldier in the newspaper article. That meant there would be people out looking for him. The sooner she got him inside and hidden the better.

"We're nearly there." The downstairs sitting room lights were still on. "We'll go in through the back door."

Grace cringed when the door creaked. She cursed the rusty hinge thinking everyone would hear their arrival.

"You made it." Moira was waiting for them in the kitchen.

Moonlight shining through the window was the only source of light and Grace hadn't seen Moira standing at the bench. She jumped with fright; her nerves frayed. She inhaled deeply, attempted to slow the beat of her heart, thumping loudly and rapidly in her chest.

"Where are the others?" she asked.

"In the sitting room, listening to the radio."

"Right, Ben, we'll hide you up in Captain Boyle's room." Grace thought they'd better keep moving before anyone else arrived in the kitchen.

"Captain Boyle?" Ben went white and his lips trembled. "I haven't come this far to be thrown to the dogs."

"It's alright, he's away at the war, he won't be back anytime soon."

"What about getting cleaned up first?" Moira asked. She pinched her nose between thumb and forefinger as if she was back in the pigsty.

"Good idea," Grace agreed. "I'll run the bath. I'll pretend it's me who's going to have one. You go and get some of Captain Boyle's clothes."

"Or I could just help Ben have a bath," Moira suggested. "I'm sure his back will need scrubbing. Won't it, Ben?"

Grace clenched her teeth. A small growl brewed in her throat. She was not going to allow Moira to bathe her Ben. Her Ben? He wasn't hers but he certainly wasn't Moira's either.

Ben laughed quietly. "Thanks for the offer but I think I can wash my own back."

Moira disappeared upstairs and returned with her arms laden with shaving gear, a hairbrush, and an assortment of men's clothes which Ben eagerly took and disappeared into the bathroom.

Fifteen minutes later he re-emerged, no longer looking old enough to enlist. Clean-shaven, his round face was boyish. The fear in his eyes had been replaced by a hint of cockiness. He now resembled an obstreperous teenager, not a man off to fight for his country. If Grace was having doubts before, his youthful innocence confirmed she had no option but to ensure he didn't have to fight.

"We'll get these washed for you." Grace took the scrunched and dirty army uniform from Ben.

"If I never have to wear them ever again it will be too soon."

"Of course," she said. "Sorry. I wasn't thinking."

"I'm sure Captain Boyle won't miss his clothes," Moira said. "He probably won't even remember he had them when he finally gets back. We should burn your uniform." Her face lit up. "A ceremonial incineration. Destroy the evidence."

"Good idea." Grace agreed but was anxious Moira's enthusiasm would get them into trouble. "Maybe just in the coal range, not a bonfire as big as a search beacon to draw everyone's attention to the very person we are trying to conceal. We'll worry about it tomorrow. Best get you upstairs and hidden for now."

The trio tiptoed up the stairs to Captain Boyle's room. The moon gave enough light to see that a huge four poster bed dominated one wall with a freestanding wardrobe on another. The dark timber of the furniture and brown velvet drapes and eiderdown created a masculine domain. Moira picked up a photo from the dresser; it was an image of a handsome man in uniform and she wolf whistled as loudly as the secrecy of their mission would allow.

"Captain Boyle would have been quite a catch if he wasn't away at war," she said.

Grace sighed. Moira's pursuit of men seemed never-ending.

"Better not put the light on, or draw the curtains," Grace said. "Make sure no-one can see that you're in here."

Ben lay on the bed.

"I won't," he mumbled half asleep.

Chapter Eight

Nel had bacon crisping on a rack above the coal range. Its aroma filled the kitchen to welcome the land girls when they came in.

"Good morning, ladies," Nel greeted them cheerfully. "Isn't it a lovely day?"

"Yes," Grace replied. "It's a beautiful morning out there."

"And there's mail for Betsy." Nel waved the aerogramme about before passing it over to Betsy. "From R Flavell. Isn't that your fiancé?"

Grace felt as excited for Betsy as she looked herself. Betsy blushed as she turned the aerogramme over and over in her hands.

"Open it! Open it!" Nel urged excitedly.

"Yes, what are you waiting for?" Moira asked.

"What if it is bad news?" Betsy chewed her lip.

"Well, you won't know until you open it."

Betsy turned the aerogramme over again, picked carefully at the corner and cautiously unfolded the precious letter.

"He's on a ship," Betsy said as she read. "Bound for the Middle East." A tear trickled from the corner of her eye.

"He's all right, isn't he?" Grace placed a comforting hand on Betsy's arm.

"Yes," Betsy replied. She looked at the postmark on the aerogramme. "At least he was three months ago when he wrote this."

"He'll be fine, dear." Nel patted Betsy's other arm. "He'll be just fine; you wait and see."

"He promised to write again soon." Betsy sighed.

"We'd better tuck into breakfast, get the jobs done and then you can write back to him," Grace suggested trying to lift Betsy's mood. "This bacon smells delicious and I'm starving."

"Bugger!" Duncan hobbled into the kitchen. "Why didn't you wake me? It's after eight."

Five sets of eyes turned his way as he pulled a flannel dressing gown on over his pyjamas and knotted a cord tie at his waist.

"I was just about to bring your breakfast through." Nel placed buttered toast, a poached egg and two rashers of bacon on a tray next to a steaming pot of tea. She lifted the tray to suggest Duncan should return to his bed.

"I'm here now, best put it on the table," he replied taking his usual seat. "Right, how has everything gone? Have the cows been milked? Has the milk been separated? Have the pigs been fed? Have you checked on the sheep? Do they need moving? Who's taking the milk to the factory? Have you collected the eggs?"

Duncan's torrent of questions was greeted by a line of blank faces. Grace took the lead and responded.

"Cows milked. After breakfast, we'll separate the milk, won't we Betsy?" Grace looked at Betsy for confirmation and Betsy smiled and nodded. "Then we'll take the milk to the factory."

"And I'll check on the sheep," Moira volunteered.

"And Alice has already fed the pigs," Grace continued.

"Yes, Moira and I fed the pigs this morning." Alice gave Moira credit for their joint efforts. "I can collect the eggs after breakfast."

As hungry as Grace felt, the image of Ben smiling as he devoured bacon and eggs, meant she left some of hers, grabbed another piece of toast and made a sandwich.

"I'll save this for later," she said.

"I'll do that too," Moira said, with a conspiring wink.

Grace glanced nervously around the table, certain that the others would be aware of their secret. She relaxed a little seeing everybody was focused on their breakfast.

"Right then, the dew should have dried off the paddocks by the time you've had breakfast and finished those jobs."

Duncan took a bite of his toast and washed it down with a mouthful of tea. "Then it will be time to turn the paddocks of hay that Pete cut yesterday. You'll have to do it with pitchforks. They're in the back of the implement shed. Just walk around the rows and turn all of the grass over so the green side is face up."

Duncan made it sound easy. Grace hoped it was. Her arms were still aching from the ploughing.

"What about the seeding?" Grace had moved Ben because they were meant to be seeding today.

"Hopefully I'll be good enough to do that myself tomorrow," Duncan said. "I can't risk getting that wrong or we'll have no winter crop."

Grace rolled her eyes and saw Nel do the same. Whether it was for the same frustration that she felt, Grace wasn't sure. She wondered whether Duncan thought just her, and the other land girls were useless or women in general.

Mrs Terrill arrived at the Whipsnade homestead the same time as Grace and Moira.

"Good morning. I thought you ladies would be hungry with all the physical work," she said, noticing their sandwiches. "I've baked you some scones."

She placed a basket on the bench and lifted the tea towel covering her baking. The aroma of fresh scones made Grace's mouth water.

"Thank you," she said and smiled, certain that Ben would appreciate the scones as well. She just had to get them to him without Mrs Terrill's knowing.

"I haven't got time to stay today," Mrs Terrill said. "Our Women's Institute have an outing arranged. We're catching the train over to Timaru and I must get home to get ready."

Grace tried to disguise her relief with a smile.

"Have a good trip," she said, filling the kettle to make a hot drink. "Thank you again for the scones."

Grace and Moira waited a few minutes after Mrs Terrill had gone before they prepared a breakfast tray. Grace brewed a pot of tea, sliced, and buttered a scone and put her and Moira's bacon and egg sandwiches on a plate. Moira found an opened jar of blackberry jam an added a generous dollop to each segment of scone.

"A meal fit for a king," Moira joked.

There was more food on the plate than Ben had had for a while.

"It should help him get his strength back," Grace said.

Grace carried the tray upstairs and Moira opened the bedroom door. Ben scooted to the side of the bed and looked ready to escape out the window.

"Just us," Grace called when she saw the look of terror on his face. "Bringing you breakfast."

Ben sat back on the bed and pulled the bed clothes up around his shoulders.

"It's okay," Moira said. "You don't need to hide."

Grace cringed. Her teeth clenched as she put the tray down on the bedside table and poured Ben a cup of tea. Moira's voice took on a different tone when she flirted and she was using that tone now. Grace wondered if she was just irritated by Moira's actions or was she jealous? Jealousy would mean that Grace had feelings for Ben. It couldn't possibly be that; she'd only just met him.

Ben had no choice but to let the bedclothes fall to take hold of the cup of tea Grace offered.

"Is there no-one else here?" he asked.

"No," Moira said. "We've got the place to ourselves."

"But you'll still have to be careful, stay alert. You've risked too much to get caught now." Grace wanted to refocus on the reason why Ben was here. "And we've got work to do so we will leave you to enjoy your breakfast."

"Come on, Moira." Grace took Moira's hand and ensured they both left.

It was ten o'clock before Grace, Betsy and Alice arrived at the first hay paddock, each with a pitchfork in hand.

"Better get started," Grace suggested, looking at the rows which stretched away into the distance. "I think there's another paddock, after this one."

"We'll take a row each, shall we?" Betsy asked. "Then we can walk along together and chat."

And so, they began, pitchfork in under the pile of cut grass, pick the bundle up, flip it over, step forward and repeat. The women settled into a steady rhythm and were halfway down the first row when Betsy started the chatter.

"Looks like it's going to be another nice day,"

"Yes, much easier to farm in the sunshine," Grace replied. "Are you enjoying it so far, Betsy?"

Betsy laughed. "Apart from getting up with the roosters, getting cow poo on my face, spilling the milk, falling into bed exhausted and then repeating it all again the next day. Yes, I'm loving it," she said facetiously.

Grace laughed too, she picked up another pitchfork of grass and tossed it upwards, a green and brown shower of grass shoots tumbled towards Betsy.

"That's great then!"

Betsy didn't bother to brush herself down, she stabbed her pitchfork into the ground and used her hands to throw a bundle of half-dried grass towards Grace. Then, she bent and grabbed another bundle and threw it at Alice.

Soon, all three pitchforks stood abandoned. Hay wasn't being turned, it was being tossed skyward, to float back to the ground in disarray. Laughter filled the paddock, the giggles of three young women behaving like children, turning a task into a game. Patch barked, jumped about and snapped at the shoots that fell past him. A rabbit ran out from the barbary hedge and stopped, it appeared to observe the goings on, keen ears forward, listening to the fun before it scampered off to safety. A pair of magpies, also drawn to the frivolity, left their grandstand in the Macrocarpas and hovered overhead, squawking noisily.

With shoots clinging to clothes, stuck to hair, and protruding from gumboots and overalls, Grace, Alice, and Betsy eventually collapsed to the ground and lay looking skyward until their laughter subsided.

"Not a cloud in the sky," Grace observed with a chuckle.

"There will be a big cloud over you lot if you don't get the hay turned," Moira, who'd crept up on the trio, growled.

"No need to be grumpy." Grace got to her feet, brushed herself down, retrieved her pitchfork and set off down the row. Moira was right, but it was nice to have some fun. Why had Moira taken so long to get here anyway? Grace hoped she hadn't gone back to the house and Ben.

"The gunfire sounds awfully close, doesn't it?" Betsy glanced across the paddocks towards its source.

"I can't see any soldiers." Grace realised she sounded panicky. Soldiers nearby would mean Moira wasn't the only threat to Ben's safety. She took a deep breath and tried to calm herself. "Maybe the sound is just carrying on the wind," she said unconvincingly.

Moira looked at Grace with a knowing smile. Grace's glare silently warned Moira not to disclose Ben's whereabouts. She set off with her pitchfork hoping the others would do the same and forget the army manoeuvres.

By midday they had finished the first paddock and returned to the house for lunch. The aroma of fresh baking and the warmth of the coal range filled the dining room.

"I've baked you some scones," Nel said. "Half plain and half lemonade. Here's some whipped cream and blackberry jam to go with them."

"Thank you, Nel," Grace said. "I'm starving."

"And thirsty too, I hope," Nel said. "I picked some lemons and made you lemonade."

The young women tucked into the delicious food, ignoring Duncan as he shifted restlessly in the armchair beside the coal range, a well-read newspaper folded on his lap and an empty cup of tea on the side table.

"Ahem," Duncan cleared his throat.

Moira, glanced over Alice's shoulder at Duncan. She had a mouthful of food but managed a smile before she resumed eating. Duncan struggled up out of the chair, he needed to be at the table to get the information he wanted.

"How much did you get done?" he asked.

"One paddock," Grace replied. She didn't know, and Duncan didn't indicate whether that was more or less than he had expected, but Grace was proud of their efforts. "We should get the other one done after lunch."

Duncan looked out the kitchen window.

"If this weather continues, it should be dry enough tomorrow to put it into a stack," he said. "Just make one over by the barbary hedge so there is a bit of shelter from the rough weather."

"A stack? By the barbary hedge?" Grace could visualise the barbary hedge and a pile of hay beside it but how they were going to get all the grass from two paddocks into one stack she hadn't a clue.

"Is there something or someone to help us?" Moira asked.

"There's a wagon in the implement shed. Hitch it to Jess and cart the hay to where you want the stack. There are rakes in the back of the shed too. Use them to pull the hay into a pile, then fork it onto the wagon."

Grace looked at her palms. The red welts from ploughing had been aggravated by the pitchforks and a wagon and rakes didn't seem like much help at all to prevent the welts from blistering further.

"Take a ladder with you too. When the stack gets higher, one of you will need to climb up and be the crow," Duncan continued with his instructions.

"The crow?" Betsy asked.

Grace frowned. There were birds called crows, but not in New Zealand and what did they have to do with haymaking?

"The person who stands on top of the stack and spreads the hay, that the rest of you throw up," Duncan replied.

"You should do that Alice, you're the smallest." Moira made it sound like she was looking out for Alice.

"How high will the stack be?" Alice looked worried as if being on Jess was quite high enough.

"Six, eight, maybe ten feet," Duncan said. "It depends on how much hay there is, and I can't see that from in here, so I can't tell you."

Everyone could hear the frustration in Duncan's reply, and they took another mouthful of scone to quell further conversation.

When the bottom of the lemonade jug was just a collection of pips and pith, the girls thanked Nel for the delicious lunch. The sun was high in the sky, and she insisted they didn't leave the house without wide-brimmed hats to keep the sun off their faces.

"I'll just dash back to the house to grab a scarf too," Grace said. Until she was out of view, she pretended to eat the extra scone she'd taken for Ben.

Grace made certain Mrs Terrill hadn't returned unexpectedly before she ran up the stairs calling out to him.

"Ben, where are you?"

There was no sight of him. Grace was terrified that the army had already found Ben, that she hadn't done enough to save the young man. The bed had been made, not as neat as Mrs Terrill would have done, but still the covers had been pulled up. Ben's uniform sat folded on the chair where she had left it. Captain Boyle's clothes were nowhere to be seen. She searched under the bed and behind the curtains.

"It's okay Ben, it's only me."

Ben gingerly opened the wardrobe door and stepped out from amongst the hanging clothes.

"Oh, there you are." Relief washed over Grace. "What are you doing in there?'

"Have they gone?" Ben's eyes were wild with terror.

"Who?"

"I heard gunfire." He shivered and cowered back towards the wardrobe. "I heard the sergeant yelling commands."

"Duncan said it's just an exercise, they're firing blanks, not real bullets." Grace kept her voice soft and took tiny steps towards Ben. She could see his body trembling. "Are you sure you heard the sergeant? I didn't think they were that close."

Grace wanted to hold Ben, to reassure him he was safe inside.

"I need the toilet." Ben squirmed. "I've been in there a while," he admitted, heading towards the door. "I need some food as well."

"I brought you a scone." Grace held out the offering, cream, and jam oozing from between the two halves.

"Slow down, you'll choke," she warned, as he took it and hungrily devoured the scone. Grace had heard her mother's voice give the same warning repeatedly to each of her brothers. She stood and watched Ben, delighted in the memories that his presence evoked, happy memories of her family: mother, father and brothers all gathered at the dinner table reliving the antics of the day. There was always laughter and good-hearted jesting. Grace wondered if after the war they would ever gather in the same way. She hoped so.

"I've got to get back." Grace rested her hand on Ben's shoulder. He had stopped shaking. Perhaps it was lack of food and not terror that had made him tremble. She'd have to sneak more sustenance for him. "We're turning the hay. Just stay out of sight and you'll be fine."

The land girls made quick work of the second paddock, wanting to get it finished before milking so they didn't have to return in the evening.

Moving along in a steady rhythm, Betsy swung her pitchfork into the row of half-dried grass at her feet but stopped abruptly when the curved metal tines skewered more than grass and a beheaded rat carcass, its long, skinny tail waving, emerged.

Betsy threw the pitchfork away and shrieked with terror. She stepped away from the row of grass and stood rigid, afraid to move in case there were more live rats.

Grace was immediately by her friend's side; she looked her up and down but couldn't see any visible signs of the cause of Betsy's distress.

"What happened, Betsy?" she asked. "Are you okay?"

Betsy couldn't speak. She pointed to where the pitchfork lay.

"It's only a rat, Betsy, a very dead rat," Grace reassured Betsy as she bent and picked up the pitchfork. As a child, Grace had often been taunted by her brothers with rats and mice, both dead and alive; they never smelled pleasant but they held no fear for her. "It can't hurt you."

"Are you scared of a dead rat, Betsy?" Moira laughed but kept her distance. "Ooh, I wonder where its head is? Maybe it's looking for you, Betsy."

Betsy trembled.

"Oh, the poor rat," Alice said.

"Right, Betsy, you take your pitchfork over to my row," Grace instructed, knowing they needed to keep moving if they were to get the job finished. "I'll finish this one."

"My pitchfork?" Betsy whimpered.

Grace sensed the reason for her hesitation.

"Here, take my pitchfork. I'll dispose of the rat," she offered.

"Are you going to bury it?" Alice asked. "You'll need the head if you are, you can't bury it without the head."

"Oh, Alice! Don't be so silly," Moira mocked. "It's only a rat, not a human."

Grace agreed, she wasn't going to bury the rat, but she did need to find its head. With her gumboot she removed the carcass from its skewer and fossicked around in the grass with the pitchfork. Within a minute, the gruesome sight of a bloody rat's head greeted her, its bulging, vacant eyes gave no challenge. Grace skewered the body and head together and went to the barbary hedge to toss them to a thorny grave.

Chapter Nine

"Aargh," Duncan groaned. His neck was at an uncomfortable angle, his mouth ajar and the slightest drivel of saliva escaped from the corner of his mouth.******

"Serve yourself right." Nel tutted. "If you want to go to sleep in the chair instead of your comfortable bed then you'll get no sympathy from me."

Nel grabbed the poker from the coal bucket, opened the range's creaky door and stirred up the embers until there was an inkling of orange. She fed two shovel loads of coal into the box, shut the door, and opened the damper. The air inflow quickly burst the fire into life and Nel topped the kettle up with fresh water and replaced it on the top of the range.

"But ... I needed to make sure the land girls were up," Duncan said in his defence. "They were very tired last night."

"Yes," Nel replied. "But they probably had the sense to sleep in their beds, not an armchair, so they'd feel good this morning."

"I think I need to go to the paddock today," he said tentatively.

"Duncan McKnight." Nel stood with her hands on her hips. "You are not to leave this house."

"Not to work, just to supervise."

"No," she reiterated firmly. "You'll just have to ring Peter to see if he can oversee the haymaking."

Duncan hobbled back to the passage where the phone sat on a small mahogany table. The table had a seat attached but not one that encouraged anyone to sit for long. Static was all Duncan heard when he lifted the receiver and cranked the handle on the side of the Bakelite phone.

"Working?" he said to indicate his need for a clear line.

"Duncan, good morning," greeted the operator. "How are you this morning? Beautiful day, isn't it?"

Duncan ignored her idle chatter. "Could you put me through to Peter please."

There was no reply from the operator, just the three short and two long rings that would indicate to Peter the call was for him. Each house on the party line had its own distinctive ring tone but there was always the risk that people, for whom the call wasn't intended, would listen in anyway.

"Peter speaking."

"Good morning, Peter. It's Duncan here. I was wondering if I could ask your help again today?"

"I've a busy day ahead," Peter replied. "What would you be needing?"

"I'm still laid up. This back of mine. Thought I'd be alright today but can't leave the house. The hay is going into the stack but I'm not sure about these land girls."

"They seem to be managing alright so far. Don't they?"

"Well, yes," Duncan conceded.

"Do you think they are too pretty for building a stack?" Peter joked, teasing his long-time neighbour.

"No! Well, yes ... I mean no." Duncan mumbled. "I'm just not certain they have the skills to build a good stack."

"It's alright Duncan." Peter laughed. "I'll call by about eleven, check on their progress and pop in to give you an update."

"Thanks, Pete."

The telephone clicked dead; and static returned to the line.

"Peter Fraser has rescheduled this year's general election." Duncan read from the newspaper while the land girls finished up their porridge. "There'll be no election until 1943."

"It was going to be my first-time voting," Alice said.

"Well hopefully the war doesn't last until then," Nel said. "And you'll get to vote soon."

Outside, with gumboots and sunhats on, the land girls set off to build a haystack.

"I'll get Jess on the way," Alice suggested.

"Great, we'll meet you at the shed and find the rakes and cart," Grace replied.

"I wonder if Roland's ship was like the one your brothers sailed on." Betsy said. "I wish I'd been there to farewell him. He would have looked so smart in his uniform with all the others."

"I'm certain he would have," was all Grace could say to comfort her.

Moira dawdled along behind and took the opportunity to have a few puffs of the cigarette she had safely stowed in her overalls pocket.

Alice quickly put the bridle on Jess and walked her to the shed. It was Jess who neighed in disapproval as cigarette smoke drifted straight towards her. The horse snorted, cleared its nostrils of the assaulting smell, and sent a glob of snot towards Moira.

"Oh, blasted horse!" Moira looked aghast at the green slime staining her trouser leg.

"Moira, please take this," Grace said as she passed a rake to Moira, halting her chance to vent further. "I think you'd better put the smoke out before we get to the hay paddock. We don't want a fire."

"Here, take this," Moira, without any politeness, immediately passed the rake to Betsy. Moira took one last long drag and blew the smoke straight into their faces in protest. She nipped the hot end of the smoke off, stubbed it into the ground with her gumboot and placed the remainder back into her pocket.

"Where should we make the stack?" Grace asked as they approached the paddock.

"Duncan said over by the hedge," Betsy replied.

"Wherever makes for the least amount of work to move all of the hay," Moira suggested.

The four managed to finally agree on a spot beside the hedge but close to the fence dividing the two hay paddocks. Using the heavy, wooden handled rakes they created a rectangle of hay, twenty-foot long and ten foot wide.

For the next two hours the women raked and forked. Grace and Betsy raked the hay into small piles around the paddock, Moira and Alice followed with the horse and forked the piles into the cart. Then they returned to the stack and forked the hay onto the stack. It was a slow laborious process which saw the haystack steadily grow. There was little time for talk and little energy to do so. Haymaking was hard work.

The stack was about two-foot high when a truck's horn sounded.

"That must be the neighbour, Peter." Grace stopped and stretched her back as she eyed the truck being driven across the paddock.

"Hello, ladies." Peter tipped his hat. "Heard you might need a helping hand."

Grace bristled at the thought of Duncan believing they couldn't cope but welcomed the extra hands as she was feeling weary and there were still cows to milk this afternoon.

"I'm Pete and this is Bill and Fred," Peter continued as two men jumped down off the truck's tray.

"Hi, Bill and Fred, I'm Moira." Moira adjusted her scarf and smiled. "Your helping hand would be lovely," she purred.

Bill grinned, a Cheshire cat grin that indicated he'd found an entire vat of cream.

"Well, hello, Moira." He wolf whistled, took Moira's hand in his and turned it palm up, wincing at the sight of the large red welts. "It looks like we've arrived just in the nick of time. Let me save you from that rake, my dear. I'm, Bill, by the way."

Moira looked happy to surrender her rake to Bill. Grace imagined she would have been happy to surrender much more than just her implement. The sleeves on his shirt were rolled up and revealed tanned, muscled forearms and hands that weren't scared of hard work. A pipe protruded from his shirt pocket; Bill wouldn't complain about Moira's smoking. His stubbled, square jaw framed a face that was used to being outside. Crow's feet etched out from dark brown eyes. A man who smoked and laughed a lot might be just what Moira needed. Grace judged him to be in his forties, a bit older than Moira was probably used to but it didn't stop her flirting.

"Where did you spring from?" Moira asked.

"I'm Pete's neighbour, on the other side. Fred lives across the road from Pete."

"So, you own a farm?" Moira's eyes widened.

"Just a small one," Bill answered. "I hear you can drive. You drive Pete's truck and I'll load it with hay. We'll leave these others with the horse and cart."

Before anyone could object, the pair jumped into the truck and drove off to the hay on the other side of the paddock. Grace and Betsy looked at each other and shrugged their shoulders; little that Moira did surprised them.

That left five of them and the horse and cart.

"I'll direct Jess and you two can load," Alice suggested to Grace and Betsy who both nodded in agreement. Forking would be a welcome break from raking and it seemed Alice was the best at getting Jess where she needed to go.

"That leaves us Fred," Peter said, "to rake up around here and add it to the stack."

It didn't take Bill long to have the back of the truck piled high with hay. He stabbed his fork into the heap and climbed back into the cab with a broad grin.

"Right, we'll take this lot back to the stack," he said. "If you back the truck up when we get there, it'll be easier to unload."

Everyone was at the stack when they arrived; Moira had to back the truck with an audience, avoid the horse and cart and stop before she hit the stack, in case the truck's hot exhaust caused a fire in the dried grass. She gulped. The gears grated before clunking into reverse. Slowly and tentatively, she backed the truck up.

"Stop!" Fred yelled, surprising Moira who jumped on the brakes.

"Impressive!" Bill laughed and climbed out of the truck.

At lunchtime, Nel turned up with a bacon and egg pie, freshly cooked pikelets, some apples and more cold lemonade.

The food looked and smelled delicious. Everyone was ravenous so there wasn't an opportunity for Grace to put some aside for Ben.

"Are you going to the dance?" Moira asked as they all sat around enjoying their lunch.

Bill folded and stuffed a whole pikelet into his mouth and looked skyward as if expecting an answer from above.

"You should, Bill," Peter urged. "It'll be good for you."

"Yeah, Joan and I will be going," Fred added. "Get your old dancing shoes out. Bill's a bit of a twinkle toes. You should see him, ladies."

Bill smiled at his mates.

"A dance would probably do me good." He blinked, retrieved a handkerchief from his pocket and blew his nose. "But it wouldn't be the same."

Grace noticed the change in Bill, laughing one minute, quiet the next and if she wasn't mistaken on the verge of tears.

"Are you and Duncan going, Nel?" Peter asked.

"No-o-o." Nel laughed. "I'm too old for shenanigans like that and Duncan can't even walk at the moment, let alone dance. But all of these lovely ladies will be there."

"Plenty of dance partners to choose from then." Peter downed the last of his lemonade. "Thank you for a wonderful lunch, Nel. We'd best get this stack finished."

"You're most welcome, Peter," Nel replied, packing the plates, glasses, and leftovers into her basket. "Thank you for your help."

"Tell Duncan, we're building a mighty fine stack for him." Peter turned to Nel before addressing the rest of the group. "Who wants to be crow?"

"Alice does," Moira replied. "She's the smallest."

Alice scowled at Moira.

"True, it is easier if you're smaller. Are you okay with that, Alice?" Peter asked. Alice hesitated and looked at the stack which was already at head height.

"I guess so," she replied tentatively. "It's about the same height as Jess and I've managed her. I'll be able to see everything and everyone."

Alice's eyes had the same flittering movement Grace had seen the day they'd signed up for the land girls; the look that said she'd rather be elsewhere.

"Good," Peter said. "Grab the ladder will you, Fred?"

Fred rested the wooden ladder on the end of the stack and held it while Alice climbed up, cautiously, one rung at a time.

"The stalks will be slippery," Peter yelled. "Dig the fork into the hay to brace yourself."

"I wish I was this tall all the time." Alice looked around the countryside. "The view's pretty good, like a patchwork blanket of paddocks, stitched together by brown fences and green hedges and dotted with animals."

Grace almost wished she'd volunteered to be the crow. With her height she'd be able to see even more than Alice.   Even from the ground she had a clear view of the Southern Alps rising majestically but without a cloak of snow after the recent rain.

"There's a huge line of soldiers marching down the road," Alice pointed.

Grace gasped. "Are they coming here?"

"Looks like they're coming this way."

Ben. They were coming to get Ben. Grace turned towards the house, her feet itched to run and make sure he was safely hidden. She turned back, she couldn't run off, she'd have to explain and that would mean giving his presence away. She'd just have to hope he'd stay safely hidden.

"Here it comes," Fred yelled before he hoisted a fork load of hay up to the top of the stack.

With the hay, came dust. Alice sneezed. The sneeze caught her unawares and she nearly toppled over. Alice grabbed hold of the fork and held on tight. When the dust settled, she set to work spreading it out over the pile. She'd just finished when Peter tossed up a load. Then the truck was back and Bill was forking hay faster than she could spread. There was a brief respite when the truck left before the horse and cart arrived. Alice managed to straighten up, stretch her back and catch her breath.

She stood back out of the way, stabbed her fork into the stack to ensure she didn't fall over the side and dared to look down. In a short space of time the stack seemed to have grown another foot. Alice looked out over the hay paddocks to see how much still lay on the ground.

"Another couple of feet and we should be finished," said Peter, answering Alice's unspoken question.

"So, do you like to waltz or quick step?" Moira asked Bill as they drove off.

"Both," Bill forked a load of hay onto the truck. "Used to go to every dance the village hall hosted. Sometimes went into Geraldine too."

"Will they have a band at the dance?"

"Yeah, some of the locals that haven't gone off to war." Bill smiled. "They do a pretty good job. I might be able to dance but I've never got the knack of playing an instrument."

"What do they play? Oldies or modern music?"

"Both." Bill climbed back into the truck. "We'd best head over to unload."

Bill stood on the back of the truck to toss the hay; the stack was too high to reach the top from the ground. While it was unpredictable where the hay would land, Alice tried to keep to a system, building each layer progressively in a clockwise direction.

Peter glanced at his watch as Grace and Betsy arrived with the last load. It was two-thirty, just in time to get the stack finished before milking.

"Great job, everyone," Peter said. "Duncan should be pleased."

"Thanks for helping us," Grace replied as she piled the rakes and forks into the cart. "We'd better take this gear back and get on with milking."

"What about me?" Alice yelled from the top of the stack. "I can't see the ladder."

"Over here." Fred stood the ladder against the side of the stack. The highest rung was still a couple of feet below the top of the stack.

"Where? I can't see it." Alice clung onto her fork. "I don't want to get too close to the edge."

"Here, I'll help you." Fred climbed up the ladder.

"I'm scared," Alice whispered.

"Slide the fork down over the side and come over here." Fred spoke calmly, reassuringly.

Alice tried to take a step but couldn't. She started to cry.

"Sit down," Fred directed. "Good. Now crawl over towards me. It's okay, you can't fall... That's it, hands and knees. Good, nearly there... Now turn around and I'll guide you onto the ladder."

Grace couldn't see Alice but imagined her terror. She thought the tiny woman was such a contradiction. She had the strength and stamina to plough all day long but was scared of dark places and now apparently heights.

, Grace called out.

"That's it, a little bit further and you'll be on the ladder," Fred encouraged.

By now, the rest of the group had gathered.

"Almost there, Alice."

Alice edged her foot back, stretched it out, searching for the ladder.

"I've found it," she said with relief when she felt the solidity of the ladder beneath her toes.

"One rung at a time, Alice," Grace said.

The group clapped when she had hold of the ladder. Fred moved down a couple of rungs, but his body continued to shroud Alice's, ensuring she didn't fall.

"I'm right now." Alice sounded braver than she looked.

Fred climbed down and stood at the bottom, holding the ladder to ensure it didn't move. Alice methodically shifted one hand then the other, one foot then the other. At all times, at least three parts of her body touched the ladder. Rung by rung she descended until both feet were on the ground and she sighed with relief.

"Thank you," she said politely.

Grace and Betsy placed comforting arms around Alice and walked her away to Jess. Moira lingered behind.

"Bye for now." Moira farewelled the men with a smile and a sashay of her hips. "I look forward to seeing all of you at the dance."

Chapter Ten

"Where have you been, lass?" Nel asked when Betsy re-entered the kitchen looking like a drowned rat. Nel had just positioned the butter churn on the kitchen table ready to embark on the first of her rainy-day chores. "Was there bad news?" She noticed the tremor in Betsy's hand as she passed the bundle of envelopes.

"I don't know," Betsy replied quietly. A wet tendril of hair fell over her face, and she did nothing to push it away.

"Don't worry dear, everything will be fine." Nel patted Betsy on the hand. She yanked the rubber band off and flicked through each envelope. "Bill, bill, another bill. Duncan takes care of those when Captain Boyle's gone. Letter! Addressed to me!"

Nel's excitement was short-lived. She recognised the fine handwriting on the front of the envelope and it wasn't William's. She flipped the white envelope over, confirming from the return address who the sender was.

"From my sister," she explained. "It's lovely to have a letter from her but ... one from William would be better. I'll read it later."

There were more bills which Nel added to Duncan's pile. The very last envelope in the pile was brown and carried 'On Her Majesty's Service' in type written letters across the top. Nel looked at Betsy who stood quietly wringing her hands.

"Mr D McKnight," Nel read to whom the letter was addressed. "Surely it's meant for both of us. It'll be about William and I'm not going to wait for Duncan to get here."

Betsy was lost for words. She swallowed hard and wrapped her arms across her chest, giving herself a comforting hug.

Nel ripped open the envelope and scanned the contents of the single typed page.

"He's coming home! He's coming home!" Nel repeated excitedly. "Forty-eight hours leave after the first fortnight's training. I'll get my boy back. I'll have to plan a special dinner. That's the weekend of the dance, he'll be able to escort you young ladies."

She was grinning with anticipation until she looked across at Betsy's forlorn face. "Oh, I'm sorry, dear. Perhaps it will be Roland's turn next time."

"They're not going to send Roland home from the other side of the world for forty-eight hours. It'll be forever or never." A single tear ran from the corner of Betsy's eye. Never was forever.

"It's all right dear," Nel pulled Betsy into her arms and patted her back. "Did Duncan have another job for you?"

"He didn't say anything."

"Well, I've just the task when you're feeling out of sorts," Nel moved over to the butter churn, added some cream to the wooden barrel and replaced the lid into the top. "Take a coat, duck back to the house and get changed into some dry clothes. Then come back here and start turning, dear and don't stop until you've made butter."

Grace pulled the door to Captain Boyle's room shut and turned to walk across the landing.

"Who are you talking to?" Betsy asked coming up the stairs to change.

"What? Who?" Startled and looking as guilty as she felt, Grace stumbled over her words. "No-one. No-one here but me."

"What were you doing in Captain Boyle's room then?"

"I wasn't." Grace didn't like lying to her friend. "Well … umm, I thought I heard a noise. I just looked in but there's nobody there. Must have been the army exercises outside."

"Grace. The army have hunkered down in this rain. I know that look. You're hiding something."

"Never mind. You've got enough of your own worries. Look at you. You're soaked. And … and you've been crying. What's happened? We'd better get you changed."

Grace opened the door to their shared bedroom and disappeared inside, forcing Betsy to follow.

"Here you are," Grace grabbed a clean shirt from Betsy's drawer. "Put this on."

"Grace! I'm twenty-two." Betsy took the shirt. "Thank you, but I can dress myself."

"You don't want to catch a chill." Not like Ben. It had been his sneeze that had earlier drawn Grace into Captain Boyle's room. That and the piece of toast and jam, all she'd been able to take at breakfast without looking suspicious. It clearly wasn't enough. Lack of sustenance on his days on the run and sleeping out in the open had taken its toll on Ben. He'd caught a cold. Grace planned to get some lemons off the tree and make him a hot drink with honey. She thought she'd check the liquor cabinet in the lounge. A nip of whisky would be good for Ben too. That's what her mother would have done when she or her brothers succumbed to winter bugs. It was the only time she condoned the consumption of alcohol. "Now, tell me what's made you cry."

"William has forty-eight hours leave. The same weekend as the dance. Nel's so excited."

"I thought you'd be happy about that too." Grace tried to keep Betsy talking. "Why tears?"

"The last time Roland had forty-eight hours leave I looked as happy as Nel too. He'd given me this ring." Betsy fondled the small gold band on her finger and continued wistfully. "He said it was a declaration of his eternal love. We didn't have time to make it official. He promised we would do that as soon as he got home. We went to a hotel in the city. Booked in as Mr and Mrs Flavell. The concierge didn't question us." Betsy blushed. "Those forty-eight hours, Grace, they were the most beautiful two days of my life." She closed her eyes and inhaled deeply. "I can still feel him, taste him, smell him. Surely it's not asking too much for Roland to come back to me."

Grace wrapped her arms around Betsy, like a mother bird sheltering a hatchling beneath its wings. She absorbed the sobs that shook Betsy's body. She wanted to reassure her everything would be alright but no-one could make promises like that. There was no set date that the fighting would finish and everybody would return home. No guarantee that anybody would return home, only wishful thinking. That thought tightened her resolve to protect Ben. To save him from having to go where Roland and her brothers had already gone. Grace waited until Betsy's breathing had calmed before she spoke.

"You like William though?"

"Yes," Betsy replied. "But I'm engaged to Roland."

"I know that Betsy, and I'd never suggest you be anything other than faithful to Roland. Just let William be a friend who makes you happy. Surely there is no harm in that."

Betsy broke away from Grace's embrace and dried her eyes on the clean shirt.

"I guess you're right." Betsy stood, inhaled long and slow, pulled her shoulders back and exhaled to release all her worries. "I'd better finish getting changed. Apparently, I've got some butter to make."

Achoo!

Betsy's head popped up, she stared at Grace, her wide eyes asked the unspoken question – who sneezed?

Achoo!

"That wasn't you," said Betsy. "Moira and Alice aren't here, neither is Mrs Terrill."

She headed for the door, seeking the source. Betsy stopped on the landing and waited. Grace followed; she had no choice. If Ben sneezed again, he'd be found, and Grace would have to convince Betsy not to dob him in.

A third sneeze echoed from Captain Boyle's room. It was like three strikes and you're out. Betsy didn't knock, she stormed into the room.

Pillows had Ben propped up in the bed, the flannelette pyjama top he wore, hung loosely, its vertical stripes almost prison issue but in shades of grey. His eyes were glassy, his nose red and his face prickly with regrowth.

Betsy gasped, stopped in her tracks, and stood motionless; mouth agape as she pondered the sight. "Captain Boyle," she said. "Excuse me for barging in. I didn't realise you were home. You don't sound well, sir."

Ben looked from Betsy to Grace and nodded in affirmation. He wasn't well.

It was a natural assumption for Betsy to make. She hadn't met Captain Boyle and hadn't seen his portrait. Grace considered continuing it, adding to the lie to keep Ben safe but the implications whirred through her mind like a movie: Betsy would tell the McKnights, Duncan would insist on seeing Captain Boyle, Mrs Terrill would want to care for her employer. That lie couldn't continue. Grace would have to make Betsy a party to the secret, complicit in the concealment of Ben. She hoped the look she gave Ben, reassured him he would still be safe.

"He's not Captain Boyle," she said.

"Who are you then?" Betsy folded her arms across her chest. "What are you doing in here?"

"His name is Ben," Grace said. "He's unwell and needs our help."

Betsy slowly nodded as she assessed the information. She scanned the room, saw the discarded clothes on the end of the bed and a neatly folded uniform on the chair.

"Are you from the army? A returned soldier?" Betsy moved in closer to the bed and studied Ben. "You aren't one of Grace's brothers, I'd recognise them."

Defeat was creeping up on Grace. She'd have to disclose Ben's secret to her best friend and trust Betsy would help. She was about to do so when a noise on the stairs caught her attention.

"Well, well," Moira said. "What are we up to in here?"

She came into the bedroom with Alice in tow. At the sight of four women, Ben pulled the blankets up until his baby-blue eyes peeked gingerly over the top.

"Oh, you're not looking so good, Ben," said Moira. "Grace isn't doing that great a job of mothering you, is she?"

"You know about Ben?" Betsy asked.

"Yes." Moira didn't say 'of course' but she meant it. "Grace's runaway soldier she's trying to save."

"The runaway soldier that was in the newspaper?" Alice added to the flurry of questions.

"Possibly," Grace conceded.

"You don't look very well," Alice said. Another sneeze caught Ben by surprise and droplets showered the bed cover.

Moira jumped back. "Well, I for one, don't want to catch your bugs so we'd better get you better and on your way." She turned to leave.

"Where are you going?" asked Grace, anxious that they were going to surrender Ben to the authorities.

"To the sitting room. A dose of whiskey will help kill the bugs and I just happen to know where there's a ready supply."

"And I'll go get some lemons from the orchard," Alice said.

Grace began to relax. Alice's offer to help made her complicit in the crime whether she was aware of it or not. Grace inhaled and looked across at Betsy, her wide eyes asking the unspoken question, would Betsy help or hinder?

Long silent seconds ticked by while Betsy looked from Ben to Grace and back to Ben. Grace could imagine the questions that would be whirling through Betsy's thoughts; she'd asked and tried to answer them all herself, over and over. In the end it was literally a matter of life and death and she'd chosen life.

Eventually, unable to wait any longer, Grace said, "Well?"

"I'd be devastated if Roland was in the same position, not that he would be, but if no-one offered to help him then it would be a precious life destroyed. There is enough of that happening without my help."

"So?" Grace asked. "You'll help us hide Ben?"

"I don't really have a choice, do I."

Grace hoped that was a statement and not a question.

"I'll go and put the kettle on and have a look in the cupboard for some honey."

"Thank you, Betsy." Grace pulled her friend into a hug.

"Then I'd better go and churn the butter."

"You won't say anything to Nel, will you?" Grace believed Nel would agree with what they were doing but the more people that knew of Ben's presence, the riskier it became.

"No, I'll keep your secret, Grace."

Ben quietly watched as his fate was decided. When Betsy left the room, he finally lowered the bedcovers.

"Perhaps I should just go," he said. "I don't want to get anyone into trouble."

"No!" The word had left Grace's mouth before she could tone down its forcefulness. "No," she repeated in a softer, more rational voice. "We need to get you well first, otherwise you'll be caught for sure."

Grace had never given up nursing a sick or injured animal until it either recovered or died. She wasn't about to stop caring for Ben, if he didn't recover and was caught and court martialled, he might as well die.

"Here we are." Moira was back with a crystal decanter and a matching whiskey tumbler. She poured a generous amount into the glass and passed it to Ben. "Get that down you and you'll be right in no time. It'll burn the bugs off your throat and put hairs on your chest."

Did Ben have hairs on his chest? Grace's eyes lowered. The flannelette pyjama top was buttoned up and failed to answer the question. Why was Grace even interested in whether Ben's chest was hairy? The answer had no relevance to his health but she couldn't stop the images that played through her mind like a stilted movie. She pictured all of the men in her life that she had seen without their shirts. There weren't many but the hairless chests appealed far more than those where even a smattering of short curly strands grew. She hoped the old-wives' tale wouldn't ring true.

Ben's cough brought her back to reality. The whiskey reddened his cheeks and made his eyes water. Grace stepped around Moira and patted his back.

"There, there, you'll be alright." She sounded like her mother again but that was better than thinking about Ben half naked.

"This will help sooth your throat." Alice returned and handed Ben a cup. "It's the biggest cup I could find, full of lemon juice, warm water and honey. I can get more honey if it's too sour."

When the coughs no longer wracked Ben's body, he took the cup from Alice and sipped the remedy.

"I got an egg too. How do you like yours done? I'll go and cook it up."

Grace was grateful for Alice's enthusiasm but worried she'd gone too far.

"Won't Nel miss the egg?" she asked.

"I'll just say there were only three."

It was another lie to add to the growing list. An egg would be good though; easy for Ben to eat and it would give him some much-needed protein.

"Poached would be great," Ben said between sips. "On toast if you could."

Grace sighed with relief as Alice departed for the kitchen again. Keeping Ben safe and healthy was going to get easier with the land girls united in the cause.

"Anything unusual to report?" Duncan asked as they were finishing dinner that night.

It was a routine question but each of the land girls froze, mouths open, forks suspended mid-air as a red flag of guilt coloured their faces.

Silent seconds ticked by while Grace gathered her wits and cleared her throat.

"Why would there be anything unusual?" she squeaked.

If Duncan had noticed the high pitch of her voice, he didn't react.

Grace looked at the other land girls one by one, conveying a silent message for them to stay quiet. Alice fidgeted nervously, her mouth agape as if she was about to confess all. With her finger on her fork, Grace raised both in front of her mouth and ssshed as quiet as she could.

"No reason," replied Duncan. "Sometimes animals can get caught out with the changeable weather. We just need to be more alert and rescue anything that's got itself into trouble."

Grace smiled. That's exactly what she was doing.

"We'll be sure and keep an eye out, won't we girls?"

They all nodded in agreement.

"It's hard work looking after ev-er-y-thing." Moira smiled at Grace as she took another piece of bread and piled it high with vegetables. "I'll take a snack for later, if you don't mind, Nel?"

"Me too," Alice added, nodding enthusiastically.

"Certainly, ladies," Nel replied. "You take as much as you like. Duncan, are you working these ladies too hard?"

Betsy and Grace each made a sandwich as well. Ben was going to have more food than he could eat.

"Well, Nel," Duncan seized the opportunity to vent. "If you stop insisting that I stay at home and rest, then I'll be able to take a man's share of the load."

Chapter Eleven

Duncan declared his back was better, he got the seed sown and then insisted that the sheep needed to be drenched. He, Grace and Patch set off in the truck to round the sheep up and herd them into the yards while Moira and Betsy milked the cows and Alice fed the pigs.

It hadn't rained for a few days now and the free draining ground had a thin slither of dust which the sheep's hooves rustled into a low-lying cloud. Packed into the yards, their bleating had a sense of dread as if a memory lodged in the brain said nothing good came of being in the yards. The combined cacophony pierced the country air.

Duncan whistled and yelled, ordering the dogs this way and that. If they couldn't get around the herd or through the wooden fences, they would clamber over the top of the sea of wool, drools of saliva swinging from their jaws. Grace wasn't exempted from Duncan's orders either. It was as if his frustration at being couped up in the house was exploding.

"Shut the gate," he yelled at her when the dogs had chased the last of the ewes through.

The sheep pushed back; not wanting to be confined without food, they sought to escape the pens. Grace had to lean on the gate, with her hip she held it closed long enough to be able to slip the iron hook through the catch.

The last of the lambs to be weaned had sneaked in with the ewes so it was necessary to run the flock through the race and separate them out. Duncan didn't trust Grace to know which was which, so he stood at the gate to draft the lambs into a separate yard while she chased them up.

"Can you whistle?" Duncan asked.
Grace gave her best wolf whistle.
Duncan shook his head.
"Not like that, the dogs won't move to that. Like this." Duncan demonstrated two short shrill whistles and the dogs barked in response.

Grace tried to emulate but only a weak hiss escaped her lips.

"Have a look in the woolshed. There should be a shepherd's whistle hanging on a nail by the light switch."

The woolshed door creaked as Grace turned its rusty handle. The smell of sheep, wool, excrement and stale sweat filled the space where light filtered in through cobweb covered windows and nail holes in the corrugated iron walls. The wooden grating floor, worn smooth by the trampling of hooves over many years and oiled by the lanolin from the sheep's wool, revealed some of the flock who'd sought shade underneath. Their bleating echoed around the empty building. Grace scanned the area searching for the light switch. It was on the wall beside the shearing platform and she retrieved the whistle hanging beside it.

Back out in the sunlight, shepherd's whistle in her mouth, Grace practised two short whistles. The dogs responded. It worked. She smiled and took her place at the back of the yards. It didn't take long to run the rest of the sheep through, and the small yard then held some thirty lambs.

"We'd better dock this lot while we're here," Duncan said. "The rest of last year's lambs have already been done; these are just the tail enders. You wait here, and I'll get the elastrator."

Grace had no idea what an elastrator was, but she did as Duncan said, and waited by the lambs. While the lambs wriggled their tails, her thoughts wandered to Ben. He seemed to be occupying her every spare moment. The whiskey and the lemon and honey had worked and between the four of the land girls, they'd been able to sneak a lot more food. Grace sensed his growing restlessness but the terrifying sound of gunfire and the rumble of tanks was keeping him housebound. Mrs Terrill had come and done her cleaning, thankfully not in Captain Boyle's room so Ben had gone undetected. If they needed to move him, the woolshed looked like a viable option.

Duncan returned to stand on the other side of the fence, the elastrator in one hand and a jar full of green rubber rings in the other.

"Right," he instructed as he put one of the rings on the prongs of the elastrator. "Pick a lamb up from behind, hold it under its front legs and rest its butt on the fence, I'll do the rest."

The first lamb bounded away from Grace. She tried again thinking she would grab a handful of wool, but the wool was too short, and the lamb slipped through her fingers. Third time lucky she thought as she grabbed at the lamb closest to her. She wrapped her arms around its middle, but it kicked, bleated in her ear and squirmed its way free.

"We'll be here all day at this rate," Duncan said. "Here, swap places."

Grace detected his annoyance and quickly climbed the fence to take the elastrator. With the skill gained over many years Duncan easily caught a lamb. He held it on the top rail of the fence, one arm around its chest, the other spreading the lambs back legs and holding its tail.

"Now, squeeze the handles of the elastrator, that will stretch the rubber ring. Hold the handles tight and then thread the tail through the ring." Grace did as she was told. "That's right. You'll feel in the tail, three joints from the anus. Let the handles go and release the ring so it stays at the third one. That'll leave the lamb with sufficient tail to prevent issues."

Grace didn't know what issues the de-tailing would prevent but did as Duncan said and released the rubber ring. The lamb bleated loudly and kicked out. A thump to Grace's belly expelled any remaining thoughts of Ben. She needed to concentrate, or she'd be losing a limb as well.

Duncan dropped the lamb in the next pen so he could grab another one. It jumped this way and that, trying unsuccessfully to free itself from the tightness around its tail. The lamb sat down, bleated, stood up, bleated again and unable to find relief in either position, flopped down on its side in the corner of the pen.

"It'll be alright soon," he said. "When the blood supply to the tail is cut off by the rubber, the end of the tail will die and fall off. It usually only takes a week."

The next lamb Duncan grabbed was a ram lamb, so it wasn't just the tail that needed ringing.

"We'll need to do these too," he advised, holding the two testes between his fingers.

Grace imagined her brothers' quips about rendering a poor male sexless. She tried to convince herself it was just a lamb and wouldn't feel a thing,. She closed her eyes and wondered if she could do it without looking.

"Ouch!" Duncan yelled. "The sheep, not me, you, stupid woman."

"Sorry... sorry... didn't mean to," Grace apologised. "I'll hold the lambs, you do this."

Grace put the elastrator on the fence post and jumped back into the pen. She took the lamb from Duncan and held it tight, almost in a comforting cuddle. She closed her eyes as Duncan carried out the deed. She said a silent sorry to the lamb as she placed it in the other pen.

"You think this is bad, when I was a lad, we'd nick the scrotum with our pocketknives and rip the balls out with our teeth." Duncan laughed at the memory. "Mountain oysters they were called – a fine delicacy when fried up."

Grace was grateful her brothers hadn't forced that treat on her. She'd never enjoyed oysters from the sea, and she had no plans to try mountain oysters any time soon. To her relief the next half a dozen lambs were ewe lambs.

"We'll leave the lambs here overnight."
Duncan put the lid back on the jar of
rubbers. "They won't be able to reach
the ewes for a feed, but they'll be able
to hear them. Less stress that way. In a
couple of days, we'll come back and put
the sheep through the trough."

The drenching trough was to the side
of the yards, sheltered by a barbary
hedge. It was more like a drain than
a trough, wide enough for a single
sheep and about twenty-foot long with
a concrete ramp at either end for entry
and exit. Some of last week's deluge
still sat in the bottom of the trough.
The woolshed's water tank had enough
to fill the remainder and Duncan had

come over early morning to set the hose running. It would take a few hours to fill to the depth required. Drenching entailed the sheep swimming the length of the trough to ensure they were sufficiently doused.

When Duncan returned home for breakfast, the land girls were already enjoying Nel's hearty porridge and chatting excitedly.

"The dance is next weekend," Moira reminded the group. "Has everyone worked out what they are going to wear?"

"Unlike you, I only brought a couple of dresses with me," Grace replied. Grace had spent most of her childhood in hand-me-down shorts and trousers. It wasn't until she started work, that dresses became her normal attire. "One of those will do."

"What about you, Alice?"

"I'm not sure that I'll go," she replied.

"Oh, you have to go Alice," Moira said. "You can't stay on the farm all the time."

"I can fix a dress up for you, if that is what you need," Grace offered.

"And William will be home to escort you all there and back." Nel's excitement at the return of her son, if only for a little while, was growing with each passing day. "I'll cook you all a special tea and Duncan won't growl."

Duncan's brooding look gave Nel an answer.

"I'll see," was all Alice chose to say.

"What about you, Betsy?" Moira asked. "I know your dear Roland won't be there, but you can't hide away in a closet until he returns. A girl is allowed to have a little fun."

"I'll see." Betsy opted for the same noncommittal reply as Alice.

Moira shrugged her shoulders.

"Well, I have a beautiful floral dress with a flared skirt which billows out when I'm swinging around the dance floor on the arm of a man. I plan to finish the farm chores early, soak in a long hot bath to get rid of these smells." Moira sniffed at her hands before continuing. "I'll paint my finger and toenails and curl my hair. You mightn't care but I intend to be the belle of the ball."

"Women," Duncan muttered and shook his head. "Such a kafuffle you make of a simple dance." He kept his head down and quietly ate his porridge.

By the time everyone arrived at the woolshed after breakfast, the trough had sufficient water for Duncan to add the bluestone and nicotine sulphate which would kill any sheep parasites. He sprinkled the granules on top of the water and as they soaked in, the drench turned its tell-tale blue.

"Moira, do you think you can take the truck and make sure all the gates are set up to let the sheep into the paddock next to where we put them the other day."

Moira saluted Duncan with a big smile on her face and was gone before he could change his mind.

"Grace and Betsy, stand beside the trough and use these to push the sheep along." Duncan, had retrieved two long wooden handled tools from the woolshed. "Keep the sheep down in the drench so they get fully dosed."

Grace and Betsy nodded and took up position beside the concrete walls of the trough.

"Alice, you can stand at the end and open and shut the gate." Duncan pointed to the gate at the far end of the trough. "Don't let the sheep out unless they're all drenched. We'll need to put them back through if they aren't covered from head to toe."

Duncan waited until Alice was in position before he opened the gate to the first pen. The sheep, who had been without food for a couple of days now, were eager to escape and dust swirled into the air as they jostled for position in the race. Duncan let them through, one at a time into the trough. They splashed, thrashed and bleated as they realised, they needed to swim to the other end.

Bent at ninety degrees, Betsy had to stretch down to reach the sheep.

"I wonder if this is what the trenches look like," she said. "I hope they're keeping Roland safe and aren't full of water."

"Perhaps you'll get a letter again soon and he'll let you know," Grace replied. Duncan let a few too many sheep in at once and an over-enthusiastic animal tried to mount the ewe in front of it, forcing a spout of blue drench skywards. Unfortunately, Betsy's concentration was on Roland, not the sheep and she copped a chest full of the drench.

"You'd better hose yourself off," Duncan suggested. "The drench won't do you much harm, but the blue will probably stain."

"Brrr," Betsy shivered. "Teach me for not focussing on the task again. First cow poo and now this."

They stopped briefly for lunch when Nel arrived with egg sandwiches and a bowl of plums..

"Just a few plums. I picked them on the way over" she said. "They're William's favourite so I wanted to leave some for him."

"Wash your hands at the hose," Duncan said. "Don't touch your eyes if you've got drench on your hands. They'll get sore."

They were already sore thought Grace. Drenching was laborious work. She'd spent the morning with sweat running down her forehead; it merged with the dust particles stirred up by the sheep and the filth that didn't catch in her eyebrows seeped into her eyes. Trying to rub them dry only served to add more grime from the back of her hand. Grace didn't care how cold the hose water was, she poured it over her head and hosed her face clean. She relished the trickles that ran down her back and between her breasts.

"The army doesn't seem to have worn the soldiers out yet," Moira said. "I could hear the gunfire out the back of the farm."

"Are they here at Whipsnade?" Grace hoped she succeeded in keeping the panic she felt from her voice.

"I didn't see them, but they sounded as if they were fairly close."

"Twill keep them going until they are sure they know a ," Duncan said.

That was a comforting thought for those that wanted to be soldiers but not for Ben who needed the army gone so he could come out of hiding.

The group were soon back onto the job. Nel wanted to do some more baking for William, so she left them to it.

"Shall we go for a swim in the river?" Moira suggested as the last of the sheep exited the drenching trough.

"Do we have time?" Grace asked. She would love to cool off in the river. "We've still got to milk the cows."

"Just a quick one," Moira replied.

"You'll have to shut the sheep into the paddock first," Duncan reminded her "Moira, take the dogs and your whistle and chase them up the race. You did open the gates, didn't you?"

"Yes," she answered. "I'll see you girls there, just down from the house."

"Be careful," Duncan warned Grace. "The river can be deceptive; the flow is usually quite strong. I'm going home for a cup of tea. A wash in the wash-house tub will be enough for me."

"I don't have any togs," Betsy whispered to Grace when Duncan was out of earshot.

"Neither do I." Grace laughed. She was planning to swim as she always did with her brothers. "Just wear your bra and knickers. They'll soon dry out."

Alice's cringe didn't go unnoticed by Grace.

Chapter Twelve

When all the sheep had gone, the trio left the yards and headed to the river. It was cool under the shade of the willow trees lining the riverbank. The wind rustled the small green leaves of the weeping branches which dared to dangle toward the water. A small area of gravel had built up between some boulders and Grace stopped there. She removed her gumboots, her overalls and shirt quickly followed and she draped them over a boulder.

Betsy and Alice stood wide-eyed and gape-mouthed.

"Come on, you two. You look as if you've never seen a woman's body before." Grace laughed as she dipped her toe in the cool water.

"If only we had a body like yours," said Betsy, her hands on her hips she always complained were too wide.

"You have a beautiful figure, Betsy. I'm sure Roland would agree."

Betsy coloured and Grace knew she'd triggered a memory.

"And Alice, you're so petite," Grace said.

"Yes, but ..." Alice hesitated, her eyes flittered nervously, and she went quiet.

"But what?" Grace asked.

Alice bit her lips, raked a hand through her thick hair as if it was annoying her. She opened her mouth to speak, looked everywhere but at Grace and stayed silent.

"Your underwear," she eventually muttered.

"My underwear?" Grace looked down at her lace bra and silky underwear. They weren't at all practical but once she'd been professionally fitted and found them so comfortable, that was all she had worn.

"Mine are plain, sensible, practical," Alice said. "A white cotton bra and knickers that nobody would look twice at."

Grace struggled to understand how underwear, lace or otherwise, had any bearing on Alice's look of terror. She sensed something must have happened in Alice's past, something that had left her insecure and frightened. She was too tired to solve the problem now, Grace wanted a swim.

Just as Duncan had warned, the river was flowing quickly and it wasn't as clear as Grace would have liked. The rapids had stirred up the river's muddy bottom and the water was a murky shade of grey. Nor was it as warm as Grace would have liked. She edged out into the river, feeling for rocks with her feet, when she was knee-deep and the water was gushing past, Grace decided it was safer to just sit down where she was.

"I thought you were having a swim Grace, not a paddle," Moira remarked as she joined the group and began stripping off. "And you two, still fully dressed, are you too scared to get in?"

"I'm in far enough to cool off," Grace said. "The water isn't that warm."

Betsy and Alice looked at one another and shrugged. They turned their backs on Moira and Grace and gingerly began to undress.

"I don't think it's safe to go too far out, Moira," Grace warned as Moira waded out past her.

"Like most things around here," Moira said. "The water is dirty. It'll do more harm than good to my hair." Moira found a submerged boulder and sat down to let the cool water wash around her.

Eventually, Alice and Betsy dared to join them.

"It'll be time to milk the cows before you two get wet." Moira scooped up a handful of water and flicked it in their direction.

Betsy squealed and immediately sat down where she was, the water was only ankle deep, but it was enough to cool her down. Alice didn't want any more of Moira's idea of fun, so she followed suit.

The land girls spent another ten minutes soaking up the sunshine and lowering their body temperatures in the water before it was time to leave and move onto the next farming chores – cows needing to be milked and pigs needing to be fed.

Ben was standing by the window, gazing longingly at the countryside when Grace brought him a meat sandwich for dinner. He turned and smiled.

"Thank you," he said, taking a bite of the sandwich before moving over to the bed. He sat down and patted the bed beside him. "Have a seat, stay a while, please."

After the day of drenching, all Grace wanted to do was crawl into bed but Ben's baby-blue eyes implored her to stay.

"I'm going a little stir crazy confined to these four walls. Tell me what's been going on in the real world."

"We've been drenching all day, running the sheep through a trough until they're covered in blue dye. It's back-breaking work and Duncan's a hard taskmaster so the only break we got was for lunch. Then we had to milk the cows." Grace ran her hands down the sides of her torso, dreaming of a soak in a hot bath. She listened to herself moan and silently growled. Ben had wanted cheering up and all she was doing was being negative. "At least we got to go for a swim in the river in between."

"A swim." Ben licked his lips at the thought then took another bite of his half-eaten sandwich. "I might have to sneak out to the river myself."

"Not in the daytime." Grace panicked at the risk of Ben being caught. "And the river runs really fast. It's not safe to go by yourself."

"It's coming up to a full moon," Ben said. "We could go for a moonlight swim tomorrow night."

Grace heard the 'we' but wasn't sure who Ben meant, just the two of them or Ben and all the land girls. A selfish wish that it was just the two of them made Grace want to change the subject. Then she remembered; she was meant to be taking care of Ben, not dreaming about having a moonlight swim with him.

"Swimming won't be any good for your cold," she said in a motherly tone. "We should wait until you are better."

"I'm much better and will be even better tomorrow," Ben replied.

If Ben was better, then he'd be leaving. Grace wanted him well, but she didn't want him to leave. There was a tug of war between her head and her heart and neither side seemed to be winning. Grace couldn't stifle a yawn. She needled her aching shoulder muscles with her knuckles.

Ben swallowed the last of his sandwich. "Meanwhile I could give you a shoulder rub."

"A what? Oh, no, I'm okay." Grace's denial was hollow, and Ben ignored it.

He stood, nudged Grace to swivel on the bed so he was facing her back. Strands of Grace's hair had escaped the clips holding them. Ben deftly rearranged the clips so that Grace's neck was left bare. One strap from her overalls conveniently sagged down over her shoulder and Ben pushed the other to do the same. The thin fabric of her shirt wasn't a barrier to his skilful hands. He rubbed, kneaded, and probed, pushing his thumbs into muscles that resisted his touch. Eventually they surrendered and softened.

Grace closed her eyes, absorbed his touch, and fought thoughts that she had no control over, thoughts of Ben's chest, his eyes, his lips; thoughts that brought a tingling deep inside her. She sighed with contentment.

"You're more than okay," Ben said as he expertly alternated his thumbs climbing up the vertebrae in her neck. When he could no longer feel any tension, he leaned down and placed a single kiss on

Grace's neck. "Thank you for all you have done for me," he whispered into her ear.

Betsy still had the light on when Grace returned to their shared bedroom. She noticed the dreamy look on Grace's face.

"What have you been up to?" she asked.

"Oh, Betsy," Grace flopped down, lay as spreadeagled as her single bed allowed and closed her eyes against the light. "Ben just gave me the most divine shoulder rub."

"He must be feeling much better then," Betsy said. "He'll be going on his way soon."

Grace's eyes flew open. She didn't answer Betsy. Instead, she opted for a conversation in her head. One side said, yes, he is much better and he was only going to stay until he recovered, and you hardly know him so it will be fine when he leaves because you've got so much farm work to do and then when your training is finished, you'll be assigned to another farm and it could be miles from here. The retort came swift and strong – but he does have baby-blue eyes that implore you to get lost in them, there is a feeling that you can't ignore, a warmth that you haven't felt before, it's like a switch flicking on whenever you are around him and then when he touches you, well you have no explanation for the tingling sensation that starts from your heart and permeates every cell in your body.

"I think Ben and I are a bit like you and William," Grace admitted.

"Well, I'll repeat your advice back to you, Grace. Be careful, be very careful, my dear friend."

"I want to come to collect William from the train station on Friday." Nel stood with her hands on her hips and a determined look on her face.

"Oh darn, I'd forgot it was this week he was coming," Duncan said. "I guess you women won't want to do anything other than essential chores on Saturday so you can get yourselves ready for the dance. We'll have to crutch the sheep tomorrow then.

The rams are due to be put out and the ewes need to be crutched before tupping to help ensure a good pregnancy rate. We've always done it in March. A little later this year, with everything going on but it needs to be done and done now before the weather packs up. Autumn is often unpredictable in Orari. Cold snaps arrive without warning. All this rain lately, means lush, green grass which was great for feed but also good for dags."

"Ideally the sheep should be in the yards for twenty-four to forty-eight hours before crutching – to ensure they are dry and their bowels are empty," Duncan continued explaining. "Twenty-four will have to do. Grace and Moira, you seem to be pretty good with the dog and whistle, you can round the sheep up and bring them to the yards."

Grace didn't comment but she smiled. Duncan wouldn't admit it, but he had just complimented her and Moira and was going to entrust them with an important task.

Moira insisted on driving the truck and Grace conceded, knowing that she needed all the practice she could get. Fortunately, Duncan stayed back at the house so didn't see the three bunny hops the truck lurched through before they left the yard; nor the near miss when Moira nearly drove into, rather than through the gate. Grace had to grab hold of the heavy steering wheel and yank it down so the truck wheels turned sharp enough to get between the two gate posts. The trip didn't get any smoother as Moira seemed to find every rut and pot hole on the way to the paddock.

"Are you watching where you're going?" Grace asked, one hand braced on the dash and the other gripping the door handle.

"I was just thinking about the dance." Moira glanced over at Grace and hit another rut bouncing them both off the seat. "Who I'd dance with – William, Jake, Bill, Fred and Bob. I hope there will be others there too."

"If we make it to the dance," Grace said. "I'm sure you can dance with all of them."

"Jake is the best looking of them but if he's got two left feet ... well, you know what they say ..."

"No." Grace didn't want to encourage Moira, but it seemed she was unstoppable anyway. "What do they say?"

"If a man has rhythm on the dance floor." Moira giggled. "They usually have rhythm in other activities."

Grace coughed. "Pull over here," she said, grateful that they had reached the paddock where the sheep were grazing.

"William seems besotted with Betsy but when he realises, he's not going to get anywhere with her, her being engaged and all, I'm sure he'll be up for some fun." Moira stopped long enough to climb out of the truck. "And then there's Bill. If I want someone to rescue me from all of this farm work, Bill might be a better option."

"Come on, Patch." Grace had the shepherd's whistle and was ready to round up the sheep. "I can't believe you've had enough time to even think about them all. We'd better get on with this, Duncan will be waiting."

Patch barked excitedly, his tail wagging. Grace blew the whistle. It made a faint rustling sound but nothing like the command Duncan had taught her. She tried again, and the whistle squeaked. Her third attempt was successful, and Patch ran off around the perimeter of the paddock to the back of the herd.

"Well-a-go, Patch, well-a-go." Grace lowered the pitch of her voice and imitated Duncan and Patch responded with a bark, crouching on his haunches to eye up any stubborn sheep.

"Lucky, he knows what he's doing.' Moira laughed. "Because that sounds nothing like Duncan."

Grace huffed. "I'll go this way, you'd better head around that way, to make sure we get them all."

Half an hour later all the sheep had been herded from the paddock. The women, red-faced from their efforts, climbed back into the truck and followed Patch and the sheep down the track to the yards where Duncan was waiting for them.

"Right, we'll have to run them through the race again," Duncan said. "Dagging is shitty work. We don't want to have to dag anything we don't have to. You take the end gate, Grace. I'll yell yes or no.

Yes, and we put the sheep in the side pen. No, and we let them go."

Duncan had that impatient look again, so Grace was wary about asking questions. But she had no idea what 'dagging' was and was here to learn.

"What's dagging?" she asked.

Duncan did give that look, that sideways glance with a rolling of his eyes as if she was stupid.

"Sheep don't have the advantage of toilet paper," he replied sarcastically. He coughed and reminded himself he was meant to be training the land girls. "Sometimes the faeces will stick to the wool around the backside which can result in internal parasites or even worse flystrike. Hopefully, with the drenching we will have killed both, if they existed and by dagging we will help prevent future infestations. When the shit sticks to the wool it is known as a dag and when we cut them off, it is known as dagging."

Grace concluded dagging was probably worse than docking. She saw Moira look at her fingernails. She moved to the gate, hoping that Duncan would yell 'no' more times than not.

Despite having had the best sleep ever after Ben's massage, standing in the heat of the morning, it was difficult for Grace to concentrate when Duncan's instructions seemed counter-intuitive. If she heard a yes, she had to close the gate to ensure the sheep went into the side pen. If she heard a no, she had to open the gate and let them back out to the pasture. There was the odd time when she heard a 'no' and closed the gate which unfortunately just meant there were more sheep to dag.

Thursday's breakfast was hurried along by Duncan who wanted everyone at the woolshed by 8.30 a.m. He had already sharpened and oiled up the hand shears to ensure they would be straight into it.

Duncan got the dogs to bustle the first lot of sheep up the ramp and into the shed, ten into each pen behind a shearing stand and the rest into the bigger pens. He wasted no time in dragging one from the pen and onto the shearing platform to demonstrate what he wanted the land girls to do. It was a large old ewe with a backside covered in pendulums of poo. Duncan was used to the earthy aroma, the stench of digestion and decay that the dags gave off but the land girls all covered their noses.

"If you tuck one of the fore legs behind your thigh, the ewe won't be able to move," Duncan explained as he went, the ewe's head resting in his groin. "We're just crutching today so you just have to remove all of the shitty wool from around the ewe's back end. Make sure the blades are parallel with the sheep's body and be careful not to nip any of its genitals or teats. We're trying to make it easier for mating not worse."

Duncan made short work of the crutching and took the opportunity to have a close-up inspection of the ewe's important bits. He opened the gate behind him to release the sheep down a chute and back into the yards below.

"Now I want each of you to have a go. We have four sets of shears. We'll see who is the best and whoever can't manage it will have to be the rousey and collect all the dirty wool up, sort it and scoop it into the wool bags."

When Alice bent over the animal, its face was right beside hers and unblinking grey eyes taunted her. The sheep flopped to the side and Alice had to drop the shears to get it back in position. It was then a struggle to retrieve the shears. Grace and Betsy had finished their sheep before Alice had even started. Moira was taking her time;

not wanting to appear too quick nor to be last and assigned to handling the filthy wool.

"Well, Alice, it looks as if you are the rousey." Duncan jumped down off the shearing platform and set a wool sack up in the rack. "Sort through the dags, those mostly wool can go in the wool sack to be sold. The rest can be collected over here, we'll put them on the compost heap later."

So, the tasks for the morning were set. Nobody was happy. Groans of protest were muffled by dags rattling on the wood, sheep bleating at the intrusion, and the grating of metal on metal from the shears. The stench didn't improve, it pervaded the stuffy atmosphere of the shed and infiltrated the pores of the women's hands. There was no energy spare for serious conversation or idle chatter.

Duncan spent the morning helping with any feisty sheep the women couldn't manage on their own and sharpening the blades of their shears. If there were any nicks or cuts on the sheep—and there were a few—Duncan would inspect closer to confirm the damage was superficial and didn't result in the removal of a teat or something else life threatening.

He kept an eye on all the sheep while they were being crutched, looking out for any obvious deformities that would prevent or hinder their breeding. Captain Boyle always wanted to maintain a high-quality flock and

Duncan worked to ensure he met his employer's standards even if he wasn't about.

Moira refused to touch the excrement, she whipped it off with the shears and kicked it aside with her gumboots. Whenever anybody's pen was empty, she was quick to exit the shed and whistle the dogs to chase some more sheep up. Any opportunity for fresh air eagerly taken.

Alice had no such luxury; her hands now bore a green tinge and she held the bundles of dags at arms-length to limit the stench. The pile for the compost heap was steadily growing and the wool sack was half full.

Grace's height and long limbs allowed her to easily hold the sheep and operate the shears. She quickly became confident and was onto her third pen of sheep well before the others.

"What's up with this one, Duncan?" Grace asked. The udder of the sheep she'd just finished crutching and still held between her legs, was swollen and the nipples enlarged.

"Bugger!" he replied. "Looks like the ram got in early and this one is about ready to lamb, better leave her in the yards so we can keep an eye on her."

Duncan took the sheep from Grace and manhandled it back outside into a separate pen. In-lamb ewes, this far advanced, wouldn't normally be subjected to drenching and crutching.

"Nel is here with lunch," Duncan announced. "Finish the sheep you're on, wash up and get something to eat."

Duncan's voice startled Betsy.

"Aargh!" she screamed. Blood spurted from a cut on her finger.

Duncan grabbed the sheep before it had a chance to escape and finished the crutching.

"There will be some plasters in there." Duncan pointed to a cupboard mounted on the wall. "Best wash up first though, you don't want an infection."

"Over here, Betsy," Nel called from beside the tap. She rinsed the wound for Betsy and dried it on her apron. "Just a scratch, we'll put a plaster on, and you'll be fine."

"Too much blood for just a scratch," Betsy said. "Silly me, I was daydreaming about Roland again. Picturing him waiting at the altar, ready to put a ring on my finger. Now all I've got is a cut."

"Hold it above your heart, dear," Nel continued. "That'll stem the blood flow."

Betsy followed Nel's motherly instructions and the blood flow soon abated enough to get the plaster on.

"Egg sandwiches again today," Nel announced, passing around the tin to the rest of the party when they exited the shed.

Nobody cared what the sandwiches held, they just wanted sustenance and eagerly devoured the offering until the tin was bare.

"Another couple of hours and we should be finished," Duncan advised between a mouthful of tea and a bite of sandwich.

There was a collective sigh from the land girls, anguish that they had to return to crutching for another two hours but relief that it was only for two hours and no more. This wasn't a task that any of them would write home favourably about.

"Well done." Duncan glanced at his watch and noted his time estimate wasn't too far out. It was now just after three. "That's the last of them. Moira, you can take the truck and head the sheep back up to their paddock. Alice, if you get the horse, you can get the cows in for milking and then bring the cart back here for the dags to go on the compost heap by the pigsty. Grace, you can go set up the cowshed and Betsy can give me a hand to clean up the shears. No ... second thoughts, Betsy, you set up the cowshed and Grace clean the shears. We don't want any more chopped fingers."

Moira was gone before Duncan could change his mind about her task. With a whistle in her mouth, she was barely out the door before the first shrill command to the dogs was issued. They barked in reply and soon the sheep were jostling for position to be first back to the paddock.

Alice didn't move with any such enthusiasm.

"You alright, Alice?" Grace asked.

"I was hoping I'd handled the last dag but no." Alice rubbed her forehead with the back of her hand. "Now I've got to shovel them onto the cart and then again onto the compost heap. I don't think I'll have any energy to do anything after that."

Chapter Thirteen

Alice's stomach grumbled loudly. The sun was sinking down behind the Southern Alps by the time she finally made it to the compost heap with the cart laden with dags.

"Nearly finished, Jess," she said, patting the horse before she retrieved the shovel. She sat down on the small concrete wall at the end of the pigsty to rest a moment and catch her breath. She closed her eyes and rested her head and hands against the handle of the shovel.

"Thought, I heard someone," Moira said barging through the door of the pigsty with a wheelbarrow full of dirty hay from the pens. "What are you doing? There is no time for slacking off. I've had to feed the pigs and clean the sty all by myself. Again!"

Startled, Alice leapt up, she tripped on the shovel and fell face first into the compost heap.

"Serve you right." Moira dumped the wheelbarrow load and went back into the pigsty.

Alice didn't have the energy to immediately push herself up and off the heap. Combined with the odour of sheep shit, the stench of pig poo now permeated every part of her. Her tears fell freely.

Through the blur of tears, Alice caught a glimpse of pink and gold amongst the waste. Curiosity got the better of her and she sat up to get a better look and retrieve the item. Alice reached over and took hold. A small limb, half buried, came away in her hand. She recognised it – a piglet's hind leg, a dead piglet's decomposing limb cast aside without a care on the compost heap. Alice screamed and threw it away in disgust.

With a few minutes to spare before dinner, Alice ducked back over to the woolshed to check on the ewe they had left in the yards. She quietly approached the wooden railings. There were no lambs yet. The fidgety sheep walked uncomfortably around and around the small pen, stopping frequently to paw at the dirt. Tufts of wool clung to the wooden railings where the ewe had rubbed to ease her discomfort. A clear mucous discharge showed the lambing had started. Alice sat quietly in the adjacent pen to keep an eye on the proceedings.

The sheep's loud bleating woke her, just as a tiny lamb covered in afterbirth fell to the ground. The ewe quickly tended to her new-born, licking the yellowish film from its wool. With natural instincts and wobbly legs, the lamb went in search of its first feed, before the ewe had finished its ministrations.

Alice clapped her hands at the successful outcome and headed back for dinner. She'd come over later and put the sheep out into the paddock so the ewe could eat.

Moonlight lit the way for Alice to return to the sheepyards after dinner. Expecting to see one recovering ewe and a bouncy lamb she was shocked to see two lambs on the ground and a third hanging limply from the rear of the sheep. The sheep's muted bleat evidence of its waning energy. Alice hesitated at the railings for a few minutes, waiting for another contraction to give the lamb the final push it needed but the sheep just turned uncomfortably on the same spot.

Slowly, tentatively, Alice climbed the rails.

"It's okay, girl," she said quietly. Alice's clean, but stained hands, were bare and she had no gloves. Whatever she did was going to have to be done without protection. "Never mind, I can't let the lamb die."

Alice delicately reached for the end of the mucous, wrapped her fingers around the slimy fluid and pulled it away from the lamb's tiny face. As she had watched Duncan do with a piglet, she put a finger in the lamb's mouth and ensured it was clear and then did the same with the small nostrils. When no further contraction came, Alice put two hands on the lamb's shoulders and gently pulled downwards. The small bundle fell with a thud to the trampled earth.

Alice stepped back to the railings, expecting the sheep to tend to her offspring. However, it was the two healthy lambs who stood, latched onto her bulging udder, and bunted to encourage the milk flow. The ewe ignored the lifeless third lamb. Alice picked it up, oblivious of the bloody placenta. As Duncan had done with the piglet, she blew breath into the lamb's mouth and gave its chest a slap. She watched for movement. Nothing. Alice desperately tried again, three breaths and a slap, three breaths and a slap.

"Come on, little lamb, you can do it," she encouraged, searching for any sign of life.

She repeated the three short breaths and a slap. The tiny lamb tried to lift its head but was too weak. Alice watched the small chest rise and fall; it was shallow breathing, but it was breathing. The lamb was alive.

"You need a drink don't you, little lamb and I don't think your mum is going to be any help with that."

Alice scraped the placenta off with her hands then cradled the little animal in her arms.

"I'll keep you warm," she said. "Duncan will know what to do."

"I've got a new lamb." Alice stood in the washhouse and called out to Duncan who was sitting in his armchair listening to the nightly war report on the radio. "It needs a drink. Shall I get some cow's milk?"

"Why isn't the new lamb getting milk from its mother?" Duncan asked. "I hope you haven't removed it from the ewe unnecessarily. We don't have time to interfere with Mother Nature around here."

"It's the one in the yards, she's got two others as well," Alice explained. "I found this one, nearly dead, I resuscitated it, like you did with the piglet, and it survived but it's not very strong. If only we could feed it."

"Very well then." Duncan conceded. "We have no choice, the sheep wouldn't take the lamb back now, not with your smell all over it. Bring it inside by the coal range. Nel will get you some milk powder and a bottle."

Alice kicked her gumboots off and came through into the kitchen.

"What have you got there, Alice?" Nel asked as she wiped her hands on her apron.

"I've got a new lamb. It needs a drink." Alice looked down at the little lamb to check that it was still breathing.

"Oh, it is a little 'un." Nel inspected the bundle in Alice's arms. "We keep a box with some hay on hand. It's in the washhouse cupboard with the bottle and teat. I keep the milk powder in here. We don't want the mice getting into it."

Nel put the box in front of the coal range and busied herself making up a bottle of milk. She dribbled milk on the inside of her wrist to test its heat and added a little cold water to cool it. She reached out to take the lamb. Alice clutched the lamb tighter.

"I'll just feed it first," she said.

"Is the ewe dead?" Nel asked.

"No," Alice replied. "There are two other lambs, the ewe rejected this one."

"Hope you know what you've got yourself in for." Nel tested the milk again and handed the bottle to Alice. "That should be right now, dear, give the mite a drink."

Alice offered the rubber teat to the lamb as she cradled it in her arms.

"Oh, you can't do it like that dear, the milk will go into its lungs, and it will drown." Nel took the bottle back. "Put the lamb in the box so it's sitting up. Rest it on the side of the box if it's too weak."

"I can't kill it." Alice looked horrified. "I've got it this far."

She followed Nel's instructions, took back the bottle and soon had the lamb suckling on the teat.

"Not too much for its first feed. Better to be little and often when they are first born," Nel continued. "Just watch its stomach, when it starts to bulge, you'll know it's had enough."

Just as Nel had said, the lamb's stomach which had been concave quickly bulged out. Alice removed the bottle and sat it down on the floor. The lamb lay its head on the hay and dozed off.

"You're a right Florence Nightingale, aren't you?" Duncan observed from the comfort of the chair.

"I don't think so, it's just a little lamb," Alice said, colouring from head to toe.

"Well, Doctor Doolittle then, prefers animals to humans."

Alice nodded in agreement.

"When will it need feeding again, Nel?"

"It will let you know, my dear," Nel replied. "Probably four-hourly for the first couple of days and then four times a day for a couple of weeks. It is a bit of a commitment I'm afraid."

"That's okay, I don't mind."

"You may do, by the time it's weaned." Duncan laughed. "I've lost count of the number of orphan lambs we've had to mother over the years.

"Don't tease, Duncan," Nel chastised. "You'd better clean up, dear."

Alice gave an apologetic look to Nel and exited to the wash house to clean up the remnants of birth stuck to her hands and clothes.

Chapter Fourteen

With her towel tucked under her arm, Grace was as ready as she would ever be to go for a night-time dip.

"Ben and I are going for a swim."

"I thought he had a cold." Betsy didn't look up from the shoe box of letters she cradled in her lap.

"He's feeling much better." Grace believed Ben despite his still frequent use of a hankie. "Did you want to come, Betsy?"

"No, thanks, I don't want to be your gooseberry."

Grace winced at the bite in Betsy's reply. "Are you angry with me?"

"No, but I do think you are setting yourself up for heart break." Betsy sighed as if the weight of the world was on her shoulders. "Who am I to stop you from doing that? I have enough of my own. I'll just stay here and re-read Roland's letters."

"I won't do anything silly, Betsy, I promise."

"Sometimes, Grace, lust makes us do things we have no control over."

"I'll see if Moira or Alice want to go." Grace thought having a chaperone might please Betsy.

Moira was in her room tending to her fingernails, or what was left of them after the day of crutching.

"Are you up for a swim, Moira?"

"I haven't got time for swimming," Moira groaned. "No man will be attracted to a woman with farmer's hands. I have to salvage what I can before the dance."

"Do you know where Alice is?" Grace asked.

"She's off rescuing some sick lamb. What is it with you two? She's rescuing animals, you're rescuing soldiers? I just want someone to rescue me."

Grace ignored the question and went to get Ben. Secretly, she was glad she had him to herself.

"I'll just do a final check," she said directing him to wait in the back porch. "You wait here."

She waited until Alice's tiny silhouette disappeared into the farmhouse and then whispered that the coast was clear.

The moon hung suspended between the stars lighting up their path across the lawn. They crept behind the camelia bushes in the garden, and wove in and out of the fruit trees in the orchard. Grace checked there was no-one at the illuminated windows of the farmhouse to see them as they snuck past to follow the track down towards the river. Ben's ankle had healed so they made quick work of the short walk, staying quiet until the rushing water camouflaged their voices.

"It's so great to be outside," Ben said. Eager to be in the water, he wasted no time in stripping off his shirt.

Grace couldn't help but notice the spattering of hair on Ben's chiselled chest. There was a fine, dark trail that led down to his waistline. She sucked in a breath and turned away. Despite the light breeze that brought a coolness from the south, she could feel her body temperature rising. She wanted to imagine where the trail of hair led but she needed to follow Betsy's advice and be careful.

She removed her shirt, folded it carefully and lay it across a dry rock. When Grace looked up, it was Ben's naked back that faced her. He'd rolled up his discarded clothes and was ready to get into the water. His white buttocks, untouched by the sun, glowed in a shimmer of moonlight. Grace stood, mesmerised by his physical presence. He wasn't as big as her brothers in stature. Anatomically he was the same but he was different. He wasn't her brother.

"Ahem," Ben turned, holding his hands over his groin, he smiled at Grace. "Are you coming in or are you going to stand there all night?"

Grace blinked and went scarlet from head to toe. She hoped the moonlight wouldn't reveal her mortification at being caught out.

"Yes, you go in, I'll join you soon." She turned her back to Ben, undid her trousers and stepped out of them. She was grateful to have her lace undergarments and could now understand Alice's reaction. Lace was glamourous; plain, white and practical was dowdy and now was not the time to be looking anything less than beautiful. But should she remove them and swim naked like Ben? Betsy's warning echoed in her ears—sometimes lust makes us do things we have no control over. Grace left her bra and knickers on and carefully picked her way across the rocks to join Ben in the river.

Standing on the rocks at the edge of the water, she didn't feel cold, but goose bumps peppered her arms and prickled her limbs and torso. Ben was submerged up to his shoulders, about ten foot from the river's edge. Even in the semi-darkness Grace could feel his eyes on her as she dipped her toe into the water.

"Oh! It's a bit chilly," she squealed. It was a lie; the water was bloody freezing. Grace was torn, she wanted to be in the river with Ben, but the thought of her warm clothes held her in limbo.

"Bracing," Ben said. "Makes you feel alive. Come on, you'll get used to it."

Grace wasn't sure she'd get used to anything when Ben was around. She slowly edged her way into the river, feeling the riverbed with her feet, wrapping her toes around the stones, one step at a time. She sucked in a breath as the water level rose up her body, puckering her skin into a mass of goose bumps. She felt her nipples harden and imagined they'd be visible through her bra. Swimming had been much easier with the girls in the light and warmth of the sun.

She was nearly beside Ben when a rock moved unexpectedly. Grace lost her footing and fell forward. She waited for the impact, her body smashing against the rocks, but it never came. Instead, Ben's arms wrapped around her and pulled her into his chest.

When Grace dared to open her eyes, Ben's face was inches from hers.

She was rendered speechless by the intensity of his gaze; she closed her eyes to surrender to whatever came next. He brushed his lips against hers, lightly as if testing the taste. Grace hoped he liked it, she wanted more. Her lips parted in anticipation.

Gunfire pierced the night. Amplified by the still of the evening and echoing against the riverbanks it sounded as if Grace and Ben were caught in a volley. Ben went rigid, his eyes wide with fear. His arms, that moments before had held Grace protectively were now thrashing about in the water as he spun left and right, searching for the source of the noise.

"What the hell?" Ben sunk down into the cold water until only his head and the whites of his eyes were visible.

"It'll be the army doing a night exercise." Grace sought to bring some calm.

"They haven't done one before." Ben's retort came as quick as his breathing. "What if they know I'm here? What if they're looking for me? Trying to scare me out of hiding."

Ben looked terrified. Grace couldn't let him surrender. All of her efforts to save him would be for nothing if he gave into his panic. She put her hands on his shoulders, hoping her touch would be enough to return him to a rational state. Eventually his eyes ceased their anxious flitting and settled on her.

"We'd better head back," she suggested. "We'll creep back the way we came, and nobody will know."

From over to their left an indiscernible command was bellowed into the night. It was delivered with force but at a volume that indicated the army exercise was some distance away and in the opposite direction from the house.

"They're over there a way." Ben pointed and then crept towards the opposite riverbank. "Stay low and follow me."

When the water was too shallow to conceal them, he hunched down and scampered across the rocks, grabbed his clothes, and ran to the cover of a willow tree whose weeping branches provided a curtain behind which they quickly dressed.

It was as if Ben had become the soldier he didn't want to be, the fear was banished and a steely demeanour fixed upon survival had taken its place. He took command and manoeuvred back through the orchard. A morepork cooing into the night was nearly their undoing as they left the safety of the last apple tree and tripped on a tree root. They crouched down, regrouped their thoughts and listened to ensure no-one bar the cheeky nocturnal bird was about. They crept into the garden with stealth, lingering in the shadows only long enough to ensure the path was clear.

Ben didn't speak again until they were safely back in the house.

"That was bloody stupid," he growled.

Grace placed her hand on his arm. The aura of the kiss was lost but she didn't want everything to be gone.

"It will be alright," she said. "Nobody saw us."

"But how could I risk everything for that." Ben's head hung low as he shook it from side to side. "I'd better get back up to the room and stay out of sight until I can leave."

Grace watched his back as he disappeared up the staircase. She too shook her head, thinking perhaps Betsy was right.

"Oh, William. It's so lovely to have you home." Nel was wedged between Duncan and William in the front seat of the truck for the trip home from the train station. Her eyes welled up when she saw William step down off the train in his full uniform: khaki trousers with the straightest of creases, a jacket with four large pockets and belt, and a side cap. "You look so grown up in your uniform."

"Don't get too excited, dear, it is only for the weekend." Duncan tried to temper Nel's enthusiasm.

Nel gave her husband a sideways glance, ignored his comment and kept chatting to her only son.

"So, tell me all about it, what is it that you do at training camp? Where do you sleep? Do they feed you well? Who does your washing? Have you made any new friends? Did you eat all the biscuits I gave you? I've baked some more."

"Mum," William laughed. "One question at a time."

"Well, what do you do at training camp?

"We march a lot, around the field, in full uniform, packs on our back, rifles on our shoulders, sun or rain, we march."

"What good is that going to do you? Fancy making you do that in the rain." Nel tutted. "Don't those officers know you could catch a chill."

"It's training for when we go overseas. Who knows what the weather will be like?"

"Have you fired a gun yet, son?" Duncan asked.

"Only at targets, nothing else. Every day we have to strip them right down and reassemble them. We have to know how to keep the guns in good condition in the battle fields."

Nel went quiet. The reality of war was suddenly much closer to home.

"There's a dance tomorrow night in the Orari hall," Nel said to change the subject. "You will be going, won't you? The land girls need an escort and I've offered your services."

"Betsy, Alice, Grace and Moira," William recited their names. "So, how are the land girls going?"

"Your father, the silly man, you know how he hurt his back, well he had to have a few days lying flat in bed and the girls managed fine, they even got the haystack built."

William wolf whistled. "That's impressive."

"Ahem," Duncan interjected. "They did have help from Peter, Bill and Fred and they had had a week of teaching by a very good trainer."

"Oh, Duncan, you won't admit it, but I heard you, just the other day, say Grace was pretty good with the whistle and dogs."

"Farm work is still man's work," Duncan said. "Even if there is a war on, you won't convince me otherwise."

"Grace?" William asked to steer his mother back to talking about the land girls.

"She has four brothers, but you wouldn't know it," Nel replied.

"Why wouldn't you know it?" William asked.

"Well, you'd think with four brothers she'd be a bit of a tomboy but no, she's as graceful as her name. Very assertive at the same time though, you wouldn't be able to boss that one around."

"I'll be sure and remember." William laughed. "The others, how are they going?"

"Moira, the redhead," Nel replied. "She still paints her fingernails and dresses up her overalls. Bless her, one day she might realise it's pointless on a farm."

"Still smokes," Duncan said with a grunt.

William had enjoyed a few roll-your-owns at training camp. Everyone got a ration of tobacco, the powers that be, reckoned it was good for calming the soldiers' nerves.

"Alice, the little one," Nel continued. "She'll do anything and everything you ask of her even to her own detriment. We have to keep an eye on that one."

"She's good with Jess and Patch," Duncan added. "But she's rescued a lamb so now we've got the hassle of feeding the damn thing."

"Alice is feeding it, Duncan." Nel defended.

"It's great that she's good with Jess," William said. "There are horses at training camp, but I haven't been assigned to that division, so it's travel by foot for me. And Betsy?"

"Betsy. Betsy," Nel repeated with a sigh. "She would have been perfect for you, my son."

"And ..." William held his hand out, palm up, prompting his mother to continue.

"She's quite quiet, not shy, more reticent, I think. With the right man, I'm certain she would blossom."

"I'd like to have the opportunity to make her blossom," William muttered under his breath.

"Poor thing," Nel continued. "Her fiancé enlisted and has already been sent away to fight in this horrid war. She's pining away waiting for news from him."

"Your mother means she is distracted and keeps making mistakes." Duncan pointed out the facts, as he saw them.

"You might have met him in training camp, William, the fiancé I mean,"

Nel continued, ignoring her husband's negativity. "Roland Flavell is his name."

"Betsy did tell me about him. Doesn't ring a bell though but there were three thousand men in the mess sometimes. You couldn't possibly know everyone."

"Well, I've got a lovely roast ready to cook for tonight, so you'll be able to see all the girls again at dinner." Nel patted her son on the leg and smiled contentedly.

"The lads were planning to go into Geraldine." William saw the disappointed look on his mother's face. "But I'll catch up with them tomorrow night at the dance."

"So," William said when everyone had filled their dinner plates. "I hear I am taking all you ladies to the dance tomorrow night."

"I won't be able to go now," Alice announced.

"Why ever not, Alice?" William asked.

"I've got the lamb to feed," she replied. "Nel, I mean, your mother said it would need four-hourly-feeds for the first couple of days, so I'll have to stay home."

Grace thought of Ben. He wasn't as needy as Alice's lamb, but he too would require some food – tonight and before they went. She had deliberately piled her plate with more than she could eat and had a serviette on her lap. Her plan had been to sneak some of the delicious mutton and vegetables to Ben in the serviette but sitting next to Duncan she hadn't dared to risk it.

"You can feed it before we go and again when we get home," William said.

"We don't want to have to leave the dance early for the sake of a lamb." Moira scowled at Alice across the table. "I, for one, will have a full dance card and don't plan on leaving until after the very last dance."

"And what about you, Betsy, will your dance card be full, or will you save a space for me on there?" William smiled at Betsy.

"Oh ... um ... I don't have anyone on my dance card."

"Well, you do now, please save the first and the last and every second one in between for me."

"Oh, I couldn't possibly do that." The words Betsy spoke didn't match the message her eyes were conveying. "I'm sure there will be lots of young women wanting to dance with you."

Grace looked over at Moira, who obviously believed she'd be the belle of the ball.

"I'll be sure and save one for you too, William," Moira said placing her hand on William's arm.

William lifted his knife to cut some meat. The subtle move forced Moira to remove her hand.

"Thank you for the delicious meal, Mum," he said to change the subject. "We don't get food like this at training camp."

"What have they been feeding you, dear?" Nel asked.

"Mince, mince and more mince; fried, stewed, savoury and patties. There are usually some vegetables for good measure, but you can't always tell what they are." William laughed.

"That sounds terrible." Nel tutted. "I've made you some biscuits, perhaps I'd better make something else as well."

"At the end of a hard day's training you're so hungry, you'd eat anything," William replied.

"Speaking of eating, do you ladies need to be taking a plate to the dance?" Nel asked the land girls.

"Yes, we do," Grace replied. "We'll have to make something tomorrow in between milkings." There would be a chance to make something for Ben.

"I'll take care of that for you, if you like," Nel offered. "I can make some sandwiches, a pie and some pikelets."

"Ah ... um." Grace hesitated, disappointed that the opportunity was lost but not wanting to appear rude. "That would be wonderful. Thank you. You are so kind."

At the head of the table, Duncan observed the goings on.

"Remember when we used to go dancing, Duncan," Nel reminisced with a faraway whimsical look, like she was wishing her life had turned out different.

"You always liked me to twirl you around the dance floor like a spinning top," Duncan said. "But I preferred the slow songs so I could hold you close."

"You sentimental old fool." Nel rolled her eyes and giggled like a bashful schoolgirl.

"How are you planning to get to the dance?" Duncan asked.

"I thought we'd give Captain Boyle's Plymouth a run."

"I'm not sure that's a wise move," Duncan spluttered. "Captain Boyle would be livid if he returned to find his pride and joy Plymouth car scratched or worse, dented."

"Well, we can't all fit in the front of the truck," William proceeded to justify the use of the Plymouth. "We can't have the ladies on the back, not in their best dresses. And we can't make two trips, that would use up too much precious fuel."

It was like a conversation between one of Grace's brothers and her father. The son could see his father beginning to waver, so he persisted, knowing he would win.

"It will be better for the old car to have a run. We don't know how long before the captain returns. The petrol will go off anyway, if it isn't used."

"Oh, alright then," Duncan conceded. "But you'd better be careful."

"Speaking of dresses," Grace nudged Alice. "Do we need to be going home early to alter one for you, Alice?"

The lamb poked its head up from the box and gave a high pitched 'baa'.

"Sounds like I need to feed the lamb first," Alice replied. She finished the last few mouthfuls on her plate and excused herself from the table.

"Oh, isn't it cute." Betsy hadn't noticed the lamb before. "It sounded like it was calling out for its ma."

"Well, I'm its ma at the moment," Alice said as she made up another bottle.

"Have you given it a name?" Betsy asked.

"We don't name the livestock on this farm," Duncan interrupted with a stern look. "It is best not to get too attached to those that are likely to end up in the works."

Grace could tell it was too late; Alice was already attached. The little lamb needed her and she needed the lamb. Just like Ben needed Grace and she needed him. Alice put herself between Duncan and the lamb and offered the bottle. It easily latched onto the teat and stood in the box to bunt at the bottle as it would have done its mother. The lamb's tail wriggled in happy contentment.

"Where are you planning to keep this thing?" Duncan asked.

"I could keep it in my room," Alice suggested wanting to protect the lamb and not let its presence annoy anyone else.

"Captain Boyle would definitely not allow that. Maybe in the washhouse."

Alice had been in the washhouse at the Whipsnade homestead – it was all cold, dark concrete.

"Doesn't it need to be by the fire to keep warm?" she asked tentatively.

"Perhaps you should leave it here for the night again," Nel suggested, seeing that Duncan and Alice had opposing views about the lamb.

"I'm not getting up to feed it," Duncan declared.

"I'm not getting up to feed it either," William added.

"I'll feed it," Alice squeaked. She was starting to panic.

"Yes," Nel stood, rested her hands on her hips and announced her solution. "Alice can stay here as well and then she'll be able to get up and feed it and everyone will be happy,"

"Well, you'd better not wear yourself out over a lamb," Duncan said. "There are other more important jobs to be done tomorrow."

"I won't," Alice promised.

"And it's only here for one night," Duncan decreed. "You can set up a pen in the shed and give it some hay to sleep on. It needs to get used to being outside, it'll be back in the flock with the others as soon as its weaned."

"I will," Alice agreed.

"And the rest of you had better get an early night too. Just because there is a dance tomorrow night doesn't mean there isn't a day of farm work to be done before hand."

"Are you all right, Grace?" Nel asked. "You've hardly touched your food."

"I might save it for later, if that's alright. I'd better get Alice's dress sorted first, then I'll eat."

"I can put it in the oven to keep it warm for you."

"No!" Grace gasped, scared that her reaction would give her secret away, she calmed herself before she spoke again. "No, it'll be fine cold. It's delicious. Thank you."

"Very well then," Nel shrugged. "I'll just put it in a bowl for you. I don't want to risk my best china getting damaged."

Chapter Fifteen

"They're going to find out about Ben, you know." Betsy waited until her, Grace and Moira had reached the big house before she issued her warning.

"You won't tell William, will you?"

"No," Betsy replied. "You'll give him away yourself if you keep reacting the way you did. You're as jumpy as a March hare."

"I know," Grace conceded. "Nel caught me by surprise. It's so hard to get food for him."

"Well, you could let us help you. A little bit from everyone will look better than a whole heap from you."

"You'd do that?" Grace was so grateful that the land girls had agreed to keep the secret, she hadn't considered asking for more help.

"Yes, we would." Betsy nudged Moira. "Wouldn't we, Moira?"

"I suppose so," Moira agreed. "I don't think Alice will be much use to you though. She'd probably bring him lamb's milk."

"Thanks ladies." Grace sighed with relief. She went to the kitchen to fetch a knife and fork. "I'll just take this up to Ben."

Grace knocked quietly and pushed the door open. The waning moon still gave sufficient light to see Ben's form under the bed covers. He didn't stir when she put the bowl down on the bedside table and only gave a slight twitch at the jangle of the knife and fork. She noticed his hair had grown, curls that disappeared with the army number one haircut were winding their way into a wavy mess. Eyelashes longer than any man deserved, were obvious, now Grace wasn't besotted with the closed baby-blue eyes that they framed. She stepped back, unsure if their quivering was an involuntary sign of the terror of a dream or Ben's eyes were about to flutter open. Either way she didn't want to frighten him further.

"Ben," she whispered. "Ben, I've brought you some food."

He groaned, stretched an arm upward and slowly opened his sleepy eyes. A smile crept over his face as he focused.

"An angel," he said. "An angel come to save me."

Grace blushed. "Are you alright?" she asked. "You were in a deep sleep."

"I've been sleeping most of the day."

"Is your cold back? Perhaps we shouldn't have gone for a swim."

"I think I'll be fine."

"I've brought you some food." She stepped forward and picked up the bowl and cutlery.

"Thank you." Ben sat up in the bed and took the plate. "Hopefully, this will perk me up. Sit down. Tell me what you've been up to today. It's boring in here with no-one to talk to."

"I can't stay long." Grace sat on the side of the bed. "I've got to fix a dress up for Alice for the dance tomorrow night."

Ben's eyes went wide as he finished chewing a mouthful of meat. "You're going to a dance?"

"We all are." Grace realised 'all' didn't include Ben, as much as she wished it did. "Sorry, I mean all the land girls are going. Do you like to dance?"

"I have been called twinkle toes in my time." Ben chuckled.

"Perhaps we could have a dance down in the sitting room when I get back," Grace suggested.

"That would be great. I'm sick of this room." Ben gulped down another mouthful. "How are you getting to and from the dance?"

"William is going to take us in Captain Boyle's Plymouth."

"William!" Ben's eyes were now wide with panic, not wonder. "Who's William?"

"He's Duncan and Nel's son. He enlisted and has been away at training. He's got leave for the weekend."

"You won't tell him about me, will you?"

"No, Ben, you're safe here." Grace hoped she sounded as convincing as she wanted to.

"Make sure the others keep quiet too."

"I will," Grace promised. It was an oath she sincerely hoped she'd be able to keep.

"Which dress do you think I should take in for Alice?" Grace was scanning the half dozen dresses in the wardrobe she and Betsy shared. They hadn't been able to convince Alice to come home after dinner and try one on to see what needed to be done, she was too worried about leaving her precious lamb.

"Probably better to be one of mine," Betsy replied. "Yours would be a long dress on Alice, you're quite a bit taller."

"Which one are you going to wear?"

"Oh, I don't know." Betsy sighed.

"It'd better be something comfortable, if William has things his way, you're going to be dancing all night."

"But, Grace, I'm engaged; I'm in love with Roland, I'm not going to do anything to jeopardise that."

"Betsy." Grace sat down and took her friend's hands in hers. "Talking to William, even dancing with William or anyone else at the dance, is not going to jeopardise what you have with Roland."

"But I'd feel like I was being unfaithful."

"I'm sure that's the last thing William would expect you to be. He seems like quite a gentleman." Grace stood back up and returned to the wardrobe, she needed to get the alterations done or they would be up half the night. "Well, I think you should wear the blue floral one and I'll just nip in the green one for Alice, it'll match the colour of her eyes."

"Decision made then. Thank you. What about you, what are you going to wear?"

"I'll wear my navy dress, the one with the satin bows on the sleeves." Grace sat down on the bed with her sewing kit and the dress.

"I'm sure Bob will think you look gorgeous in that."

"Bob?" Grace had been absorbed with thoughts of Ben; she'd forgotten Bob.

"Dairy factory Bob," Betsy reminded Grace. "Your date for tomorrow night."

"Oh him, he's not my date," Grace replied, as she pinned an inch-wide tuck down both side seams of the dress.

"Are you wishing Ben was your date?" Betsy asked.

"No!" Grace snapped. The thread missed the eye of the needle.

"You seem a little too touchy for there to be nothing between you."

"I was just trying to thread the needle."

"If you concentrate on that instead of Ben, then it should be quite easy."

Grace had to concede Betsy knew her too well. She couldn't help it, images of Ben holding her as they danced around the sitting room disrupted her concentration. She hoped being so close to him would lead to another kiss.

"Now you've gone all dreamy-eyed. Grace, what have you done?"

"Nothing."

"What are you planning to do?"

"Nothing."

"Good, leave it that way, he will be gone soon. Remember."

Grace looked across at Betsy and sighed. "I know you're right, but it's a bit like you and William. Something happens when I'm around Ben and I can't stop it."

"Just concentrate on getting him fit and healthy so he can be on his way or I'm going to have to be taking care of you."

"I'll try."

Grace turned her attention to the seams of the dress, removing the pins as she hand-stitched down both sides. The light wasn't very bright in the bedroom so she didn't think her sewing would have passed her mother's inspection, but it only needed to hold for one night, then she'd unpick the stitches and return Betsy's dress to normal.

"There that will have to do," Grace said as she held it up for Betsy to see. "If it's still too big, Alice will just have to wear a belt."

"Maybe Alice will catch the eye of some handsome young farmer," Betsy suggested.

"She may well do but I think he'd have to work pretty hard to catch her eye." Grace hung the altered dress back in the wardrobe. "She seems more interested in the animals."

"You'd best be up and getting those cows in for milking." Duncan's loud voice startled Alice who'd been trying to sleep in the armchair.

The lamb bleated, as it had done, several times in the night. Alice stretched and yawned. The chair wasn't designed for sleeping in. She wiped the sleep from her eyes and peered at the clock on the wall. It was only two hours since the last feed.

"Not this time, little lamb." She patted the lamb on the head. "You'll have to wait until I've finished my other jobs."

Alice quickly toileted and splashed some cold water on her face before leaving the house. The lights were already on at the cowshed. Her gumboots lay on the backdoor step where they'd been left yesterday in her panic to get sustenance for the lamb. She scanned the paddock for Jess while she blindly righted the boots and stepped into them.

"Ouch!" she yelled. Something sharp in her left gumboot stabbed her foot. She removed the boot and sat down on the concrete step. In the half light of the morning, there was nothing to be seen or felt on the sole of her sock. Alice peered into the blackness of the gumboot. She gave the upturned boot a vigorous shake, she heard some scratching but nothing fell to the ground and the culprit of the stabbing eluded her. Thinking she must have imagined the jab; Alice pushed her foot back into the gumboot.

"Ouch!" She removed the boot. Clinging to her sock was a Weta, its spiny limbs hooked into the woollen threads. "What are you doing hiding in my boot?"
she asked rhetorically, as she carefully removed the insect and placed it in the garden.

"Always stand your boots up," Duncan said from the wash house. "The little critters are often looking for shelter."

"Thank you," Alice said. "I would hate to squash anything."

Alice returned to the house after fetching the cows and then feeding the pigs, to feed the lamb before having breakfast herself but the lamb and its box were no longer beside the coal range.

"What happened?" Alice screeched. "Did something happen to my lamb?"

"No," Duncan replied. "I've just put it out in a pen in the shed."

"That's cruel," Alice muttered. "I'll go and feed it then."

"No," Duncan looked at the dark shadows under Alice's eyes. "You'd best feed yourself first. The animal will be okay for half an hour."

Alice sat down at the table and tucked into a plate of scrambled eggs on toast. She followed them with a cup of tea, adding extra milk to cool it down.

"Thank you, Nel," Alice said as she placed her dirty dishes in the sink.

"Slow down, girl," Nel replied. "There's no need to be rushing."

"But I need to check on the lamb," Alice explained as she started to make up a bottle of milk.

"The lamb will be fine." Nel chuckled. "Your dedication is admirable but just remember it will be back in the paddock with the others soon."

Alice found the lamb nestled on a pile of hay in a pen at the front of the implement shed. She climbed the railings and knelt down to offer the bottle to the lamb. It drank greedily, bunting the bottle to hurry the milk flow, its tail wriggling happily. When the bottle was empty, Alice sat down on the hay and let the lamb climb over her. It bunted its head under her armpit, seeking an udder where there wasn't one. It sniffed at her face; its tiny pink nose brushed against her cheek. A constantly wriggling tail battered at Alice, making her giggle.

Alice returned to the shed several times during the day. After the last feed, she lingered, sat down, and played with the lamb.

"Much as I'd like to spend the night with you little lamb, I'd better go." Begrudgingly, she gave the lamb a hug and climbed out of the pen.

"Where have you been, Alice?" Grace asked as Alice entered the house. She didn't wait for an answer but headed upstairs to take pikelets and scones to Ben, yelling to Alice as she went. "The bath water will be nearly cold. You'd better hurry."

Alice hadn't bathed since last Sunday and it had been an eventful week. If she was going to wear someone else's dress then she'd better get clean. She stripped off and climbed gingerly into the tepid water. This was one occasion when it was good to be petite. In the long deep bath, Alice could lie down and completely submerge. When her hair was wet, she lathered in a squeeze of shampoo, gave her scalp a good massage and then lay back down in the water to rinse the shampoo out. Using a wet flannel like a scrubbing brush she cleaned her face, arms and legs. When she felt clean Alice lay back, rested her head on the end of the bath, closed her eyes and inhaled deeply.

Thump! Thump!

"Are you finished in there?" Moira yelled. "You'd better hurry up. We have to go soon. We don't want to be late."

Alice jolted up, splashing water up the sides of the bath, her moment of rest had come to an end.

"Coming," she replied. She wrapped a towel around herself and ran upstairs to get ready.

At the sight of Grace, dressed ready for the dance, Ben wolf whistled, until he realised the possible impact of the noise he'd made. He slapped his hand across his mouth and resorted to a whisper.

"You look beautiful."

"Thank you." Grace wasn't used to such compliments. Her brothers had never been so kind.

"I'd ask you to save the last dance for me but I'm not feeling so good." Ben blew his nose with one of Captain Boyle's handkerchiefs.

"Your cold's back?" Grace had another reason to regret the moonlight swim. "I'd better stay home and make you a lemon honey drink."

"No, you go on your way and have a fun time. I will be fine."

"Are you sure?"

Ben sneezed, blew his nose loudly and waved Grace away.

Ooga! Ooga! William, smartly dressed in his army uniform, gave two loud blasts on the horn of the Plymouth as he pulled up outside the Whipsnade homestead to pick up the land girls. The car had started first turn of the key and William, after further cautions from his father, had carefully backed it out of the garage. When he saw the four women exit the house, William placed his army cap on his head and stood beside the car like a true chauffeur to open the door for his passengers.

"Madam," he said with a posh voice as he ushered Alice into the back seat. "Thank you for joining us tonight, Dr Doolittle. I trust your patient is well fed and asleep awaiting our return."

Alice giggled, wearing the dress that Grace had altered for her, she too was now caught up in the excitement of the occasion.

"Grace. Grace, with the bows." William waved her into the car. "Wrapped up like a present for some handsome gentleman."

Grace looked back up at the window where she hoped Ben would be safe until she returned. He was the only man she'd like to give herself to but that wasn't going to happen. She climbed into the back seat next to Alice. Betsy was next in line and William stood still to admire her from head to toe.

"Ah, beautiful," William put a hand up to halt Betsy and dashed to the garden where he picked a pink rose flower. "A flower as sweet as you," he said, presenting the bloom and ushering Betsy to the front seat. "A front seat in the chariot for one so fine."

Betsy turned pink, two shades darker than the flower. She smiled as she slid onto the leather seat in the front of the Plymouth.

When William turned back around for the last of his passengers, he was nose to nose with Moira. He stepped to the side and indicated for Moira to hop into the rear seat. She ignored his hand signals, stepped around him and climbed in next to Betsy.

"Front seat for me, driver." Moira laughed. "I don't want to miss a thing."

William stood, mouth agape for several seconds before shaking his head.

"Well, I'd better get you ladies to the dance," William said. "First stop is the farmhouse."

Betsy had to scuttle across the front seat to make room for Moira which meant when William climbed into the driver's side, his body touched hers. She glanced back at Grace and brushed her hand across her brow as if she had a temperature.

Grace just smiled. Betsy's sigh was audible when the car stopped, and William climbed out.

"Just got to collect the supper plates," he said.

Nel came out holding a basket, a checked tea towel covered the treats she had prepared, minus the few that Grace had already taken for Ben. William placed the basket in the boot.

"Oh, just look at you all, so pretty," Nel said. "We should get a photograph. Duncan! Duncan, get the camera and bring it out here please."

It was several minutes before Duncan responded to the yelling and exited the house with a Kodak Brownie in hand. By this time Nel had organised all the land girls into a line, positioned William in the middle of the row and stood them at the front of the Plymouth.

"Aren't they beautiful, Duncan?" Nel asked rhetorically. "Quick, take a photograph."

Duncan obliged, capturing a black and white image of the five smiling young people.

Chapter Sixteen

"How exciting," Moira said. "Look at all the cars here already."

William pulled the Plymouth onto the grass verge outside the Orari Hall. He quickly climbed out of the car and opened Alice's door, before rushing around to the other side to open the door for Grace and Moira.

"Like a true gentleman," Grace said. "Thank you, William."

William offered his arm to Betsy to escort her to the hall. Moira linked onto William's other arm. So Grace decided she'd do the same and offered her arm to Alice. All the girls giggled with the excitement of the occasion.

An archway of Ponga fronds decorated the entranceway and either side of the stage, where seats and a microphone were set up for the band. Strands of coloured lights were strung down each side of the hall above rows of seats. It seemed that one side was occupied by the women while the men gathered in small groups on the other. All eyes turned to the front door as the group entered. The grapevine had circulated the news that four young women had arrived at Whipsnade to learn how to farm and everyone was eager to see them.

"Here you are, ladies." William directed the land girls to some empty seats. "I'll just go and get the supper out of the car."

"I'll help," Moira offered.

"I can manage. Thank you, Moira. It's all in one basket." William sighed.

Grace sat down. "We'd better rest up before the dancing starts."

Betsy and Alice joined Grace and gradually those that had been eyeing them up lost interest and carried on with their conversations.

"Aren't we going to go and introduce ourselves?" Moira asked as she joined the others. Nobody replied. "Well, I'll take that as a no. At least, I can check them out from here."

Slowly the hall filled: couples, separate groups of men and women, young and old, men in uniform, men in trousers and open neck shirts, women in fitted dresses, and women in flared skirts. The patchwork of colours was matched by a medley of voices echoing around the hall.

"There's Jake and Bob," Betsy said as the two men from the dairy factory entered the hall and waved.

"They've got a bit of a swagger," Moira observed. "They might have had a few too many already by the looks."

"Duncan said no alcohol was allowed at the dances."

"Best I keep an eye on them then," Moira said. "They've probably got a secret stash outside."

The hall's piano had been pushed in from the wings. The pianist lifted the lid and ran his fingers over the ivory keys. The other musicians followed, they sat down and took up their instruments ready to check they were in tune. The band members all wore matching black suits, white shirts and bow ties and looked smart for a collection of locals at a country hall.

William returned with the basket, taking it through to the kitchen where the hall committee members thanked him for his contribution.

"Aren't you a bit greedy, Will?" Paul asked as William left the kitchen. Paul had signed up too and they'd become good friends at training camp. He leaned in close, the couple of beers he'd enjoyed beforehand evident on his breath, and slapped William on the back

"They'll put it on the tables at supper time," William replied. "You can have some then."

"Not the food." Paul chuckled. "Will McKnight with four women. You can't possibly manage all of them on your own."

William laughed. "Just the good looking one in the blue floral dress will be more than enough for me." William caught Betsy's eye across the hall and smiled.

"Looks like she's keen." Paul gave William an elbow nudge and a wink.

"Come, I'll introduce you," William said to his friend, but their walk across the hall was thwarted.

"Testing. Testing." The hall committee president checked the microphone was working. "Quiet please," he continued, waiting for the din to subside so he could say a few words of welcome.

The drummer gave an impromptu drum roll which had the desired effect of hushing the last of those still chatting.

"I'd like to welcome you all to the Orari Hall, to the first of our dances for 1941. It is wonderful to see some new faces amongst the familiar. We acknowledge the efforts of those who are absent due to service. We must also honour the memory of those who have made the ultimate sacrifice in the name of King and country. If we could please observe a minute's silence as a token of our respect."

Heads were bowed and silence swallowed the hall for sixty seconds.

"Thank you," the hall committee president continued. "I believe tonight's band is going to start the ball rolling with a Gay Gordon. Please take your partners and form a circle."

Grace sat back as the men rushed from the other side of the hall, a stampede of shoes belting across the wooden floor. The women outnumbered the men by nearly two to one so she thought their rush was unwarranted.

"Betsy." William, having abandoned Paul without another word, stood in front of her with his hand extended. "Please may

I have the pleasure of your company for this dance?"

Betsy blushed. She glanced at Grace beside her, and Grace nodded in response to her unasked question. Yes, she could, and should dance with William. Betsy stood and tentatively placed her hand in William's. He turned and ushered Betsy onto the dance floor, smiling from ear to ear.

Jake soon followed and collected Moira, Bob shadowed Jake and Grace was also escorted to the dance floor. That left Alice who crossed her legs, busied herself smoothing the skirt of her dress and fidgeted nervously.

Alice could almost glimpse her reflection in the shiny black shoes that appeared before her. She had no option but to look up at the man in uniform standing expectantly in front of her.

"The lucky last of the land girls," Paul said to Alice. "William was going to introduce us, but I see he is busy, so I'll have to do it myself. Paul, Paul Tanner, at your service, Miss?"

"Alice." Alice chewed the inside of her lip. "Just call me Alice."

"Will you please join me in the Gay Gordon, Alice?"

Alice looked to her right–the row of chairs was empty. She glanced to her left, there were a few women, but they were at the far end of the hall. It appeared nearly everyone but her, including women who'd coupled with women, were on the dance floor. There wasn't any way to politely turn Paul down.

"Thank you," she said and timidly followed him into the circle. They took up position in between Grace and Bob, and William and Betsy.

Grace saw Alice's spine go rigid when Paul's arm brushed her neck. The petite woman was clearly uncomfortable. Grace couldn't fathom why.

The music began. Side by side everyone went, forward, two, three, four, reverse, two, three, four, forward, two, three, four. Grace never saw Alice make eye contact with Paul and it wasn't because she was bewitched by Bob, whose breath smelt like a brewery. His slurred words were accompanied with spits of saliva and it was safer to stay as far away as possible.

Each step Grace took was with toes elegantly pointed. The same couldn't be said for Bob who managed to tread on her toes several times.

The men twirled their partners around under their arms. Alice's cringe was visible as Paul pulled her into his body and they spun in circles around the hall together. The twirling finished, and the women were sent onto their next partner.

Bob mouthed an apology to Grace and then moved on. Grace shrugged and smiled at her next partner, one of the soldiers returned home on leave. It made no difference to Grace whether they were soldiers, farmers or factory men, she wasn't looking at them as anything other than dance partners. Her thoughts were about the young man back at Whipsnade farm.

"Hello, Dr Doolittle," William said to Alice. "I see you met Paul. Nice fellow, isn't he?"

Alice ignored the question. "I thought you were going to spend the night dancing with Betsy."

"I very much intend to," replied William. He glanced back at Betsy as he twirled Alice under his arm, caught her eye and smiled.

"You know she is engaged," Alice reminded William.

"So, I've been told," he said. "Several times now. I'm an honourable man, Dr

Doolittle. I wouldn't do anything to hurt someone I care about."

William spun Alice onto her next partner.

Moira danced the Gay Gordon with frivolity. Where others stepped with gentility, Moira skipped. When the men twirled their partners three times, Moira pirouetted until her skirt billowed and revealed glimpses of skin that others kept demurely covered. When the couples spun graciously together, Moira encouraged her partners to double the tempo.

Following their earlier conversation, Grace assumed Moira was critiquing the men, if they couldn't keep up with her, or didn't have rhythm then they wouldn't make it to her dance card. Moira's smile indicated those who passed the unwritten test; Bill seemed to be one of them.

When the music finally wound down, the men escorted the dance partners they ended up with back to their chairs. Idle chatter filled the hall as the dancers caught their breath and waited for the next dance.

"Something slower for you now," announced the saxophonist. "A snowball waltz with hall committee chairman and secretary to begin, please."

The locals laughed. The chairman and secretary, Mr and Mrs Potts were a couple from the village who'd been married for nearly forty years. They eagerly took to the floor. Despite being twice the age of most in the hall and with bodies no longer slim and lithe, they made a dapper couple. When the music began, Mr Potts led his wife gracefully around the dance floor, they moved as one, gliding across the floorboards, an inspiration to those sitting at the sides.

The music stopped again. "Please take another partner," came the call from the stage.

The couple separated. Mrs Potts turned and strode decisively across the floor to select William.

"William McKnight, my favourite student," she said. "You've grown into a handsome young man. I hope you can still remember everything I taught you at primary school."

Mr Potts approached Betsy and soon had her smiling with his skill on the dance floor. When the music stopped again, Betsy was obliged to pick another partner. She paused in the middle of the dance floor, she scanned the row of men, hesitated then walked over to Grace.

"Please join me on the dance floor, miss," Betsy giggled as she put her hand out to Grace.

"Get me next time," Moira demanded, wanting to get back into dancing.

"I'll be the man," Grace said taking control, as the music restarted.

"I didn't want to choose a man and have him misinterpret my intentions," Betsy said as they twirled around. "And the soldiers' uniforms remind me of Roland.

Life would be so much easier if he was here."

"You were looking at William like you wanted to choose him."

"But the whole point of a snowball waltz is to get someone different."

"But you were looking at him." Grace spun Betsy around to their left to avoid another couple.

"Grace, stop teasing." Betsy giggled. "It's hard enough to second-guess my thoughts and words without you making fun of me."

"Looks like Moira is latching herself onto Bill." Moira was being twirled around in Bill's arms.

"He seems to be one of the better dancers here."

"And out of his farm clothes, cleanshaven and smartly dressed, he is quite the catch."

Betsy laughed. "Now you're eyeing up the men and I thought your eyes were only for Ben."

"And you're making fun of me now." Grace looked over at Alice. "We need to find some fun for Alice, she's looking all lonely sitting over there by herself."

"Now that you're rested, we'll liven it up with a Lindy Hop," came the announcement from the stage as the music wound down.

"Or we could just join her for a rest," Betsy suggested.

The pair left the dance floor while Moira smiled mischievously at Bill.

"You up for this?" she asked.

"Of course," Bill replied. "I couldn't disappoint a charming lady."

There were only half a dozen couples on the dance floor when the band launched into the fast-paced swing music, others were happy to sit and admire the athleticism of those on the dance floor. Each couple improvised their own moves, swinging and spinning, jumping and jiving, twisting and twirling. Bill and Moira shimmied across the floorboards, feet, knees, hips and arms flexing and gyrating in time to the music. He grabbed her by the waist and swung her up to his left until her red toe peepers soared above his head. Bill lowered Moira to the floor but her shoes only touched the wooden planks for a split second before he swung her up to his right. Another touch to the floor and Moira was hoisted up in front of Bill, her skirt billowing. Bill spread his legs and swung Moira down sliding on the floor between his legs. She whooped loudly, her face flushed, glowing with heat and happiness. As a finale, Bill pulled Moira back through his legs and hoisted her up in the air. When she came to a rest it was with her legs wrapped around his waist. Moira gave a squeal of delight and raised her arms in a victory 'V'.

The music stopped. Those sitting out the dance cheered, whistled, and loudly applauded, excited with the display.

"Phew!" Bill said as he lifted Moira back to the floor. "I think I need some fresh air after that."

Moira grabbed her clutch purse from the seat beside the girls. "We're just going outside for a smoke."

Bill collected his jacket; Moira hooked her arm through his and they were gone before anyone could respond.

"I do hope Moira is careful," Alice said, a worrying frown crinkling her forehead.

"I think we'd be wasting our time worrying about Moira," Grace replied. "I'd say she's had plenty of experience looking after herself."

"She does seem to find it very easy to relate to men," Betsy said.

Grace laughed. "That's one way of describing her behaviour."

"But you can't dance like that and not expect the man to get ideas." Alice's voice was shaky.

"I think Moira wants them to get ideas."

Alice kept looking at the door, the whites of her eyes wide with terror. Grace leaned over and put her hand on Alice's knee.

"It's okay, Moira will be all right."

Alice shivered and sat straight-backed in the seat. She didn't make eye contact with Grace or Betsy.

"Are you okay, Alice?" Grace saw the same frightened bird look again. "Has something happened we should know about?"

With a shake of her head, Alice brought her focus back.

"No," she said, too quickly for Grace to believe. "Nothing you need to worry about."

The only conclusion that Grace could draw was that something had happened, and she resolved to find a way to discover what.

"If it makes you feel better." Grace stood and moved to stand by the window. "I'll keep an eye on them."

The hall lights cast a dim glow through the window to where Bill and Moira stood in the shelter of the hedge at the side of the hall. Clouds shrouded the moonlight but Grace could make out the pair standing in the semi darkness. She watched as Bill put a lit match to the tobacco in his pipe and drew in a few puffs until he was rewarded with glowing embers. Moira then leaned in to the flickering flame to light her cigarette.

"They're just having a smoke," Grace reported to Betsy and Alice as small tufts of smoke rose into the night.

"That's all right then," Betsy said.

"Bill's taking his jacket off now."

Alice gasped.

"It's okay, Alice," Grace said. "That wind, it's blowing straight from the Alps. Moira's rubbing her arms, like she's cold. Anyone would be after all that dancing."

"They sure were energetic."

Over by the cars, Grace could make out a group of young men. They were taking turns to swig from shared bottles of beer being passed around. She couldn't hear their banter, but their smiles showed they were having fun. When she looked back to Moira, she stood alone swallowed by the broad shoulders of Bill's double-breasted jacket.

"Bill's gone."

"He hasn't come back inside."

"There he is," Grace said. "Looks like he's got a bottle of beer."

Bill flicked its lid off on the fence post and offered Moira the first drink. She gulped down several large mouthfuls.

"And it looks like Moira's not a stranger to drinking either." Grace's life seemed rather sheltered compared to Moira's. She'd tasted beer but her brothers insisted she drink from a glass and not the bottle like them. She even tried smoking, behind the caretaker's shed with the other girls at high school but her only puff ended in a coughing fit she wasn't keen to repeat. And Grace knew she was a good dancer, but the Lindy Hop; she'd never dreamed of learning it, let alone dancing it with a man she'd only met once before.

"Oh, no." Grace watched Moira move closer to Bill, lean against his side, and rest her head on his shoulder.

"What's happened?" Alice rushed to stand beside Grace at the window in time to see Bill wrap his arm around Moira's waist and pull her closer. He rested his chin on Moira's head, drank from the beer bottle, and looked skyward at the stars where dreams and memories lay.

"What's he saying?" Alice demanded.

"Sorry, Alice, I can't lip read."

"I should hope not," Betsy said. "They are adults, they are entitled to some privacy."
Grace pulled away from the window. "Yes, you're right. Best we leave them alone."

Chapter Seventeen

The band were playing a foxtrot when Bill and Moira re-entered the hall. Purse and jacket were quickly cast aside and they took to the dance floor. In the absence of a trumpet, the saxophonist led the slow sultry number as couples glided gracefully around the hall.

"They're back again," Grace observed. "And looking quite comfortable in each other's arms."

"So are Betsy and William." Alice pointed to the pair dancing on the opposite side of the hall.

"They are just friends though." The words were out of Grace's mouth before she could retract the falsehood. It was the same as her and Ben. To the outside they were just friends, but thoughts and feelings smouldered, threatened to burst into uncontrollable desire. "William knows her situation." And Grace knew Ben's situation, he was leaving, he had to leave, he couldn't stay in Captain Boyle's room for ever. The thought that Ben might have chosen tonight to leave, when everyone else was distracted by the dance, left an aching chasm in the pit of her stomach.

From the foxtrot, the band went into a jive. The older couples more familiar with the ballroom dances of old took the opportunity to rest, leaving the quick, quick, slow, slow steps to the younger ones.

Jake and Paul strode decisively in a line, straight across the hall to stop in front of Grace and Alice.

"Grace," Jake said, bowing like a gentleman. "A dance, please?"

Grace saw Alice shrink into the seat as she registered Paul's intentions would be the same. She wanted to take Alice as her partner, to save her from the anguish that having a man so close obviously caused.

"Sorry, I've twisted my ankle," Alice said. "No more dancing for me tonight."

The noise that escaped Grace's mouth was a laugh and a cough blended to disguise her shock at Alice's ability to lie so believably, and admiration for her clever excuse. Grace moved away with Jake, content that Alice could keep any unwanted men at bay.

Jake was definitely a better dancer than Bob but his hand, supposed to be at her waist, seemed to slide down. The move was so subtle, Grace was unsure if it was an accident or deliberate. Uncomfortable with his fingers splayed across her buttocks she grabbed his hand and lifted it back to her waist. Then it seemed the space between their bodies was squeezed out, leaving their chests touching. Grace pulled back only to find herself gradually edged in closer. She was glad when the music came to an end. When the band announced a rumba would be next, she excused herself from Jake. He didn't need any encouragement from the suggestive moves of that dance. She passed Moira and Bill on her way back to the seat.

"A rumba?" Moira asked with a sashay of her hips and a suggestive smile.

Bill answered by coming to stand behind her, his hands on her hips, his front touching her behind, his breath on her neck. The music started and everyone watched as their hips moved as one, swivelling from side to side. Bill took Moira's hand and spun her out beside him only to then twirl her back into him, torso to torso, face to face. They stared into each other's eyes. The passion was palpable. The music continued and so did their dance. It was a display of unfulfilled desire and they seemed oblivious to the eyes watching them, unaware of the murmurings around the hall.

"Tut, tut, how can they do that in public?"

"They might as well be having sex."

"Bill's wife will be turning over in her grave."

"That's one of those land girls. I wonder if she's any good at farming."

Sitting the dance out, Grace, Alice and Betsy heard the comments from the locals.

"Nothing Moira can do will shock me now," Alice said.

A final spin as the music finished, flung Moira back into Bill's arms. Touching, their chests rose and fell in rhythm as the pair regained their equilibrium.

"And now, to get you all back on the dance floor before supper, we'll dance the Charleston," came the announcement from the stage. "Come on everybody, no partners required."

"Come on, you two," Grace urged Betsy and Alice, who were sitting wide-eyed, mouth agape beside her. "No partners required."

"Sorry," Betsy replied. "I'm just shocked. I don't think I could ever dance like that, even with Roland."

"I wouldn't go saying anything, if I was you," Alice warned. "Moira will let you know it's none of your business."

Moira, her arm wrapped around Bill's, smiled as they passed the trio.

"We're just going to get some more fresh air before supper," she said.

"I bet that's not all they are going to get," Betsy muttered.

The supper room was hectic. Chatter that had been muted while the dancing was on, exploded into full voice. Plates were eagerly filled with pastries, pikelets and scones, slices of Louise cake and wedges of sponge, with lavish dollops of cream. Cups of tea were poured, and milk generously added. Country hospitality was at its best and appeared exempt from wartime rationing.

"What a lovely supper," Grace remarked to Betsy and Alice.

"Moira had better hurry up," Betsy replied. "Or there will be none left."

"She's probably not even hungry for food." Grace laughed.

"I know what I'm hungry for," Bob spoke with innuendo as he stumbled up to the trio.

"Well, you've obviously had too much to drink." Grace smelled the alcohol on Bob and nudged him away with her elbow. "You'd best get some food into yourself."

"Oh Gracey, don't be like that," Bob slurred. "You're saving the next dance for me, aren't you?"

Grace hated being called Gracey. A kick in the shins had stopped her brothers from calling her anything other than Grace. She was tempted to do the same to Bob. Instead, she chose to ignore him and turned her back.

"What's up, mate?" Jake came to Bob's side. "Lucked out there, did you?"

"You can talk," Bob replied. "Where's the redhead?"

"Don't know, don't care." Jake shrugged his shoulders.

"Oh look, there she is." Bob laughed and pointed to Bill and Moira as they came into the supper room. "Looks like you're too late. Bill beat you to it, Jake."

Curiosity made Grace turn back around. Moira's flushed cheeks and Bill's ruffled hair confirmed they'd enjoyed more than fresh air outside. The Orari locals all seemed to be sizing up the pair as well. Bill and Moira helped themselves to several savouries and tried to ignore the eyes cast their way. Grace pricked her ears and listened into their conversation.

"I've so enjoyed tonight, Bill." Moira lay her manicured hand on Bill's forearm. "I'd love to spend some more time with you."

"The dance hasn't finished yet." Bill looked uncomfortable. "Would you like a cup of tea?"

Before Moira had a chance to answer, Bill left, went to the servery, and collected two cups of white tea.

"Not that hot, I'm sorry." Bill quickly downed the cup of lukewarm tea. "We must have been outside for too long."

"We can go outside again if you like." Moira's offer came with a suggestive smile.

"Excuse me." Bill leaned across, gave Moira a peck on the cheek and turned to leave. "I need to visit the gents."

Moira was left standing alone in the supper room.

A group of local women standing to the other side of Grace drew her attention, their whispers still audible above the chatter.

"What would his wife say?"

"Poor Miriam."

"It hasn't been a year yet."

"Shouldn't Bill still be in mourning?"

"Not chasing some floozy."

For Moira's sake, Grace hoped she and Bill would soon be old news, surpassed by something grander and more exciting and no longer the object of the village gossips.

"Betsy." Alice glanced at her watch. "Where's William?"

"I'm not his keeper, Alice," Betsy snapped then realised her over reaction. "Sorry. I think he's outside with the other soldiers. He's been gone a while."

"I hope he's not drunk like Bob," Grace said. "He's meant to be driving us home. If he can't, I'll have to drive the Plymouth and I don't think Duncan would like that."

"I need to get home soon." Alice checked her watch again. "The lamb needs a feed."

Grace laughed. "You and your precious lamb."

Alone in the supper room, Moira downed the last dregs of her now cold cup of tea. The band restarted with a slow number. Placing the cup and saucer on the table, Moira moved to the doorway and scanned the hall. Bill was nowhere to be seen.

"Have you seen Bill?" she asked Betsy and Alice, who were sitting out the dance.

"I saw him go that way a while ago." Alice pointed to the front door.

"Did he come back?" Moira was beginning to get frantic.

"I haven't seen him."

Moira scanned the dance floor again. "He might still be in the toilet," she muttered before heading in that direction.

Moira wasn't bold enough to go into the men's toilet but listened quietly at the door. She relaxed at the sound of a man's cough, the flush of a toilet and a running tap and stood back to allow Bill to exit. But it was William who burst through the door.

"What are you up to there, Moira?" William asked, leaning on the door frame for support, the few beers he'd had having gone straight to his head. "Waiting for me, are you?" he joked.

"No, actually I was looking for Bill." Moira tried to peer around William.

"Nobody else in there," William laughed. "Nobody would want to be, just at the moment."

"He must be out smoking his pipe," Moira turned to go outside and search.

"Wait up." William moved to follow Moira. "I'll come with you."

Moira didn't wait. She dashed back around to the side of the hall but there were no puffs of smoke to signal Bill's presence. She hugged her arms around herself.

"His truck's gone." William came up behind Moira. "He must have gone home."

Moira burst into uncontrollable sobs.

"It's alright, Moira." William wrapped his arms around her. "Bill probably just has an early start in the morning."

"We kissed. I thought he liked me," Moira said between snivels.

"I'm sure he likes you."

"I thought he was a gentleman. A gentleman would have said goodbye."

"Come on, Moira. We'd better get you back inside, it's cold out here." William put his arm around Moira's shoulder and led her back inside the hall.

"What?" Betsy exclaimed through clenched teeth. She gripped the wooden seat. Her knuckles whitened but her face grew red as a hot rage engulfed her.

"What's happened? What's the matter, Betsy?" Grace saw Betsy's bulging eyes and turned to see the source of her anguish. Grace shook her head in disbelief. Moira had abandoned Bill and was now latched onto William. Grace was stunned. Did the woman have no scruples whatsoever?

"I'm sure it's not how it looks, Betsy," she said.

Betsy gritted her teeth and looked away. "It's none of my business if it is exactly how it looks. William and Moira are adults, and their actions are nothing to do with me."

Grace gave Betsy's back a comforting rub. She knew her friend was just being stoic when inside she was deeply hurt.

"Would you like to dance, Moira?" William asked. "It'll help take your mind off things."

Moira ran her fingers under her eyes, careful not to smudge her mascara while she removed any evidence of her tears.

"Come on," William encouraged. "You never did give me that dance you promised."

"Oh, alright then." Moira was cold, and a dance would warm her up.

The number of dancers had thinned, many choosing to head home straight after supper, leaving plenty of space for William and Moira to join the slow waltz. William's dancing decorum had been left outside with his second beer. He pulled Moira close, wrapping his arm firmly around her waist and rested his forehead on hers. Moira closed her eyes, absorbed the heat emanating from William and relaxed into his hold, too emotionally drained to consider the implications of her actions.

"William isn't the gentleman I thought he was." "And as for Moira, I have no words a lady would use to describe her."

"I think we'd better go home after this dance," Grace said to the others.

"Yes, I agree," Alice replied for totally different reasons.

Grace glanced at her watch. It was eleven o'clock and they would have to be up again at six in the morning. The thought made her feel tired and she covered her mouth to hide her gaping yawn.

When the band wound the song down, William led Moira over to the other land girls.

"Looks like you three have had enough dancing, shall we head home?" he asked.

None of the women looked at William, all eyes were focused on Moira with varying degrees of animosity. Nobody answered the question as they eyed her hands looped around William's arm.

"Right then." William squirmed uncomfortably. "I'll just grab Mum's plates and we'll be off home. I'll meet you at the car if you like."

"I'll help you get the plates." Moira turned towards the kitchen.

William didn't refuse Moira's help this time and the pair quickly walked across the hall.

"There's Bill's jacket." Moira picked it up from where it was abandoned over the back of a seat. "Something terrible must have happened for him to leave without taking his jacket."

Grace, Betsy, and Alice found the Plymouth unlocked.

"If she wants him, she can have him." Betsy hurried to climb into the back seat. The leather was cold as she slid over and sat behind the driver's seat so she could avoid eye contact with William.

The boot lid shut with a thump and William and Moira climbed into the front seat.

"All aboard?" he asked but got no reply. "Right then, best get you all home."

The rumbling of the Plymouth's engine as it laboured along the tar seal road back to Whipsnade was the only noise that disturbed the silence of the night, inside and outside the vehicle.

Betsy stared into the darkness, pierced only intermittently by the lights of farmhouses where the occupants were still awake. Grace reached over and held Betsy's hand. She could her friend's tension and it didn't ease.

When William pulled the Plymouth up outside the Whipsnade homestead, Betsy didn't wait for any act of chivalry from him, she let herself out of the car and headed straight up the path to the front door.

Grace paused, contemplating who to help: Betsy who'd stormed off or Moira who was slumped into William's side, her head resting on his shoulder.

"Goodnight," William called out to Betsy. The only response was the shutting of the front door and a sleepy murmur from Moira.

"I'd best go and feed the lamb." Alice climbed out of the car and rushed inside to change into her farm clothes.

"Yes, Dr Doolittle needs to attend her patient," William said. "I'd better put the car away."

"What about Moira?" Grace asked.

"Unless you want to carry her up the stairs, I'll have to."

Grace looked up at the house. There was no light shining from Captain Boyle's window, not that there should be, but she wanted some signal that Ben would still be there. If William didn't need her help, then she'd check on Ben before they got back to the house.

"Alright then," she said. "Thank you for the ride."

"Moira!" With the car safely in the garage, William gave her a nudge to wake her up. "Moira!"

"What? Who? Where?" Moira struggled to determine where she was in the darkness of the shed.

"We're at home now," William replied. "Are you okay to walk?"

"Yes! Why wouldn't I be?" Moira slid across the seat and climbed out of the car. Then she stopped. "Where am I? It's so dark. Turn the lights on."

"We're in the car shed. There are no lights. Just turn to your left and walk straight ahead."

The car shed was home to the Plymouth and a family of spiders that had spun an intricate network of webs among the wooden rafters and from dwang to dwang. Moira walked with her hands splayed out to her sides, one on the side of the car and one on the wall of the shed.

"Aargh!" She walked straight into the interlaced threads of a spider's masterpiece strung from the rafter to wall. The silken sinews stuck to her skin and clung to her hair. Moira froze, too panicked to move any further.

William rushed to her aid. "What's wrong? Are you hurt?"

"There ... there's something on my face," she said through sobs.

William helped Moira out of the shed and in the moonlight could see the cause of her distress.

"It's just a cobweb." William laughed and wiped the web from Moira's face. "We'd best get you inside, I think."

Chapter Eighteen

A shaft of light slithered under the door of the bedroom Grace shared with Betsy. It signalled that Betsy was still awake and Grace had time to check on Ben. She crept over to Captain Boyle's bedroom and quietly turned the door handle. Her heart beat so loud she felt it would surely give her presence away. The niggling feeling that the room would be empty, that Ben would have left, seemed to be the only reason why it thumped so rapidly.

She pushed the door slowly, apprehensive at what would be revealed. Darkness greeted her. She imagined Ben had pulled the curtains but told herself that was silly; she'd seen them open, and he wouldn't do anything to give his presence away.

Grace closed the door behind her and waited until her eyes adjusted to the darkness. The silhouette of the room's furnishings gradually came into focus but she still couldn't make out Ben's presence. She tiptoed closer to the bed. Her ears heard him before she could see him curled up in a foetal position under the covers. His breathing was raspy, mucous rumbled in his throat as his blocked passages struggled for air.

Grace exhaled a huge breath she hadn't realised she'd been holding, and a slow smile crept over her face. Ben was still here. She pressed her hand to her heart and felt relief wash over. The feeling was quickly replaced by concern. He wasn't well, and she was doing a poor job of looking after him.

She headed to the door, eager to get down to the kitchen to make another lemon honey drink. The sound of William and Moira on the landing stopped her. She put her ear to the door and waited until she was certain it was safe to leave undetected.

The door to Moira's room was open, light and laughter flooding onto the landing. Grace couldn't risk going downstairs yet. She'd have to wait until William had gone. For Betsy's sake she hoped he'd leave sooner rather than later. Until then, Betsy needed Grace's help more than Ben.

"Are you alright, Betsy?" Grace asked as she closed the door to their bedroom.

"I'm fine. I'm just tired."

Grace was unconvinced but decided not to push further. She undressed in silence and climbed into her bed.

"We'd best get some sleep then."

"I think I'm a bit wound up for that yet." Betsy sighed. "I'm so angry."

"Why angry?"

"Moira's total lack of morals. William's response to her."

"You don't have any control over how they behave. You said that yourself."

"Well, I'm angry at myself too, for that very reason. Why am I even thinking about William?" Betsy pulled at her hair. "Mostly … mostly I'm just angry at Roland for not being here. He should be at my side. We should be making a life together. He shouldn't be on the other side of the world in God knows what forsaken place."

Grace sat down beside Betsy and pulled her into a hug. It was meant to comfort, to ease Betsy's anger and it succeeded but it created a silence and into that void fell the noises from the next-door room. Murmurings. The voices of a man and a woman. William and Moira. William in Moira's room. Grace felt the realisation intensify Betsy's anger; her body went rigid. The murmurings became laughter, giggling in the deep of the night.

"He's in her room." Betsy's voice held both disgust and disbelief. She broke away from Grace's hug, shoved her fingers firmly into her ears, squeezed her eyes shut tight and curled up into a foetal position.

Grace pulled the covers up over Betsy and turned out the light. It would be a long night if the noises were going to continue. She hoped not. She wasn't doing a good job of looking after her friend either.

With William's assistance, Moira made it up the stairs to her bedroom, only to trip on the rug and fall face first onto her bed. She rolled over and giggled at herself.

"Moira," William laughed. "I think you need some sleep, let's get you into bed."

"Are you hopping into bed too?" Moira asked as she attempted, unsuccessfully, to remove her shoes.

"Tempting Moira, very tempting but not this time." William removed her shoes, his hand brushing her ankle as he did so.

Moira managed to stand and turn her back to William. She held her hair aside so he could undo the centre full-length zip on her dress. The teeth of the zip separated to enticingly reveal the porcelain skin of Moira's shoulders, waist, and lower back.

William sucked in his breath at the sight of her white silk underwear. He closed his eyes and shook his head. When he reopened his eyes, Moira had turned back around. She let her dress drop to the floor and lie like a fallen halo around her feet. William coughed, almost spluttered, he stepped around her and pulled the bed covers aside.

Moira slid between the cool cotton sheets. She held them open and beckoned William to join her.

"Not this time." William took the bed covers from Moira's hand and tucked them in around her and quietly left the room before she made an offer no man would refuse.

Grace woke extra early but lay still and listened for movement about the house before quietly leaving her room. The door to Moira's bedroom was ajar and allowed Grace to check who had stayed overnight. She tiptoed along the landing to peek inside. Moira's red locks lay in disarray on the white pillowcase and traces of lipstick still stained her parted lips. The dishevelled bed exposed a breast and revealed her nakedness beneath the sheets. How long William had stayed, Grace wasn't certain but at least, for Betsy's sake, only one side of the double bed was occupied this morning.

Grace's next task was to check on Ben.

"Have you come to dance?" he asked in a hoarse whisper as she approached the bed.

"I've come to see if you are feeling better."

"Not too bad." Ben tried to smile but it was half-hearted. Sweat beaded his forehead and a row of tiny droplets sat as a watery moustache.

"Not too good either." In the way her mother had done on many an occasion, Grace checked Ben's temperature with a hand on his forehead. "You've got a fever."

"But I feel quite cold."

Ben's body had been fighting the infection, sweating out the virus and his pyjamas and the sheets he lay on were damp and cold. Grace knew they needed changing but how she'd manage to do that and get them washed and dried without Mrs Terrill knowing, was another dilemma she had no solution for.

"We need to get you into something warm."

In Captain Boyle's drawers she found another pair of pyjamas and from the wardrobe, she retrieved his dressing gown. It was a heavy robe in a blue and green tartan pattern, just like Grace's father wore. She wondered what her father would have to say about the situation she'd got herself into, harbouring a runaway soldier. Being the only daughter, she had always been her father's favourite but Grace was uncertain she'd be able to twist him around her little finger this time.

"Here." Grace lay the clothes on the bed. "Better get these on."

Ben drew back the covers and pushed himself up to sit on the edge of the bed. Every movement appeared an effort.

"Whoa, a bit woozy," he admitted. "I might need a hand."

Grace had never imagined she'd be alone in the bedroom of a man she'd never met, undressing a man she barely knew but here she was, with no choice but to do so. She did have another option but it wasn't one she wanted to take. Turning Ben over to the authorities would be, considered by some, the right thing to do but Grace couldn't bring herself to do it. She pictured each button she undid as a bullet the firing squad would shoot into his chest. She wouldn't be held responsible for sending a young man to such a fate.

Sitting half-naked and vulnerable on the bed, Ben wasn't just a runaway soldier, he was a man who made Grace's insides do somersaults. Even when she knew he was in no condition to do anything physical, she wanted to wrap her arms around him, she wanted to kiss him like there was no tomorrow and she wanted him to be her first.

Fortunately, common sense prevailed. Goose bumps prickled Ben's skin and he began to tremble with cold. Grace grabbed the pyjama top, fed one arm into a sleeve, then the other and buttoned it up.

"Do you think you can stand?" she asked.

"I can do anything you want me to," Ben joked.

Grace inhaled deeply. If only Ben knew what she wanted.

"We need to get your pants off ..." Grace felt her cheeks glow red.

"Oh, Grace," Ben interrupted, before he fell back on the bed exhausted. "I thought you'd never ..."

"To put clean pyjama pants on."

"You'll have to. Sorry. Not feeling so good."

Mortified, Grace grabbed hold of the bottom of the pants legs and pulled. They came free easy, and she lay them on the floor to dry. Taking the clean pants, Grace threaded each of Ben's feet through the top. She pulled on the waistband until she had the pants up to his knees, all the time keeping her eyes on the pyjamas and not Ben.

"You'll need to help now," she said but Ben didn't reply.

He had fallen back to sleep.

Tell yourself you're a nurse, a silent conversation began in Grace's head. If you were posted to a hospital at the front, you'd have to deal with naked men every day and think nothing of it. You've seen a penis before. Your brothers all have one. You didn't get all wound up and silly when you saw their appendages.

Keeping her eyes averted, Grace pulled the pants up, with one hand either side of the waistband. Ben was a dead weight on the bed, and it was awkward to get the waist of the pants under his bottom. Without thinking, she looked to see what the obstruction was, and came face to face with Ben's cock.

"Grace!" Betsy had followed the noises coming from the next-door room. "Not you too?"

"Ah! Umm!" Grace jumped up and away from the bed. "Umm ...no, it's not what it looks like."

"I thought you'd all be full of excited chatter about the dance," Nel said. The dining table stayed silent except for the clang of cutlery on plates. The land girls were either focused on their breakfast or their eyes were averted to the ceiling. Nel checked the ceiling, there was nothing special overhead.

"Did something happen?" she asked. "William? You're not your usual happy self."

William didn't answer. He was staring at Betsy, trying to catch her eye but Betsy looked everywhere but at him.

"Very well then. I'll just wait for the village grapevine." Nel shook her head. "I just hope none of you have done anything rash or foolish you will regret."

"Well," Duncan said. "Farm work doesn't stop just because you've indulged a bit too much. Too bad if you've had a big night. You've been here a few weeks now and you're supposed to learn all facets of farming while you're here. So, I think it is time for a change around of tasks."

Moira frowned at Duncan. She'd already asked Grace to let her take the milk to the factory tomorrow morning. She planned to call in at Bill's house on the pretext of returning his jacket.

The conversation on the way to breakfast had surprised Grace. There was no mention of William being in Moira's room, in fact, Moira hadn't mentioned William at all. Grace wondered if, in her tipsy state, Moira had forgotten how she'd made it to her bed. Betsy certainly hadn't; she was just as livid. Perhaps more so after discovering Grace in a compromising position. It had taken Grace a while to convince Betsy nothing had happened between her and Ben. Eventually Betsy helped to move Ben to the dry side of the bed but she wouldn't come anywhere near him until he was fully clothed.

"From this afternoon, Alice can show Grace how to feed and clean the pigs and Betsy can teach Moira how to milk the cows," Duncan announced. "I'll keep an eye on you all to make sure you don't miss anything."

Betsy scowled at Moira. Grace knew the last thing Betsy wanted was to spend time with Moira.

"Before that though, there are some fences out the back that need fixing. We'll get the gear after breakfast and head out on the truck," Duncan informed the group.

"Do you want me to give you a hand?" William offered.

"That would be great, son. Another pair of male hands on the job would be so much easier." Duncan turned to Alice. "Has that lamb been fed this morning?"

"Yes, I gave Lulu a bottle before I came in for breakfast." Alice gulped and braced herself for Duncan's response.

"Lulu? You've named a bloody lamb." Duncan shook his head in disbelief. "The sentimentality of women. I'll never fathom it."

"Duncan!" Nel gasped. "The naming of a lamb isn't the 'done' thing, but neither is swearing at the breakfast table and on a Sunday too."

"Lulu is special," said Alice. "She likes playing with me."

"It'll be back in the flock soon enough." Duncan grunted. "And you won't know it from any other."

After breakfast, the group assembled at the implement shed to await further instructions from Duncan.

"We need a strainer post," he said. "Two of you grab one off the heap and put it on the truck. The other two get an armload full of battens each."

Grace and Betsy were quick to respond to the request, that is, until they tried to lift the post, one at each end but it still weighed heavy, and they grunted under the strain.

"Let me help you." William offered to take over from Betsy.

"I can manage," Betsy replied through gritted teeth.

The women carried the post but had to concede defeat when they reached the truck. Betsy wasn't strong enough to lift the strainer up onto the deck. Fortunately, William ignored her refusal of help and was waiting to give the strainer the last heave.

Moira and Alice added the battens. Meanwhile Duncan had gathered coils of barbed and number eight wire, a box of fencing staples and the tools necessary to carry out the repairs.

"Shall I drive?" Moira asked when they had finished loading the truck.

"No," came Duncan's unwelcome reply. "I think we need to teach one of the others to drive. Alice?"

Alice looked terrified. Whether it was terror about driving or terror about Duncan, Grace couldn't decide.

"Right then, in behind the wheel," Duncan ordered, pointing at Alice. "The rest on the back with the gear."

William jumped up onto the deck and held his hand out, first to Grace who was so slender and agile, then to Moira who held on for a little too long.

"Sit over that side on top of the posts," he suggested before holding his hand out to Betsy who had no choice but to accept.

The frisson of excitement that passed when William's large hand clasped Betsy's was visible, but Betsy pulled her hand away as fast as possible, and it was replaced by the anger Grace had born witness to last night and this morning.

There was limited space with the fencing gear on the truck. Betsy was forced to sit next to William. She wrapped her arms around her legs, tried to furl herself into a tiny bundle, and looked anywhere but at the man beside her.

Under Duncan's instruction, Alice started the truck and headed out to the paddock where the fences needed attention. The truck, its load of gear and passengers all jerked with her first gear change. The jolt ruined Betsy's good intentions. If it wasn't for William's quick hands wrapping around her shoulders, she probably would have been thrown from the deck.

"Sorry," William said, rubbing her shoulders.

Betsy heard the apology but didn't speak her thoughts. She responded with a scowl directed at Moira. It told William all he needed to know.

"Nothing happened," he murmured, loud enough to be heard over the noise of the truck but quiet enough to keep their conversation private. Betsy frowned and wouldn't look him in the eye. He put his hand to his heart. "I swear, Betsy, I swear nothing happened."

Betsy kept looking straight ahead. "Even if I believe you, it makes no difference to me. I'm engaged to Roland."

Chapter Nineteen

By the time they reached the paddock at the back of the farm, Alice appeared more confident with her driving. There were no more missed gear changes, even though she'd had to perch on the edge of the seat to reach the pedals and she'd managed to manoeuvre the truck through gates, with a few last second yanks on the steering wheel by Duncan.

"Right," Duncan said, getting everyone's attention. "We've got to dig in a new strainer at this gate, replace the broken battens and tighten the wires."

Duncan looked around the women's blank faces.

"I'm guessing none of you have done any fencing before."

The land girls all nodded to confirm their complete lack of knowledge.

"We'll work in pairs then. Grace can take the fencing pliers and remove the staples from all the broken battens. Start over there on the back fence while we fix this strainer." Duncan took the fencing pliers and demonstrated to Grace how to wrench the staples from the post. "Mind the barbs on the wire, they can be sharp and the rusty ones can give a nasty infection."

Duncan looked around the group. "Alice, you go with her. Take a bucket and pick up all the staples and bits of wood. We don't want them left lying in the paddock hidden by grass and if this war continues for too long, we will have to fix and re-use the better ones."

The bucket Alice picked up was itself being re-used; an old paint tin with a piece of number eight wire for a handle.

"Son, we need this fence to keep the rams in, so you'd better staple the new battens." Duncan's look implied the women were incapable. "We want them straight and evenly spaced."

William waited with baited breath to see which of the land girls his father would get to help him.

"Moira," Duncan started.

William's shoulders slumped with disappointment.

"You can help me fix this strainer," Duncan said. "Get that shovel off the truck, will you? It'll need a big hole; we'd better get started."

Moira grunted as she stomped away to get the shovel.

"Betsy, you can brace the battens for William. He'll show you how."

William grinned; he couldn't hide the delight that he was going to spend the morning with Betsy.

Equipped with battens, hammer and staples, William and Betsy went to where Grace and Alice had removed the first batten. William showed Betsy how to hold the batten up to the wire and brace it with her hands and feet while he climbed through to the other side with the staples and hammer. The top and the third wire were barbed, the others number eight. William held each wire in place while he hit in the staples. Every thump of the hammer reverberated through the post into Betsy. She stood rigid and absorbed the jarring.

"Relax, Betsy," William said between staples. "It's easier if you just relax."

He'd rolled up his shirt sleeves and looked calm and casual. His arm muscles flexing each time he hit with the hammer.

"I would if I thought it was safe," she replied.

With the first batten securely stapled, they moved onto the next and soon developed a routine as if they'd been fencing together since the beginning of time. Some of the battens simply needed re-stapling, others that had cracked and splintered needed replacing. Betsy quickly worked out which was which but she made the fateful mistake of looking at William. He caught her eye and winked. Betsy coloured from head to toe and lost all concentration. As she lifted the next batten into place, she snagged her finger on the barb of the wire.

"Ouch!" There was only a small cut on her index finger, but blood spurted with each pump of her heart.

William reached out, took hold of Betsy's hand, and did what he would have done, had it been his own finger. He put

Betsy's finger in his mouth and sucked. The gesture was kind but that wasn't the only message conveyed or received.

The warmth of William's tongue curved around her finger, sent any remnants of anger packing, quickly replaced by a heat of a totally different nature. Betsy gulped. She glanced around the paddock to see if any of the others were watching.

Eventually, William removed Betsy's finger from his mouth. He inspected the wound, and saw that the bleeding had eased but not stopped. He selected the cleanest edge of his handkerchief and tore off an inch-wide strip. It wasn't the most hygienic bandage but it would have to do until they got home.

"There," he said as he knotted off the cotton strip wrapped around Betsy's finger. "That should do the trick."

Seeing Grace and Alice had completed this side of the fence, the pair resumed their task, taking extra care around the barbed wire. Near the end of the first side, they ran out of replacement battens and had to return to the truck for another armful.

Moira was red-faced, sweaty and grunting with each shovel load of dirt she lifted from the post hole which was now several feet deep. When she stopped to rest, leaned on the shovel handle for support and wiped the perspiration from her brow, she saw William and Betsy approach.

"Making good progress?" Duncan asked his son.

"Getting there." William winked at Betsy.

Moira looked unimpressed.

"I think we're ready to put the strainer in. Can you give me a hand to lift it?" The two men hoisted the heavy post from the truck deck and dropped one end into the hole. It hit the bottom with a thud. "Thanks, son, we should be able to manage again now. Shovel that dirt back into the hole, Moira. I'll pack it down as you go."

"What?" Moira arched her aching back. "I have to put it all back now? How come I get all the hard jobs?" she muttered.

William and Betsy, each with a bundle of battens, returned to the other side of the paddock.

"Looks like I'm in the dog box with you and Moira. She's peeved because I didn't do anything and you're angry because you think I did something."

"You were in her room," Betsy replied in an accusatory tone.

"I just helped her upstairs. She'd had too much to drink."

"The pair of you were laughing."

"Moira tripped over, landed face first on her bed. It made her giggle and she looked ridiculous so, yes, I laughed."

"But I saw you at the dance."

"Moira was upset about Bill disappearing without an explanation."

They reached the fence, dumped their bundles of battens on the ground except for one which Betsy held in place for William.

"I like you, Betsy," William said when the second staple closed tight over the wire.

Betsy's eyes grew wide, and she released the batten to fidget with her engagement ring.

"I know you are engaged," William quickly added. "I would like us to be friends though. We can be that, can't we?"

William was ready with another staple, so Betsy had to resume her bracing position.

"You're about to go to war, William," she said. "Sadly, it seems to be near impossible to have any sort of relationship with someone who is fighting a war on the other side of the world."

"But I could write." William finished hammering. "I could write and tell you about all the places we go, all the things we do."

"I've been waiting weeks for such news from Roland. Why do you think you'd be able to do what Roland hasn't managed?"

William hooked the hammer over the top wire and took Betsy's hand in his. William rubbed his thumb gently across the back of her hand. "Please." He sounded innocent, like a child asking its mother for a treat.

Eventually, a tiny smile crept onto Betsy's face and slowly she gave a hesitant nod of assent.

"You can write," she conceded but added a proviso. "As a friend."

"Thank you." William's face lit up with delight. He leaned over and kissed Betsy's cheek. "A kiss from one friend to another."

They finished one batten and moved on to the next and the next, each smiling, each contented with what they had agreed. Writing to one another would not breach any promises made to others and would leave the door open for any opportunities for something more in the future.

"You can't tell me what to do, you know." Moira stood in the cowshed, her hands on her hips. "You don't know any more than I do."

Betsy looked at Moira, tried to decide from her demeanour whether she was talking about milking or men.

"Well, I think we'd just better stick to the job at hand."

The cows, eager to be relieved of their milk, bellowed, and jostled in the yard, edging closer to the two women.

"Okay, I'll set the milk can up and you get the cows into the bale." Betsy turned. "Watch out for Stroppy," she said as she walked toward the machine room.

"Don't call me 'Stroppy'," Moira groaned. "You're just jealous about me dancing with William. You've got the problem, not me."

Moira heard a loud slobbering beside her and turned to find a cow, its head at her shoulder, noisily chewing its cud. A green tinged, saliva covered tongue reached out towards her ear and she shrieked with horror, jumped out of the way, and yelled at the cow.

"Get in the bale, you beast."

The cow nonchalantly retracted its tongue, regurgitated another mouthful, and recommenced chewing, all while it ambled into the bale oblivious to Moira's disgust. Another cow, content in its twice daily routine, took up the second bale just as Betsy returned from the machine room.

"Hello, girl," Betsy gave the cow a pat on her rump and secured the chain behind her. A quick wash of the cow's udder and the cups were attached. Betsy leaned her forehead against the cow's side, closed her eyes and breathed in rhythm with the cow and the soothing suction of the cups.

"Oh, Roland, I hope you won't be angry with what I've agreed to." Betsy whispered to herself. "It's purely platonic. I'd tell you but I wouldn't want you to get the wrong idea when you are so far away and dealing with so much already. I wish I could see you. That mischievous twinkle in your brown eyes. I can picture your lips, your strong square jaw ..."

Betsy bolted upright on the milking stool, her back rigid with concern.

"I can't … I can't picture all of your face. I feel so disloyal. I'll have to see William after milking and tell him I've changed my mind."

In the adjacent bale, Moira gingerly washed the cow's udder and on the third attempt managed to get all four cups suctioned onto the teats.

"If you're talking to me, Betsy." Moira called out over the noises of the shed. "I can't hear what you are saying."

"Thank you, girl," Betsy said. Having hand milked the final delivery from the cow, she stood, patted the animal on the rump again and released her back into the race.

"Right, you must be finished too." Moira heard the gate open, removed the cups and reached up to push the lever to release her cow.

"You'd better flush out the last of the milk first." Before he had to take William to the train station, Duncan ducked over to the shed to check on the milking. He'd been quietly observing from the side of the shed and put his hand on the lever to stop the gate from opening. "It's not good farming practice to send an animal back to the paddock without emptying her first. It means we don't get maximum money for the milk; we don't get milk for the house and the cow can get mastitis."

Moira sighed and flopped back down onto the stool. She put the milk bucket under the cow and began pulling on her teats. Nothing happened.

"No milk, I think she must be empty," she said to Duncan.

Duncan sighed, shook his head, and crouched down beside Moira. Using the correct technique, he soon had milk spurting into the bucket.

"Squeeze and pull, squeeze and pull," he said as he demonstrated.

Moira took over. She pulled on the teats with a little more strength than was necessary, her patience wearing thin, but the milk continued to flow into the bucket. She persisted until the flow reduced to a trickle. She looked around to get Duncan's approval but he had already stood and left the shed. Moira let the cow exit the bale and turned to find the next one waiting, its head straining forward and the whites of its eyes bulging angrily. The cow mooed loudly. Moira glared at the animal. She unhooked the chain and stood to the side to let the cow into the bale.

The cow kicked out just as Moira crossed behind it to hook the chain back on. Moira's shin bore the brunt of the cow's hoof, the force of the kick dropped her to the ground. She screamed before she landed hard on the cold, wet concrete and had the wind knocked out of her.

Betsy abandoned her milking and rushed to Moira. She saw the cow was the one she and Grace had called 'Stroppy' and quickly attached the chain before it could back out of the bale and cause more strife. She grabbed the leg rope, looped it around the cow's leg and pulled hard to tie it back against the post.

Moira grimaced in pain as she clutched her shin.

"Do you think you can stand?" Betsy asked. "We'd better get you out of harm's way." Betsy stood behind Moira and hitched her forearms under Moira's armpits. "I'll help you."

Together they managed to get Moira up. She hung onto the wooden rail and tried to put weight on her foot but screamed again in agony.

"It must be broken," she howled.

Betsy crouched down and cautiously lifted the leg of Moira's overalls. Below the rim of her gumboot, blood throbbed beneath the taut skin and a purple mound rose from Moira's shin. She couldn't tell if it was broken or not but knew that Moira wasn't going to be any good to finish milking.

"I'll go get the broom. You can use it as a crutch." Betsy ran off to the machine room.

"Bloody cow!" Moira yelled.

"That's Stroppy." Betsy returned with the broom. "I did say to watch out for her."

Moira took the upturned broom and hooked it under her armpit.

"You'd better keep milking," Moira told Betsy as she hobbled away. "I'll get Nel to phone the doctor."

Moira limped slowly across the yard and over to the farmhouse.

"Help!" she yelled, opening the farmhouse back door, before lowering herself awkwardly onto the porch step.

A cool southerly was blowing and it, combined with the cold concrete step and overalls wet from the cowshed floor, chilled Moira to the bone. There was no noise from inside and no one came to her aid. She removed her gumboots, the first came easily but the boot on her injured leg didn't want to budge. She had to wrench it off and nearly passed out with the resulting pain. Moira leaned back, rested her head on the door frame and closed her eyes to the agony. She focused on long deep breaths, inhaling and exhaling to the count of four, willing her heart beat to slow.

Minutes passed. No one was home. If Moira wanted to telephone for help, she was going to have to do it herself. She manoeuvred the broom back under her armpit and pushed on the door frame until she was upright again. She made it to the passage and flopped down on the stool beside the telephone.

After the operator put her call through, there were several clicks and rings before Moira's call to the doctor's surgery was answered, only to find that he was already out on a call and wasn't expected back for an hour or two.

"Damn," Moira cursed. "Nothing's going my way today."

She hobbled back into the dining room and pulled a chair close to Duncan's armchair so that she could elevate her leg. Unconcerned about her wet and dirty overalls, she slumped down into the chair.

Chapter Twenty

Bill had been finishing a phone call to his brother when Moira's distressed voice came on the party line the neighbouring houses shared. Privacy meant he should have put the phone down, but he didn't. When he heard that Moira was hurt and the doctor was unavailable, Bill grabbed a jacket and headed to the truck.

The back door was unexpectedly ajar when he arrived at Duncan and Nel's house. Although never locked, the door would normally have been shut at this time of year when the weather was cooling. Bill went inside, closing the door after him. From the door to the kitchen, he saw Moira asleep in the chair; her dishevelled hair had fallen across her cheek and tears had reddened her eyes.

Moira stirred as Bill approached. Her eyes widened with fright until she realised who was standing over her. She shook her head to clear the fuzziness.

"I heard you needed help." Bill crouched down beside the chair. "What have you done?"

"How did you hear?" Moira asked.

"I heard you on the party line," Bill explained. "Thought I'd come and help you until the doctor arrives. Can I take a look?"

"Careful!" Moira tensed. "Don't touch it."

The contusion was now the darkest shade of purple and had grown to cover the greater part of Moira's shin.

"Is it broken?" She asked Bill.

"Well, I'm not a doctor and I can't tell without touching it, but I don't think so. How did it happen?"

"Bloody cow kicked me, the bitch." Moira made no effort to act ladylike around Bill.

"Did it happen at the cowshed?"

"No, in my bedroom," she snapped sarcastically. "Of course, at the bloody cowshed."

"I just meant," Bill spoke calmly, "that if you managed to walk from the cowshed to here, then it is unlikely that you have any broken bones. I'll get some ice to put on it."

Bill got the ice tray from the Kelvinator fridge in the corner of the kitchen and emptied half a dozen of the frozen cubes into a tea towel. He pulled the four corners of the tea towel together to form a pouch and tied a knot so that the ice cubes couldn't fall out.

"Here you go." He held the ice pack out to Moira. "This should help."

"Can you put it on please, Bill," she asked, opting for a damsel in distress persona.

Bill pulled up another chair and sat down beside Moira. He gently placed the ice pack on her shin. She hissed in a breath with the initial contact but gradually relaxed as the ice took effect, slowly easing the throbbing and eventually numbing the area.

"There, does that feel better?" Bill asked after a few minutes.

"Yes," replied Moira. "Thank you." She put her hand on Bill's shoulder and gave it an affectionate rub.

"Is there anything else I can do for you?"

"You could kiss it ... me ... better," Moira suggested.

Bill chuckled. "Even when you're hurt, you're a sexy woman, Moira. How could any man resist?"

He leaned over and brushed his lips across Moira's. Bill went to move away but she wrapped her hand around his neck and pulled him back for another kiss, this one full of passion and zest.

"What on earth is going on here?" Duncan bellowed at the scene confronting him. Bill kissing a land girl in his kitchen, in his armchair.

"Isn't farewelling William enough upset for one day." Nel wiped her eyes and finished blowing her nose before she bustled in behind Duncan to see what the commotion was about. "What is it now?"

"Moira's been kicked by a cow," Bill explained as he leapt up and stood to face Duncan. "We're just waiting for the doctor to arrive."

"Sure, you are," Duncan noted sarcastically. "Who's milking the cows then?"

"Betsy," Moira answered.

"Well, I think you'd be more use, Bill, if you helped finish the milking." Duncan rubbed his forehead. "In fact, don't you have some of your own cows to milk?"

"Ah, yes," Bill conceded. "Yes, I do. I've dried most of them off, but I'd better get back and milk the few that are left. Take care, Moira. I hope you're feeling better soon."

Bill was gone out the door before Moira had a chance to reply. It was the second quick exit he'd made in as many days.

"I'd better get to the shed," Duncan announced. "The cows could be there all night if Betsy has to manage on her own."

When Duncan made it to the cowshed there were only a few cows remaining in the yard.

"I bet they haven't been milked properly," he muttered to himself. "Production will be down."

Entering the machine room, he was proven wrong. The expected five full milk cans were lined up and a sixth was receiving milk from the line. Duncan stood at the door to the shed and watched Betsy as she went from one bale to the other and back again, greeting the cows, patting them on the rump and thanking them for their milk. It was how milking was supposed to be done. Duncan's father had taught him – be good to the cows and they would be good to you. Duncan smiled. He left Betsy to finish the task and went to check on the other land girls in the piggery.

Betsy hadn't seen or heard Duncan come to the cowshed. She'd established a routine, cleaning and setting up one cow for milking, ensuring the milk was flowing before moving to the other bale and repeating the same process. By the time she'd hand milked the first cow, let it go and got another cow started in the bale, the second one would be ready to finish. She also worked out how often she needed to change the milk cans and was feeling very proud at managing everything without a spillage. Then there was the prospect of seeing William again after milking. Betsy was looking forward to catching up one last time before he went back to training camp.

Grace, Alice and Betsy came from different directions to reach the farmhouse just on dusk. The fading sun had taken with it the last heat of the day and the women were eager to get inside out of the southerly breeze which seemed to be delivering a chill direct from Antarctica. Grace had finished feeding the pigs and cleaning out the last few sties while Alice had gone off to feed her lamb. Duncan had offered to lock the cows in the paddock so Betsy could hose down the yard. They were cleaning up in the washhouse tub when Dr Green exited the kitchen. He said 'good evening' to them and was gone in a rush out the back door before they had a chance to reply.

"What's the doctor doing here?" Alice whispered.

"Moira." Betsy didn't elaborate.

"What happened to Moira?"

"Stroppy." Betsy had no time for detailed explanations, she hurriedly washed up and went inside to see William.

"Stroppy is a cow that likes to kick," Grace explained to Alice.

Now they both jostled for the soap and water, eager to discover what Stroppy had done to warrant a visit from the doctor.

Grace and Alice entered the kitchen to find Moira in Duncan's armchair smiling like a Cheshire cat and Nel and Betsy crying. Not at all what they had expected.

"What's happened? Why are you crying?" Grace asked, rushing to Betsy's side.

"Will ... iam," Betsy replied between sniffles.

"What's happened to William?" Grace scanned the room. "I thought it was Moira that was hurt."

"William has gone back to training camp," Nel explained. "They are being shipped out next week."

Grace gathered Nel and Betsy into her arms and drew them together for a comforting hug. It was yet another repeat of her brothers going off to war. Farewelling someone with no indication of when you might see them again was never easy.

"I am hurt," Moira called out from the chair.

"But you're smiling," Alice observed.

"Doctor has just said I've got to stay off my leg for four whole days."

"Well, you're not spending them sitting in my armchair," Duncan had arrived home and growled. "I'll drive you up to the main house after dinner. The rest of you better get an early night too, we've got to finish that fencing tomorrow."

As autumn progressed the temperatures cooled and traces of snow sprinkled the Southern Alps. Alice put another layer of clothing on under her overalls and made sure she had her woollen hat and gloves for the early morning ride to get the cows. It was too dangerous to venture out on horseback until the sun decided to rise so as the days shortened, the early morning wasn't quite so early.

Alice found the pattering of raindrops on the iron roof soothing as she lay in bed at night but when they persisted into the next day and hit her face, splattering with a force that stung and left red blotches on her skin, she wished it was she who had time off and not Moira.

Alice, Jess and Patch didn't dally with their morning task, all were eager to get the job over and done with. When they arrived at the paddock, the cows were cowering in a corner, their backs to the cold driving rain. The concentrated trampling of their hooves had destroyed what grass they hadn't eaten and combined with their effluent, created a quagmire Duncan wouldn't be happy about. Alice dismounted and opened the gate and called to Patch to round up the herd.

"Way back, Patch," she instructed. "Let's hurry and get out of this weather."

Betsy already had the lights on, milk cans set up and machines ready to go by the time the herd arrived at the cowshed. She managed fine without Moira. It took a little longer but that was alright, as long as she was back at the farmhouse in time to collect the mail. The anticipation of waiting for a letter from Roland was now heightened knowing that she hadn't been able to stop William from writing to her too. He'd already left for army camp before she could tell him she'd changed her mind. Betsy felt certain something would arrive in the post any day now. That belief made plunging her hands into the freezing water used to clean the cows' udders, bearable. With the rain and mud, the udders were particularly dirty this morning and Betsy's hands were soon red and cold.

Grace was grateful to be in the shelter of the pigsty, although the noise of the rain pelting on the iron roof combined with the squeals and grunts of the pigs expecting their morning feed, resulted in a deafening cacophony. Alice joined her after releasing Jess back to the paddock with a slab of hay but the din prevented them from any interaction other than head nodding and finger pointing. When there were only a few sties left to receive their morning ration, Grace pointed to the door and suggested Alice go and feed the lamb.

The milk powder was now stored in a tin beside Lulu's pen. Since she was no longer having warmed bottles, it made sense to keep the powder ready at hand. The lamb was growing into a bonny animal.

"Don't you grow too fast, Lulu." The warm, woollen bundle was tucked between Alice's legs, its tail wriggling with contentment as it gulped downed the milk. "Duncan will make me put you back in the paddock with the others."

"Has the mailman been?" Betsy opened the back door and yelled to Nel.

"I don't know, I haven't had time to look," came the reply from behind the kitchen door.

Betsy pulled the door shut again and ran, back into the rain, down the driveway. Puddles had formed in the hollows of the metal driveway but Betsy ran through them, oblivious to the cold water splashing up the legs of her overalls. She reached the letterbox and yanked at its door, the hinges screeched in protest, perhaps a warning that her wishes were to be dashed. The letterbox lay empty. Betsy looked up and down the road for the mail truck hoping it had been held up with the weather. Despondent, wet and bedraggled, she turned and walked back to the house. Betsy trudged through every puddle she could find, stomping her feet like a child.

Nel heard the backdoor slam. Grace, Alice and Duncan were already at the table tucking into their poached eggs on toast, so it had to be Betsy.

"No letter from Roland today." Nel knew the slam meant there was no mail. "That girl needs to be patient. I'd like a letter from William, but it's only been a day and even if he'd written straight away, it would at least be the end of the week before it was delivered to Orari."

There was no rest after breakfast. No time for Grace to check up on Ben or get some much-needed food to him. While Moira convalesced, the farm work continued with three to do the jobs of four. In between milking and feeding the pigs, the fence had to be finished. Grace, being the strongest of the three, had to be on the end of the hammer. After hitting several hundred staples into the battens and fence posts, her right elbow and bicep had grown. Her elbow was swollen and sore, her bicep taut and bulging like a man's. Grace tried to give her arm a rest and hammer with her left hand but after several whacks to her thumb she gave up.

"Every time you hit the hammer it feels like a bullet piercing my heart," Betsy said.

"Luckily for us, tucked away safely on a farm you'll never have to feel the pain of an actual bullet." Grace knew it was true for her and Betsy, but Ben, he could still face the firing squad if he was found.

"But Roland and William will be right in the line of enemy fire."

"And my brothers and thousands of others."

"If William was still here," Betsy said wistfully. "He could do the hammering."

"Yes, but he's not."

"I know." Betsy looked skyward. "I pray every day that they will be kept safe. If only I could get a letter to let me know my prayers were answered."

The house was quiet when Moira finally roused the next morning. Her watch explained the silence, it was after nine, everyone else would be off doing farm work. She arched her limbs, arms up to the mahogany bedhead and legs down under the blankets to the end of the bed. The stretch pulled at the bruising and revived the memory of yesterday's events.

Moira had pulled the eiderdown up under her chin in the cool of the night and now tucked her arms beneath its feathery warmth while she contemplated the day – the first of four whole days off. Her last holiday had been Christmas. Only three months ago but so much had happened. She rubbed her hands together and felt the coarseness of her newly formed callouses, the unwelcome result of farming.

Another hour had passed when Moira stirred again. The bedding did nothing to muffle a hungry rumble from her stomach. Nobody had brought her any breakfast. She'd have to fend for herself. She found her robe and slippers at the foot of her bed and pulled them on.

She was able to put a little pressure on her sore leg, so the makeshift crutch wasn't required. She stopped by Ben's room, not bothering to knock but barging straight in, to find him standing beside a window.

"You're looking better," she said. "Planning your escape, are you?"

"I can't stay locked up in this room forever."

"True but Grace won't want you to leave."

"She's just worried I'm not over my cold properly."

"I think it's a little bit more than that." Moira laughed. "Anyway, I'm hungry. Did anyone bring you breakfast?"

"No, nothing yet, I think Grace must be busy."

"I'll go and see what's in the kitchen. Come down if you want."
Moira went in search of food.

"Oh!" Mrs Terrill nearly dropped her basket of clean but wet clothes destined for the line. "Hello, dear. I didn't expect anyone to be home this morning."

"Just me, looking for some breakfast," Moira replied.

"Mmm, not much in the cupboards here." Mrs Terrill rested the basket on a bony hip. "I was expecting you girls to eat most of your meals at the McKnights."

"The doctor has ordered me to have four days off." Moira lifted the hem of her robe to reveal her shin which was now a mishmash of blues and purples.

"Oh!" Mrs Terrill gulped. "You go and sit down, dear. I'll just get this washing on the line, and I'll be right back in to put the kettle on. I think there is still some fruitcake in the tin. It'll be getting a bit dry but with a dollop of butter, it will be better than nothing."

Ben poked his head around the kitchen door and nervously scanned the room. "I heard voices," he whispered. "Is someone here?"

"Mrs Terrill. She's just at the clothesline. You'd best make yourself scarce. I'll let you know when it's safe."

Chapter Twenty-One

Ben had no sooner disappeared out one door when Mrs Terrill came back in from outside.

"Sorry, dear," Mrs Terrill said. "I heard you but didn't catch what you said."

Moira cleared her throat. "No. Nothing. Just talking to myself."

Mrs Terrill bustled about the kitchen, the fruitcake was sliced, buttered, and put on a dainty china plate in front of Moira before the kettle whistled out its tune.

"Now, you just sit down dear and tuck into that." Mrs Terrill poured herself a cup of tea and joined Moira at the table. "Did you injure yourself at the dance, dear? You girls were all having a wonderful time."

"Were you there?" Moira had been so busy twirling and spinning that she missed seeing Mrs Terrill.

"Oh, no dear, I haven't danced in years, my knees aren't what they used to be. I saw Mrs Chapman at church yesterday. She said it was a great success. So wonderful to have all those army-boys home for the weekend. Mrs McKnight must be beside herself, having to see her only son off again yesterday." Mrs

Terrill paused to take a sip of tea. "Everyone prayed for them at church, asked God to see them safely home. It's such a tragedy, this war. But then we have tragedies much closer to home too, don't we?"

"Well, my leg isn't so much a tragedy, more just an inconvenience that has the benefit of four days off."

"Not you, dear." Mrs Terrill sighed and stared into the distance with a forlorn look. "Poor Bill."

Moira sat upright at the mention of his name. "What happened to Bill?"

Mrs Terrill shook her head, brought herself back to the present and refocused on Moira.

"Well, it was his wife really, not Bill. He is such a lovely man, a very hard worker. I've been doing his housework for him since she passed. Just to help out. I'm off there after this actually. A shame they didn't have any children of their own. He's quite lonely now I think." Mrs Terrill stopped, took another sip of tea and held her cup aloft, resting her elbows on the table. She looked at Moira and smiled. "That's right, Mrs Chapman said you were dancing with Bill. A fine couple you made, she said."

"She did?" Moira tipped her head to the side. "I heard someone saying the land girls were gold-diggers but I'm not looking to settle down yet. What happened to his wife?"

"They used to love dancing. They would be on the dance floor from the first song until the very last. That is, until she became sick. She was a very attractive woman. Bill loved her dearly. He took care of her when she could no longer take care of herself. The doctor wanted her to be hospitalised near the end but Bill insisted. She wanted to die at home, and he wanted to honour her last wish. It was a big funeral, everyone in the district came." Mrs Terrill sniffed as tears threatened. "Well, enough of sad things, the world is full of them. We need to look on the bright side. What are you going to do today, dear? Write letters to home? Some sewing? Knitting?"

Moira coughed. "I plan to soak for a very long time in a nice hot bath."

"Well, I'd better get on with my cleaning and leave you to it, dear." Mrs Terrill gathered the dirty dishes, put them in the sink and left her in the kitchen.

The remaining tea in the pot was well stewed, but cold, by the time Mrs Terrill had finished the cleaning and left the house and it was safe for Ben to emerge. Moira had only seen him in his dirty uniform or pyjamas. She wolf-whistled at the sight of him in a red-checked- shirt and brown trousers.

"I've left you a piece of cake." Moira pushed the plate towards Ben.

"I'm starving." Ben scoffed the cake and found the tin in the cupboard. The two remaining pieces were soon gone. "I'll have to go and find some fruit or something."

"I can't do that for you." Moira pointed to her leg. "It should be safe though; I think everyone is up the back of the farm finishing the fencing. I'm off to have a bath. You'll have to re-boil the kettle and top up the pot."

With the door closed and the claw foot bath three-quarters full of water, Moira lowered herself into the warm depths and reclined back against the bath, letting the weightlessness of the water lift away her aches and pains.

She massaged shampoo through her hair then bobbed her head under the water to rinse the soapy lather before repeating the process and convincing herself that no dirt nor farm odours remained.

The bath water had chilled, and Moira's fingers were wrinkled like raisins when she decided to pull the plug. She stayed in the bath until the water had drained, sending the last of her worries spiralling down the drain plug and allowing a new mission to fill her focus. Moira needed to find a way to get to see Bill again.

Back in her bedroom, she opted for a dress. No smelly farm clothes for her today. The cotton dress she chose was fitting, cinched in at her slim waist, not unflattering and baggy like her overalls. And it was green with daring patches of scarlet, reflective of Moira's own mood.

She decided to explore the house. There was no sign of Ben, neither in his room nor the kitchen. Moira assumed he must be outside stealing fruit from the orchard.

Moira opened the door to the sitting room to find the room's large east-facing windows allowed the morning sun to bathe the room in sunlight and warmth. She made herself comfortable in an armchair beside the window and gave herself a manicure. The bath had removed the accumulated grime but her fingernails were in a sorry state. There was no option but to cut her broken nails back below the ends of her fingers. With the file she evened up what was left. There was no point in putting polish on them so she moved on to repaint her toenails, at least they had been protected in her socks and gumboots.

Sitting back to allow the polish to dry, Moira remembered the Plymouth, parked unused in the garage. Perhaps, if she still felt daring in the morning, she could sneak over to Bill's in the big car and no one would know. Or if her courage failed her, she could offer to take the milk to the factory in Duncan's truck and drop into Bill's on the way back. Duncan would no doubt want her to hurry and subject her to forty questions if she took longer than expected.

A movement in the garden caught Moira's eye. It was followed by a knock at the front door.

"Don't be lazy." Moira assumed it was Ben. "Go around to the back door."

The knocking persisted and Moira had no choice but to answer the door.

Bill had removed his hat and stood on the doorstep fidgeting with its brim. "Hello, Miss Moira."

"Oh, it's you." Moira was startled. "I thought you ..." She managed to stop herself from giving away Ben's presence.

"Valerie told me you were laid up and I just had to pop over and check you were alright."

"Thank you, Bill, that's very nice of you. But who is Valerie?"

"Oh, that's right, I forgot she likes to be known as Mrs Terrill to you young ones. Old-fashioned, sign of respect and all that." The more Bill chatted, the redder his face became. "You're looking very nice, umm, I mean well," he said.

"Would you like to come in?" Moira stood to the side and waved her hand to welcome him inside.

He glanced back over his shoulder, checking that there were no witnesses to his visit and stepped over the threshold.

"I know it's not the 'done' thing for a man to visit a young single woman unchaperoned and I don't want to upset Duncan anymore."

"Duncan is up the back of the farm fencing, so he'll be none the wiser."

Moira turned and hobbled back into the sitting room. She took a seat and put her leg up on the footstool. Her dress slipped aside and revealed her bruised and swollen shin.

"Bloody hell!" Bill looked horrified. "It's not any better, is it? What did the doctor say? Did they do an X-ray? It might be broken. Don't let them tell you it isn't unless they do an X-ray to make certain."

"Thanks for your concern, Bill. Nobody else seems to care."

"They don't always get it right, doctors, you know. I've spent many hours listening to them debate what could be wrong. Sometimes when they finally reach a diagnosis, it's too late. I wouldn't trust them."

Bill had gone all glassy-eyed.

"I can walk on it, Bill, so it can't be broken," she replied. "The doctor has given me four days off, so if I stay off it as much as possible, it should be alright."

"Well, who is going to look after you for those days? Staying off it, should mean just that."

"Mrs Terrill got me breakfast," Moira said.

"Yes, she told me that." Bill rubbed his chin as he thought. "I'll ask her to get you lunch as well and I'll bring you a meal in the evening."

"Thank you, that would be wonderful of you."

"We'll have you right as rain and ready to dance again in no time." Bill smiled as he stood to leave. "I'd better get home and do my jobs. I'll be back later with some dinner. I've made a big pot of pumpkin soup, that will do perfectly."

Moira went to stand and see Bill to the door.

"No, no," he put his hand out to stop her. "You stay there, I'll see myself out."

"Can a girl have a kiss goodbye then?" Moira ran her tongue over her lips in anticipation.

Bill lent down and pressed his lips to Moira's forehead.

"I'll see you tonight," he said before hurrying off.

"Not quite what I was wanting but better than nothing," she said to the closed door.

No sooner was the front door shut and a door on the other side of the passage opened.

"Who was that?" Ben asked emerging from the coat cupboard.

"Just Bill."

"You didn't tell him about me, did you?" Ben's voice rose in pitch.

"Nearly, I thought it was you at the door, too lazy to go around the back but no I didn't."

"Is he coming back?"

"Yes, tonight." Moira smiled at the thought of it. "He's going to bring a big pot of pumpkin soup. You can have some if you like."

"Maybe." Ben looked nervously at the front door. "If I'm still here."

Ben must have spent the afternoon back in Captain Boyle's room as Moira never saw him again that day. She saw Grace when she ducked over after milking.

"How is he?" Grace asked.

"Bill or Ben?"

"Bill's been here?" Grace started to panic. "What about Ben? Does Bill know about Ben?"

"No, and I won't tell him. He's coming back over tonight with a pot of soup. I've told Ben I'll save him some."

"That's nice, thanks Moira. That'll help get him back to full strength."

"Then he'll be good to get away from here."

Betsy had, and now Moira was reminding Grace that Ben was going to leave. Their warnings fell on deaf ears.

"I'd best go and check on him."

"If he's still here. I haven't seen him since this morning."

Grace took the stairs two at a time and didn't bother to knock on the bedroom door.

"Oh, thank goodness." She stopped, caught her breath, and smiled at Ben.

"Hi Grace." He stood at the window and turned to face her. "Thank goodness for what?"

"You're still here." The words were said before Grace thought through their meaning to her and to Ben. Did she want to let Ben know that she didn't want him to leave? Could she be that selfish, thinking only of her own needs and not of him imprisoned in these four walls? "Umm … I mean …" she stuttered. "Moira thought you might have gone."

"Not yet." Ben moved to sit on the bed. "There are so many people coming and going though. If I don't go soon, I'll be discovered, and it will all be for nothing."

"But your cold?"

"I'm feeling much better now."

"Have you eaten?"

"Mrs Terrill's fruit cake."

"That's not enough."

"No." Ben ran his hands through his short hair. "Moira nearly let slip that I was here."

"She said she wouldn't." Grace thought she had the other land girls on her side. They'd promised to keep Ben a secret. "I'll have a word with her."

"It doesn't matter." Ben shook his head. "It was an accident but how it happens makes no difference to the outcome. If it's not her, it will be someone else."

His stomach rumbled loudly. He reached under the bed and grabbed an apple from his knapsack. Juice trickled down his chin as he bit into the crisp flesh.

"You've been outside again." Guilt wouldn't allow Grace to look Ben in the eye. "I'm sorry, I should have got some more food for you. I'm not looking after you very well, am I? We've been so busy."

Grace sat on the edge of the bed, exhaustion catching up with her.

"It's okay, Grace." Ben put his hand on her shoulder. "I'm not your responsibility."

"But I said I'd get you food." Grace's face lit up at the thought of a decent meal for Ben. "Bill's bringing pumpkin soup tonight."

"He's part of the reason I need to leave." Ben took another bite of apple, slurped the juice, and crunched on the flesh. "He's already been here today. I had to hide in the cupboard until he left."

"He'll only be here while Moira's got time off." Grace could hear the desperation in her voice, but she kept digging for reasons to get Ben to stay. "Just another couple of days."

"Mrs Terrill, Bill, probably the doctor will come, Duncan and Nel; no doubt they'll all want to check up on Moira. Each person is another gun closer to the firing squad."

Grace stood and moved to the window. She needed space. Space between her and Ben. Space for her to be able to sort her feelings out. She couldn't explain the emotions that Ben ignited in her, how her pulse beat a little faster whenever she thought of him. It was more than just the need to help him. There was something else that lit a fire deep inside her.

"But we were supposed to have a dance." She knew it was a feeble excuse, but it was all she could think of. "You promised me we'd dance."

Ben balanced the apple core on the side table, stood and extended his arms, an open invite to dance here and now. Grace was unable to resist. How could she when it was her that had asked for a dance. How could she when her body was drawn to his like a magnet.

She placed her fingers on his upturned palm. The involuntary shiver that ran down her spine pushed her chest closer to his. The inch that separated them seemed to contain all the air remaining in the room. Grace averted her gaze; it felt too dangerous to look Ben in the eye.

"We haven't got any music," she whispered.

"We don't need any." Ben pulled Grace's body against his and led her around the room. "We are the music."

Grace closed her eyes. The warmth of Ben's breath on her neck was like the drawing of the bow on a violin. Her heart thumped an orchestral rhythm, its tempo raced, its boom rose in a crescendo. Around and around the room they spun. Grace imagined they were at the Orari Hall. Instead of everyone watching Moira and Bill they were captivated by her and Ben.

Ben was strong, yet gentle. Grace felt protected in his arms, like she could stay there for ever. But that was the problem. Staying with Ben for ever wasn't going to happen if they couldn't resolve his predicament. He was right, his secret was bound to be revealed by someone and soon. Grace had to help him hide somewhere safe until the war ended, until his actions could no longer be considered criminal.

Images of her and Ben together filled her mind. They were going to the movies, walking hand in hand in Hagley Park, rowing down the Avon and enjoying a cold beer at the pub. The slideshow disappeared in a woosh, along with the oxygen from her lungs, when Ben lay her backwards. Grace hung suspended, her head a foot from the ground, her legs bent at right angles and Ben arched over her, his eyes looking longingly at hers, his lips parted in anticipation.

She wrapped her hands around his neck and took what was offered. The kiss was filled with the urgency they both felt, the need to explore and experience before all was lost. Grace held on; she didn't want any of it to end.

The need for air finally drew them apart. Their ragged breathing was the only sound that filled the room. Grace was speechless, dumbstruck by the feelings – physical and emotional that engulfed her. What had she done? What was she going to do now?

Chapter Twenty-Two

When Moira heard the other land girls get up for work the next morning, she simply rolled over and went back to sleep. The only task on her agenda today was to get herself looking pretty for Bill's visit. He had, as he'd promised brought pumpkin soup for dinner last night and vowed to return today with some pie.

"Good morning, Moira," Mrs Terrill greeted Moira as she came down the stairs. A quick glance at her watch assured the housekeeper it was still morning. "Good to see you are resting up."

Moira couldn't decide if Mrs Terrill was being sarcastic or genuinely cared so didn't reply.

"Don't worry if you hear more gunfire," Mrs Terrill cautioned. "The army are finishing up their training exercise with a final battle. Two and a half-thousand soldiers practicing before they head off. Firing blanks though, not real bullets."

A knock at the door halted any further conversation.

"Hello Bill. I was just about to head over to your place," Mrs Terrill said as she opened the door. "Do you need something urgently?"

"No, no," Bill replied. "I was just heading into Geraldine for supplies and wondered if Moira ... ah, I mean Miss Harvey would like to get out of the house and come for a drive."

"That would be wonderful, Bill." Moira replied, dispensing with the formality Bill seemed to think was necessary in front of Mrs Terrill. "I've got my wages to bank at the Post Office. There's nowhere to spend them around here. I'll pop upstairs and grab my purse."

"You'd best grab a coat too," Bill suggested. "It's rather cold out."

"Your coat is on the coat stand," Moira called to Bill as she went up the stairs. "I picked it up when you left the dance in a hurry. I forgot to give it to you yesterday."

Bill gulped. "Sorry about that," he mumbled.

If Mrs Terrill had an opinion about this interaction, she kept it to herself.

Bill was the perfect gentleman; he held Moira's coat out for her to slip into, stood aside to allow her out the door and rushed ahead to open the passenger door of his truck. They hadn't gone far when Bill decided to light up his pipe. The truck's cabin filled with smoke before Bill had the pipe going properly. He offered the burning match to Moira who quickly took advantage of the chance to smoke without Duncan to moan at her. Bill waited until Moira's cigarette was lit and then wound his window down a little to let the smoke escape.

Nearing the intersection close to Geraldine they had to wait for a convoy of army vehicles to pass by. There were jeeps, motorcycles and trucks, painted in the standard khaki or camouflage and filled with supplies, weapons and soldiers. At the rear were a group of foot soldiers who appeared happy enough in their uniforms, just a little weary after lugging rifles and heavy packs for the past few weeks. Their discipline hadn't waned though; all eyes looked straight ahead. The convoy made an impressive sight.

"I don't envy them. It'll be freezing camping out tonight," Bill observed.

"They've been camping outside all the time, haven't they?"

"Yes, but I reckon there's going to be a frost tonight. Brrrr." Bill pretended to shiver with cold. "Part of their training though, they have to learn how to take shelter out in the open. If they are smart enough, they'll find a friendly farmer's hayshed."

Moira would have to warn Ben, tonight wasn't the night to leave.

It was a good ten minutes before they could continue, cross the Upper Orari Bridge and head down into Geraldine. Talbot Street was a bustle of activity, cars and trucks coming and going, pedestrians waiting to cross the road.

"I've missed the busyness of the city," Moira said.

"Geraldine's not quite a city but it does have a bit more happening than Orari."

Bill parked the truck on the main street, opposite the Wood's Store.

"I should be able to get everything I need in the general store," Bill announced, turning off the engine. "If your leg isn't too sore, would you like to come in and have a look around?"

Moira didn't wait for Bill to open the door for her, she was out of the truck before he'd made it past the bonnet. He rested his hand on the small of her back and guided her across the wide road and into the store. The shop doorbell announced their arrival with a jingle.

The general store didn't have any of the glamour of the department stores in Christchurch. Its unvarnished wooden floors had been worn to a smooth finish over the years. Clothing, bolts of fabric, fresh food and groceries all seemed to have a place amongst the disarray. Pots and pans hung from the ceiling, tools and garden implements leaned against the walls. Large glass jars on the front counter held a colourful assortment of sweets: blackballs, jelly babies, lemon sherbets, barley sugars and straps of jet-black liquorice. All that was left of the dwindling stock unable to be replaced with sugar rationing.

Bill went about his business, gathering the items on his list. When he was ready to pay, Moira joined him at the counter.

"Aah." Moira pulled a thin packet from a box on the counter. "Nylon stockings," she purred.

"Just came in this morning," the shopkeeper announced. "Scarce as hen's teeth with rationing. They're using the silk to make parachutes, much more important if you ask me. They won't last long."

Moira clasped the packet tightly and held it longingly to her chest. She already had one pair of nylon stockings, but a woman could never have too many and they didn't last forever. She found the rationing coupon that had been carefully stowed in her purse and handed it over.

"Add them to my account, please," Bill instructed the shopkeeper.

"Thank you, Bill." Moira placed her hand on his arm. "That is so very kind of you."

The shopkeeper saw the gesture and looked from Bill to Moira with a frown of disapproval but kept his thoughts to himself. Bill noticed the look of judgement, but it was too late to retract his offer.

They finished their business in the store and returned to the truck with the supplies.

"I've just got one more thing to do," Bill said. "I can meet you outside the Post Office if you like. It's just down there on the right."

Moira found the Post Office easily. Before she entered the building, she glanced back to see where Bill had gone. He was across the road, walking down the footpath with a posy of fresh flowers in his hands.

"He's bought me flowers." Moira blushed. "I'd better hurry and do my banking."

A few minutes later Moira exited the Post Office, but Bill was nowhere to be seen. She walked back up to the truck, but the truck sat empty. She crossed the road and walked down to where she had last seen the man that seemed to have a knack for disappearing. Moira stood outside the cinema and scanned the area, her frustration growing.

Opposite the cinema, St Mary's Church stood proudly amongst the trees. Out to the right, under the shade of a Norfolk pine, a movement caught Moira's eye. It was Bill. He was sitting on a park bench, no longer holding any flowers and it looked like he was talking to someone.

Moira stood, openly staring, mouth gaping, in complete disbelief. She turned and walked quickly to the truck, any pain in her leg forgotten.

"Stockings for me and flowers for someone else." Tears pricked at Moira's eyes. "I can't work you out, Bill. You're two different men in one; polite and gentlemanly but dishonest and two-timing at the same time."

Moira sat back, rested her head on the top of the seat and stared at the roof of the truck.

"Brrr, it's cold out there." Bill climbed into the driver's seat and rubbed his hands together. "Did you get your banking done?"

"Yes." Moira dared not look at him

"I see they're showing Gone with the Wind at the cinema on Saturday night."

Bill turned the key in the ignition. "Would you like to go?"

"With you?"

"Yes." Confused, Bill scratched his jaw.

"Aren't you busy?"

"No," he answered. "Or I wouldn't have asked you."

"The reviews have been good. I've wanted to go." Perhaps she had misinterpreted what she had seen. "That would be wonderful, thank you."

Bill glanced back to check the traffic, waited for several vehicles to pass, and did a u-turn to head back out of Geraldine.

"We could invite the other land girls," he suggested. "They might like a night out too."

Moira smiled but it wasn't one of delight.

Alice was greeted by a blanket of ice when she left the house the following morning. The rain had stopped overnight but a frost had taken its place, painting the ground a virginal white.

"Morning, Jess," Alice greeted the horse as she approached with the bridle.

Jess neighed in response and breathed plumes of water vapour into the cool morning air.

"It is cold, isn't it?" Alice asked, her own breath clouds rising to blend with the horse's.

"Yes, it is," Duncan replied from behind her.

Alice jumped. The question had been to the horse, and she obviously hadn't expected an answer.

"Sorry to startle you," Duncan continued. "Just thought I'd better come and warn you, it being the first frost and all. Not usual for this time of year but probably Mother Nature warning us about a harsh winter ahead. You'd better take it quietly with Jess. Don't want her slipping on any ice and tossing you off."

"Oh, oh, thank you." Alice slowed her heartbeat. "Thanks for your concern."

Duncan left to check the hay. This cold spell would stunt the grass growth, within a few weeks the paddocks would turn their winter brown and the result would be a fall in the cow's milk production. They'd probably have to dry them off early, if they didn't feed out some supplements. It was a balancing act Duncan had to manage each year to ensure the health and fertility of Captain Boyle's prized herd.

Alice and Jess set off to collect the cows from their paddock. Alice listened for the crunch of Jess's hooves as they bit through the ice blanket. The noise was reassuring in the cool morning. Anything less and Alice was afraid the pair would slip and fall.

A cloud of steam rose from the herd of cows huddled together in the paddock for warmth. They were reluctant to separate from the collective and mooed loudly in protest at Patch's bark to hurry them along. Alice sat astride Jess. Exhaling, while she opened and closed her mouth, Alice managed to shape her breath into balls of steam. She smiled as the balls floated away like balloons.

"This is much better than the hustle and bustle of the city, Jess." Alice spoke to the horse as if it was human. "You're much more comfortable than those cold wooden slats of the tram seats. And as much as I don't like these baggy overalls, they are much better than my old uniform. I'd be frozen to death if that was all I had to wear."

"Speak up, Patch," she called to the dog. Alice needed to refocus on the task at hand.

Nel had bacon crisping on a rack above the coal range. The enticing aroma filled the kitchen and welcomed the land girls when they arrived for breakfast. Grace imagined Ben would appreciate some bacon so piled her breakfast plate high. It had become her practice to dish up more than she needed for herself, pretending she was taking a snack for later.

"I think we need to start feeding out some hay," Duncan said. "It's important to keep the condition on the cows in this cold weather. Alice, if you could hitch Jess to the wagon, we'll go get hay after breakfast."

The door to the kitchen opened and Moira walked in.

"Well, well, look what the cat dragged in," Duncan said.

"Duncan!" Nel growled.

"I was only joking, Nel." Duncan placated his wife. "Are you feeling better, Moira? Ready for work again?"

"Umm," Moira pondered her reply. "I am feeling better. Thank you. But the doctor did give me four days off, so I think I'd better take his advice."

"Right." Duncan didn't like taking the Doctor's advice but Nel would really be on his case if he insisted Moira ignore it. "Another day it is then."

"I just came to relay an invite to the girls," Moira said. "Bill and I are going to the Geraldine cinema on Saturday night.

Gone with the Wind is playing. You're welcome to come along."

"Oh, Gone with the Wind," Nel sighed longingly. "I've heard that is such a beautiful love story."

Duncan rolled his eyes. "Just what we need with all you women around," he muttered. "There is no way on earth I'll be going to the cinema to see a love story."

"Oh yes please," Betsy replied. "If I can't live my own love story, I'll pretend Clark Gable is my hero instead."

"That would be great, Moira, we'd all love to go." Grace gave Alice a knowing look and replied on their behalf.

"I'll let Bill know then," Moira said as she turned to leave. "I'll be back at milking the day after tomorrow."

"Would you like to stay for some food, Moira?" Nel asked. "There is plenty here."

"No thanks," Moira replied. "Bill is bringing over a pie."

Duncan cleared his throat. "I'm not your father and as long as you do your farm duties, I don't have any rights to tell you what to do in your private time but ..."

"If Moira doesn't want this lovely food." Grace interjected to save Moira from the anticipated lecture and grabbed the last two slices of bread. "I'll make a sandwich for later, if that's okay? I'm famished with all of the fencing."

"That's fine, dear," Nel replied. "Help yourself. We can't have you ladies going hungry now, can we Duncan?"

Duncan slowly nodded in agreement. He changed his focus from Moira to Alice.

"That lamb," he began. "It'll be wanting to start eating grass. You'll need to put it out in the paddock."

"But how will I feed it when it's in the paddock?" Alice's lip trembled.

"Put it in Jess's paddock for a couple of weeks. You can feed it there."

"Can it wait until tomorrow? If there is going to be another frost tonight, she'll be better in the shelter of the shed."

Duncan rolled his eyes again.

"Bring Jess over to the implement shed," Duncan asked Alice as they put on their gumboots and jackets after breakfast.

The barometer was still reading in single figures. A southerly wind had blown the rain clouds away and brought a chill that made the girls wish they were back inside soaking up the warmth of the coal range.

Duncan made quick work of getting the wagon hitched to Jess.

"Grab those pitchforks," he directed, pointing to several pitchforks leaning against the wall of the shed. The more they had the quicker the wagon would be loaded. "And the ladder. We'll need it to get on top of the stack."

Grace saw Alice cringe at the mention of being on top of the stack and she knew then and there that she would offer to climb the ladder.

"You can drive, Alice." Duncan climbed up front of the wagon next to Alice, the other two climbed on the back.

The tension in Alice's shoulders didn't ease as she flicked the reins. "Come on, Jess," she said.

Grace had noted it happened every time Alice was close to a male. Her timid persona came to the fore, she shrunk into herself like a tortoise into its shell. But Grace had also witnessed Alice's strength and tenacity. This tiny woman was a contradiction and all Grace knew was that it had something to do with men. Didn't all life have something to do with men though? Grace's own predicament, or more precisely Ben's, had turned Grace's emotions upside down.

"Park the wagon parallel to the stack."

Duncan's order was for Alice, but it shook Grace out of her reverie.

"You two put that ladder up at the end of the stack and climb up with your pitch forks."

Grace was glad the instruction was directed at her and Betsy and happily climbed on top of the stack. The first fork loads of hay landed on the wooden tray with a thud. They were sodden, after the recent rain but once Grace and Betsy broke through into the dry matter the loads of fresh smelling hay floated down gracefully. Grace remembered with delight the hay fight they'd had in the paddock while turning the crop. She considered tossing a pitchfork of hay at Alice but the serious look on Duncan's face as he spread the hay out and picked up any loose bits that escaped the wagon, told Grace he probably wouldn't appreciate any frivolous behaviour.

The cows bellowed curiously when the wagon arrived at the gate. They jostled for position, eager to be the first to test the addition to their diet. Alice directed the wagon in a loop around the paddock and the land girls left a trail of dried grass in their wake.

"Don't feed it all out," Duncan instructed. "We'll give the rest to the sheep after lunch."

Chapter Twenty-Three

"I thought you weren't coming back to work until tomorrow." Duncan eyed Moira as he buttered a slice of bread.

"Just came to deliver this," she explained, holding up the bundle of letters. "There's mail for Betsy."

Betsy dropped her knife on the table, sucked in a breath and clasped her hands to her chest. "A letter. A letter for me." Her hands trembled. "Who is it from?"

Betsy had waited and waited for a letter but now that it had arrived, Grace could see the terror in her eyes. Gingerly, Betsy reached out her trembling hand to take the mail from Moira.

"Two letters." Betsy turned the envelopes over in her hand. "No return addresses, no indication whether they are safe in New Zealand or overseas amid the fighting."

"What about the postage stamps?" Grace asked.

Betsy flipped the letters back over.

"There's a fantail on this one, that's New Zealand."

Grace remembered the old wives' tale that a fantail inside was a sign of foreboding, an imminent death. She kept her thoughts to herself.

"Foreign language on these," Betsy continued. "I don't know what country."

"Open them up, Betsy," Nel encouraged. "The news won't change the longer you hold onto it."

Betsy looked from one envelope to the other.

"I don't know which to open first? This is Roland's writing with the overseas postage. I think this one is from William. I'll open that, Nel."

My dearest Betsy it began. Betsy smiled but kept the salutation to herself.

We've finished training and tomorrow will be shipped out. Our destination hasn't been revealed yet but everyone is itching to get to the action. We are up at dawn each morning and the sunrise is amazing. I used to relish that time on the farm getting the cows in for milking when the rest of the world was still asleep. It was so peaceful and calming. Not quite so here when the commanding officer is yelling orders but I have the best of intentions to return home safely. I hope the cows are being kind to you and Dr Doolittle's lamb is growing fast. Thank my mother for the baking, which I have shared among the others in the regiment. I'd best sign off before lights out. I will write again soon and look forward to receiving your news from home.

William signed off with Take care, my dearest friend. Yours, William. Betsy sighed. Nel's eyes had glassed over. She looked at the ceiling and blinked away tears.

"Thank you, dear, it's nice to know my boy is still safe and well."

Betsy carefully folded the letter and put it in her overalls pocket, she would read it again later in the privacy of her bedroom. Then she opened Roland's.

"You don't have to share Roland's news if you don't want to," Nel said.

Betsy was quiet as she scanned the letter's contents and decided what to relay.

"The censors have blacked out most if it but wherever he is, it is hot, hot enough to sleep out under the stars. Clean water supplies are short, so they have to ration their drinking water and haven't showered in days. At least in the heat they aren't as hungry because they're all sick of their diet of canned corned beef."

Betsy slumped down in her seat. There was nothing in the letter to reassure her Roland was all right, no promises that he was safe and happy, no asking after her welfare. He had signed off 'all my love'. Betsy read the words, but they weren't enough. Not nearly enough.

"Right then," Duncan interrupted. "Eat up everybody, we need to go and move the sheep."

"You'd better put that lamb out in the paddock," Duncan said to Alice, with a hint of impatience, as they approached the implement shed after lunch. "I thought you had done it this morning."

"I forgot. Sorry," she apologised. Alice hadn't forgotten at all. She had no choice but to follow Duncan's orders now. She leaned over the side of the pen and picked the lamb up. She hugged the wriggling animal close to her chest and whispered. "Hello, Lulu. It's time to try some grass."

Jess neighed as they approached the paddock.

"I have a little friend for you, Jess." Alice held Lulu up so the animals could sniff one another. "Now you two be nice."

Alice gently dropped Lulu down onto the grass next to Jess and stood back to watch their reactions. Lulu sniffed at the grass then pranced about, springing on all four legs, excited with her newfound freedom. Without a second look at Alice, she bleated and ran off across the grass, randomly zigzagging around the paddock, her tail shaking enthusiastically.

Jess gave a disinterested whinny and resumed chomping the grass at her feet.

Alice sighed. Her arms hung limply at her side.

Duncan's shrill whistle jolted Alice out of her self-pity. The whistle was meant to get the dogs moving but had the same effect on her.

"Come on," Duncan yelled. "We've got to move the sheep."

The wind swept across the terrain as the wagon, with Alice and Betsy atop and the truck with Grace and Duncan, arrived at the paddock the sheep had occupied for the last few days. The flock had chewed the paddock down and baaed in anticipation of being moved.

"Feed the hay out in the next paddock and the sheep will follow you through," Duncan said, pointing ahead. "I'll check around for any stragglers."

In front of the gate, a belligerent sheep stood, eyed them suspiciously, stubbornly stomped its front hoof, then resumed eating. Out to its side a tiny lamb was curled up asleep. Grace walked around the pair and opened the gate.

"Oh, look at that lamb," Alice cooed. "Perhaps that little lamb needs me to feed it."

When the gate was opened, the ewe baaed at her offspring. It stood; its tiny limbs shuddered and on wobbly legs it followed its mother into the next paddock. Alice's shoulders slumped.

By the time they had done a loop of the paddock and the remaining hay had been fed out, Duncan met them at the gate, a lamb hanging limply from either hand. Alice gasped, the lambs looked dead, and she was saddened by the sight.

"Looks like it's going to be one of those years," Duncan said gruffly.

The three land girls looked blankly at Duncan, unsure what 'one of those years' was.

"Bloody lambs to feed," he continued, giving each of the lamb's a shake. "Like we haven't got enough to do."

"I'll take them," Alice offered, grinning from ear to ear. She abandoned the reins and jumped down from the wagon eager to claim the precious lambs from Duncan.

He happily handed the animals over and Alice hugged them to her chest. The lambs each emitted a quiet bleat, it wasn't much but enough to tell Alice they were alive and in need of her help.

"Just don't name them this time. Okay?" he asked seeking confirmation that the sentimental female wouldn't get too attached again.

Alice smiled but didn't reply. She climbed onto the back of the wagon and cradled the lambs in her lap whispering, 'hello Bella' to the one on the right and, 'hello Lizzy' to the other.

"Quick, we'd better get back, they need feeding," she said. "You drive the wagon, Betsy."

Duncan chuckled and shook his head. At least he wouldn't have to be up through the night feeding them.

"They can go straight to the pen. They don't need to go beside the fire."

Alice looked wide-eyed at Duncan.

"They haven't been out in the weather that long," he said. "And, they've got each other for warmth."

Back at the implement shed, Alice left the others to unhitch the wagon and put away the horse and the tools. Her focus was the lambs. She quickly made up a bottle, climbed into the pen and sat down on the hay to feed them. While one lamb guzzled down the milk the other climbed all over Alice, bunting her under the chin in search of a feed. The first lamb's stomach was soon transformed from hollow to bulging so Alice pulled the bottle from the lamb and offered the remainder of the milk to the second. Unhappy at losing her teat, the lamb stretched its slobbery tongue out in search of another. All it found was Alice's finger. Alice giggled;

the lamb's tongue curled around her finger tickled. It soon abandoned its suckling and curled up in Alice's lap for a sleep. Alice was left with a sticky, saliva-covered finger but she had never been happier.

Bill's mince pie turned out to be delicious and Moira had to curb her appetite to ensure there were leftovers for Ben.

"I'll do the dishes later," she said to Bill as she placed the plates on the bench. "Let's go to the sitting room."

They'd spent most of Bill's visits in the sitting room. On the first night, he had chosen the armchair instead of beside

Moira on the settee. Bill seemed unable to relax in Captain Boyle's formal lounge.

Tonight, Moira waited for Bill to sit first. She smiled when he opted for the settee and settled herself at his side, not touching, but close enough that she could if the opportunity arrived. They chatted away, about the weather and farming mainly. Moira carefully avoided the subject of Bill's wife.

"Shall we listen to some music?" she suggested.

There was a Columbus radio on top of a small table in the corner of the sitting room. Moira knew how to work its circular dial and pre-set buttons but feigned ignorance knowing that Bill, being a gentleman would oblige.

Static was the only noise that came from the highly polished wooden box when Bill turned the switch to on. The first of the six pre-set buttons delivered news of the war from abroad to which Bill listened intently.

"Can't we find some music?" Moira asked. "My leg is much better. Perhaps we could dance."

Bill pushed the next button. Classical music filled the room.

"Mmm, a violin amid a concerto. Not quite what I had in mind."

Moira coughed and Bill took the hint to push the next button which brought Bing Crosby crooning "Only Forever" into the sitting room. Moira saw the forlorn look on Bill's face. The music wasn't having the desired effect.

"Perhaps we should leave it for tonight," she suggested, patting the settee beside her.

"Yes," Bill agreed, turning the radio off. "I've got a big day tomorrow. I'd best be going."

"Oh," Moira pouted, unable to hide her disappointment.

"I'll try and make it over at lunchtime tomorrow," Bill offered, moving towards the passage to retrieve his coat.

"I have to go back to work tomorrow," Moira replied.

"Saturday then." Bill brushed a kiss across her forehead. "We've got the cinema. That's something to look forward to."

Before Moira had the chance to mention what she was looking forward to, Bill disappeared out the door and into the night.

Betsy made sure she'd be the first to the mailbox the next morning. She hadn't expected there to be anything for her, but disappointment still hit with a bite when the newspaper was all she could see. She snatched it from the letterbox and nearly missed the letter that was concealed underneath. The white envelope fell into the long grass growing beneath the letterbox. Betsy's heart skipped a beat when she saw the letter was addressed to her. It was William's handwriting. With the letter grasped tightly in her hands Betsy ran all the way to the homestead, up the stairs and into her bedroom where she stowed it with the others in the cardboard box under her bed.

"Is everything alright Betsy?" Grace had just checked in on Ben and heard noises in the room she shared with Betsy.

Betsy jumped up in fright. She stood rigid with her hand on her chest, her eyes wide with guilt at being caught out.

"Yes ... and you ... Ben ... is everything alright with Ben?"

The questions were successful in deflecting the conversation back to Grace.

"I think he's had a bad night. He's still asleep. If you could call it a sleep. I was just watching him and suddenly his body shuddered, his legs twitched, and his eyelids fluttered. His face screwed up and I thought he was going to yell out. He must have awful nightmares."

"He hasn't even been to war," Betsy said. "Imagine. Imagine Roland and William. Imagine what it is like for them."

"Was that another letter?"

"I thought you hadn't noticed."

"Betsy." Grace giggled. "I've known you for so long, you should know you can't keep secrets from me."

"It's from William."

"Is that why you're hiding it?"

"I feel so guilty getting letters from him. It's meant to be Roland writing to me."

"Yes, but William can write to you as a friend."

"I don't want to open it in front of Nel. She'll want to know everything."

"Is he not just writing to you as a friend?"

"I don't know. I haven't opened it. I'll wait until tonight."

"Well best we get today's jobs done so you can get back here as soon as possible."

As they walked back to the farmhouse for breakfast, Grace lit up with the idea that she could get Ben to write to her. If she couldn't keep him hidden then at least they could stay in contact until the war finished and Ben no longer had to hide. She didn't know if Ben would like the idea. She didn't know much about

Ben at all. The thought that they could reveal themselves to each other through letters sat comfortably with her.

Betsy spooned a large mouthful of porridge without thinking. The heat of the oats nearly burnt her mouth and she had to spit it back onto the spoon and blow to cool it down.

"What are we doing today?" she asked, keen to get on and get everything done so she could return to the letter.

"The truck is coming to take the baconers to the sale so we'll get them on their way," Duncan replied. "Then we will catch the weaners and shift them from the paddock to the sty."

Moira groaned. Her first day back and she had to deal with pigs.

She admired her clean, manicured fingernails, knowing that by the end of the day they would likely be chipped and dirty.

"Are you worried about falling in a mud hole again, Moira?" Alice daringly teased.

"Very funny!" Moira wasn't impressed.

The baconers were easy to get out of the sty, into the pen, up the loading race and onto the truck. The weaners took quite a bit more effort. The paddock was filled with shrieks and squeals from pigs and women alike as both ran in opposing directions. When the gate was finally shut on the last of the weaners the women's faces were as pink as the pigs' snouts.

"Right, they'll be wanting a feed now," Duncan said. "Who's on pig duty this afternoon?"

"Thank God, it's not me," Moira said. "I already stink of pigs. I don't want to add the stench of whey."

"I'll go and get the cows in first," Alice replied "Then I'll help Grace feed the pigs."

"Don't forget those lambs too," Duncan reminded. "I'll come to the cowshed; I think we need to be drying some of the cows off."

Grace looked askance at Duncan. Sometimes his farming jargon was like a foreign language. It hadn't rained for a couple of days so she couldn't understand why the cows would need drying off.

That night Betsy went straight to her room, changed into her pyjamas, grabbed the box from under her bed and climbed in between the cool cotton sheets. She turned the unopened letter over and over in her hands.

Carefully, Betsy slipped her finger under the envelope flap and opened it. My dearest Betsy it began again. Everyone is sitting topside in the sun writing to their loved ones. Betsy's heart beat quickened. The farewell was spectacular when we set sail. The wharves were packed as wives, girlfriends, mothers and fathers all came to farewell the soldiers. I was a little saddened that there was no-one amongst the crowd especially for me, but I hold happy memories of Orari close in my heart and will treasure them wherever I go. When not busy with our assigned duties, we spend the time playing cards. Some of the lads have boxing matches. It's a good way to keep our fitness up. We'll certainly need all our strength when we reach our destination. We can no longer see the green hills of home which is a strange feeling. I wonder what the terrain will be like where we land. Missing your cheery smile, William.

Grace arrived to see Betsy's smile as she folded the letter and safely stowed it back in the box.

"It was good news then?" Grace asked.

"I shouldn't let him write to me at all." Betsy coloured with guilt and rubbed her churning stomach with her hand. "When Roland comes home … if Roland ever comes home, I'll burn the letters and never talk of them."

"Until then, you hold on to whatever joy you find in them." Grace's advice was as much to herself as it was to Betsy. Until Ben left, she would find whatever joy she could with him.

Chapter Twenty-Four

"Right ladies are we all ready?" Bill arrived in his car to pick the land girls up for their night out at the cinema.

"You're looking rather dapper tonight, Bill," Moira said. "You should smile more often; it shows off your dimple."

"I'll be right with you," Grace said, ducking back up the stairs.

She found Ben sitting on Captain Boyle's bed reading a book he'd borrowed from the bookcase in the sitting room.

"We're off now," she said quietly. "To the movies, you'll have the place to yourself for a few hours. There is some food in the refrigerator, eat as much as you like, I can get some more in the morning. I picked some apples too, they're in the fruit bowl. I'll see you later."

"Thanks, Grace. Thanks for everything."

Grace couldn't help herself, she rushed over to the bed, wrapped her arms around Ben and kissed him. The book dropped into his lap, discarded in his eagerness to respond to Grace. A toot of the car horn interrupted their embrace.

"I'd better get going," Grace said. "I'll see you when I get back."

Ben didn't answer.

Clark Gable and Vivien Leigh were pictured in a passionate embrace on the large poster in the foyer of the cinema. Bill and the land girls queued for tickets and popcorn then waited in line for the usherette to show them to their seats. Bill stood aside to allow the ladies into the row before him. Moira let Grace, Betsy and Alice in first to ensure she could sit next to Bill.

The cinema was filled with the buzz of excited chatter and the crunch of salted popcorn being enjoyed as the theatregoers eagerly waited for the velvet stage curtains to be drawn and the screen to come to life.

A hush came over the crowd as the lights dimmed to signal the start of the evening. As everyone relaxed into the warmth of the velvet-covered seats, Moira placed her hand on the wooden armrest between herself and Bill. In the darkness, Bill reached over; he took Moira's hand in his and smiled.

The large speakers mounted on the side walls filled the theatre with music.
"The movie's about to start," Grace said.

"It'll be a newsreel first," Bill replied in a whisper. "They always play a weekly war review before the main feature."

Betsy sat on the edge of her seat when the image of uniformed men marching the streets, filled the screen. The narrator didn't say who they were or where they were going, just that the men 'were helping to make the country what it is – happy and free.'

"Can you see Roland or William?" Betsy whispered as she scanned the faces.

The troops boarded a ship berthed at the wharf, from every inch of the deck and every porthole they waved, smiled, and blew kisses to their loved ones on the pier below. It was just as William had described in his letter.

"I wish I'd been there." Betsy sighed wistfully.

The audience could have almost been convinced that going off to war was a giant adventure, if the newsreel hadn't continued. Images of enemy aircraft dropping bombs in Britain, buildings destroyed or on fire and frightened women and children brought the reality back to light. Prime Minister Peter Fraser appeared on the screen and declared that 'New Zealand stands beside Britain, where she goes, we go.'

Just when tears threatened, the newsreel moved onto the good deeds the army personnel still on New Zealand soil were performing, helping farmers in the Canterbury region to bring in the crops. Grace thought of Ben, perhaps he could be involved in that instead of having to fight. She'd tell him about it as soon as they got home. Anything that meant he could come out of hiding was at least to be considered.

The newsreel flickered to an end and there were a few moments when the screen stayed blank. Bill leaned over to Moira's ear and whispered.

"It's nice to hold your hand."

Moira smiled. "You can hold me anytime you want."

The music started, the orchestra playing the theme song to Gone with the Wind sounded as if it was live in the theatre. All eyes were riveted to the screen. When Clark Gable looked up from the bottom of the stairs and smiled, a communal gasp filled the cinema, every woman wishing it was she he was smiling at.

For the next two hours the audience sat engrossed in the movie, collectively gasping, sighing, and groaning in response to the antics of Scarlet O'Hara. When intermission arrived, the lights came on causing many to quickly dab their eyes with their handkerchiefs or escape to the ladies' restroom to repair their makeup in the mirror.

"Would you like more popcorn, ladies?" Bill removed his hand from Moira's and leaned forward to address the others.

"No, thank you," came the polite replies.

"Moira, would you like to go to the lounge for a smoke?" he asked.

"Yes, please." Moira stood before Bill could retract his invite.

Bill offered his arm to her as they walked up the aisle. It was the polite thing to do.

"I can't get the images of the wounded and dead soldiers out of my mind," Betsy said. "Imagine if Roland or William were amongst them."

"It's the American civil war." Grace meant for her reply to ease Betsy's worry, but she knew it made no difference which war it was. There were still going to be dead and wounded. At least Ben wasn't going to be among them. She tried not to think about her brothers.

"What about the poor horses too?" Alice's concern lay with the horses, rearing with fright when artillery fire soared past them, or fire threatened to trap them.

The movie continued for another two hours after intermission. By the time the final credits rolled, the audience were grateful to be able to stand and stretch their legs. The cinema seats that had started as comfortable had become lumpy and confining.

"Thank you, Bill," Grace said on the return trip home. She yawned loudly, raised her hand to her mouth and continued in a muffled voice. "Excuse me. I didn't realise the movie would go for so long. It's been a big day."

"You're welcome." Bill smiled at Moira. "My pleasure."

Bill, ever the gentleman, opened the car door for the land girls when he pulled up at the house. By the time he opened Moira's door the other women had gone inside. They'd turned the outside light on, there was enough light for Bill and Moira to see one another but not for anyone else to see them in the shadow of the car. Bill pulled Moira into his arms and took on a Clark Gable persona.

"You should be kissed," he recited, pulling Moira close to him. "And often, by the right person."

Bill kissed Moira, timidly at first, but like the movie actions of Clark Gable, the bolder he became. He tilted Moira backwards and devoured her lips with all his pent-up passion until they were both breathless.

"Well, I never," Moira feigned innocence in a Southern Belle accent. "I think I shall like to be kissed often by you."

Bill and Moira's laughter echoed into the night. Bill glanced over Moira's shoulder back at the house.

"Shall we go inside?" he whispered, before his boldness had a chance to escape. "I know it's not the gentlemanly thing to do but it's been a very long time since I've held a beautiful young woman in my arms."

Bill's kisses, his hands caressing her body sent tingles down Moira's spine. She didn't want to break the spell, didn't want to say, or do the wrong thing and send Bill disappearing into the night as he so often did. She revelled in his every kiss, leaned her body into his and felt his burgeoning need growing between them.

"The others might hear us," she replied. Her shoulders slumped when she realised what she'd done, offering Bill an excuse to back out before things went too far.

"Frankly, my dear, I don't give a damn."

"Thank you, Clark Gable." Moira took Bill by the hand and led him up to her bedroom.

"Blast!" Grace had been about to go and see Ben when she heard Bill and Moira's voices on the landing.

"What's wrong?" Betsy had already put her pyjamas on and climbed into bed.

"I was going to go and see Ben, but Bill is upstairs."

"Bill's upstairs!"

"Ssh, don't talk too loud, he'll hear you."

"Well, if he hears me, he can do the gentlemanly thing and leave."

"I don't think Moira wants him to leave."

"First William, now Bill." Betsy shook her head in disbelief. "Are you not concerned at all?"

"You know nothing happened with William."

"Yes, but …"

"Moira's a grown woman whose shown she'll do whatever it is she wants to do." Grace had decided the redheaded land girl was more than capable of looking after herself. "I'm more worried about not seeing Ben."

"Were you planning to do the same with Ben?"

"Betsy, we don't know what Bill and Moira are planning to do."

"I can have a damn good guess and it looks like you want to do the same with Ben."

Grace hesitated. She wanted to say 'no' but that would be a lie. She wasn't planning to have sex with Ben, but she couldn't say she didn't want to.

"Actually, I have finally listened to all of you. I know Ben needs to leave. He can't stay hidden in Captain Boyle's room for the duration of the war. It might go on for years."

"Oh, I hope not." Betsy sniffed. "I hope I don't have to wait years to see Roland."

"Even if it's only months, Ben will surely be discovered if he stays here."

"So, what are you going to do?" Betsy asked.

"I'll just have to be like you."

"Like me? How like me?"

"Rely on letters. I'll have to keep in contact with Ben through letters until the war ends. Surely, the authorities won't come after him when it's all over. There'd be no point."

"It's great that you've realised he needs to leave," Betsy said. "But I can assure you waiting for letters to arrive isn't much fun."

"But look how good they make you feel when they do arrive."

Betsy nodded and smiled, she had to agree with Grace.

"There's a slight hitch to your plan though."

"What's that?"

"You don't even know Ben's last name, do you?"

"No," Grace conceded. "I was going to see him now, to tell him my idea but I can't do it while Bill's here."

Both women went quiet, they looked at each other then turned to face the wall between the two bedrooms. Several quiet seconds passed. They sat in anticipation, as if the wall would vanish and reveal the goings on. There was no talking. If Bill was still there, and they hadn't heard him leave, then what they were doing didn't involve talking. A giggle, Moira's suggestive giggle, told them all they needed to know.

"I think you'll have to wait until the morning," Betsy said. "I'm exhausted, and I don't want to listen to them. I'm going to sleep."

She turned her bedside light out, rolled over and pulled the bedcovers up tight under her chin. Grace had no option but to do the same.

The early morning crow of the rooster roused Grace from a deep sleep. She recalled the events of the prior night as she rubbed the sleep from her eyes. As the sharpness of her vision increased so did the urgency of her need to see Ben, to do what she wanted to but was unable to do the night before. She jumped out of bed and quickly dressed, Ben's approval of her plan would keep him safe and confirm that his feelings mirrored her own. There was no point denying she had feelings for Ben, she wanted to do more than keep him safe from the war. She wanted to explore the feelings his presence evoked in her, the physical reactions she had no control over whenever she was close to him.

Once she had confirmation that they were real and shared by him, then they could work out how they could get him safely away from the farm and stay in contact until the war was over.

Grace knocked timidly on the bedroom door, it was after all early and Ben may still be sleeping. There was no answer, no noise from the bedroom.

"Ben," she quietly called as she opened the door.

The curtains hadn't been drawn but they hadn't been any other night either. There were to be no outward signs that someone was in the room. The first glimpse of sunlight illuminated the bedroom enough for Grace to see the bed was neatly made, the book Ben had been reading, closed, and resting on the bedside table.

"Ben," Grace repeated a little louder, her heartbeat quickening. She wondered what could have happened to cause him to hide again. Perhaps there had been another night-time army exercise that they had missed when they were at the movies. Grace walked straight to Ben's last hiding place, the wardrobe and opened the door.

"Ben, it's …."

She pushed aside the clothes but saw only the wooden veneer of the back of the wardrobe; no Ben. Grace lifted the bedspread and searched under the bed, she checked both sides in case the darkness concealed him. She checked behind the curtains. She stood hands on hips and scanned the room. There were no other hiding places. Ben was not here.

"What is all the kerfuffle?" Moira stood in the doorway, tying the belt on her dressing gown.

Grace looked up in surprise and was about to answer that Ben had gone but she saw Bill standing behind Moira and her mouth gaped in stunned silence. In her rush to see Ben she'd forgotten that Bill might still be around.

Bill coughed awkwardly.

"If everything is alright then," he whispered to Moira. "I'd better be going."

"Yes," Moira said as she turned. She embraced Bill and kissed him passionately.

Bill coloured from head to toe when he saw Grace had witnessed the brazen show of affection. He cleared his throat again and ducked down the stairs and out the door before anyone else saw him.

Grace shook her head. She had to refocus, to decide which was the greater of her worries at present – Moira or Ben. She decided she could do nothing about Moira, she hoped she could still do something about Ben.

"Ben's not here," Grace told Moira.

"He probably just got up early and went downstairs for food."

"The bed hasn't been slept in," Grace looked at the neatly-made bed. She looked back at Moira and thought her bed probably hadn't been slept in either.

"What's wrong?" Betsy turned up at the door, dressed ready to go and milk the cows.

"Ben's not here," Grace repeated. "His uniform is gone."

"Perhaps he changed his mind about the war and went back," Moira suggested.

Grace's nostrils flared as she inhaled deeply. Although she hadn't known Ben for long, she knew in her heart that he was just like her brother, Frankie; there was no way either of them wanted to be in the army. He'd wanted the uniform burned only they hadn't found a time or place to do it without risking being caught.

"We'd better check downstairs," she said heading purposely towards the door.

The trio were joined by Alice on the landing and headed downstairs together. They split up and checked all the rooms, meeting back at the kitchen with glum faces, Ben was nowhere to be found.

"I've got to go and get the cows in," Alice said, placing a comforting hand on Grace's arm. "I'll have a look out for him on my way."

"I'll check the cowshed before I set up for milking." Betsy gave her friend a reassuring hug. "Don't worry Grace, we'll find him, he won't have gone far."

"What if the army have caught him?" Grace asked, frowning with worry.

"Not in the middle of the night," Betsy replied. "They wouldn't be out in the middle of the night."

"They were doing training exercises the night we went for a swim. They could have been doing them last night too. We wouldn't know. We weren't here."

Grace admonished herself. Why had she gone to the movies? She should have been here taking care of Ben. If he got caught, how would she ever forgive herself?

"He might have gone back to the implement shed," Moira suggested.

"Who would choose to sleep in a cold shed instead of here?"

"I don't know." Moira shrugged her shoulders. "It was just a suggestion."

"Sorry," Grace apologised as she put her jacket on. "I'll check there on my way to the pigsty."

Unlike everyone else, Moira still needed to dress.

"I'll be right with you," she said, before disappearing back upstairs.

Chapter Twenty-Five

Morning chores were completed with everyone alert to sounds and movements that could indicate Ben was close but neither he, nor any signs of his presence were found.

"Where do you think he could be?" Betsy asked as they were washing up for breakfast.

"If I knew that he wouldn't be missing," Grace bit back. She shouldn't take her worry out on Betsy and she knew she'd have to hide it when they went in for breakfast or Duncan would know something was wrong. "We'll have to keep quiet about him now," she warned the others.

Nel had a big pot of porridge bubbling away on the top of the coal range.

"You're just in time," she said, bringing the pot to the table with a ladle to spoon it into their bowls.

To Alice's horror there were half a dozen unskinned rabbits tied in a bundle on the kitchen bench, their vacant eyes staring at the breakfast table.

"Caught them last night," Duncan explained, seeing the look of anguish on Alice's face. "Rabbit stew for dinner."

Alice sat at the table with her back to the bench and asked for a second helping of porridge. Grace's concerns weren't for Alice or the rabbits but for Ben. If he was out in the night when Duncan was shooting, he could have been injured. She needed to find him and find him fast.

"What do we need to be doing today?" she asked Duncan.

"The milk has to be taken to the factory," he replied.

"I can do that," Moira offered.

Grace imagined Moira's alternative motive would be to see Bill but that wasn't her concern.

"We'd better feed some more hay out," Duncan continued. "With this cold spell, the cows and sheep will be needing a bit extra."

"We can manage that," Grace said, eager to be able to search for Ben without Duncan around. "If you've got other stuff to do," she added, not wanting to appear too keen.

"I do, actually," Duncan said. "I've got a meeting with the regional co-ordinator for you land girls. I've got to report in on how you are going and give my recommendations for your placement when you're finished your training here."

The women all looked at Duncan with concern.

"We haven't been here that long already, have we?" Grace asked. It seemed liked they'd only been at Whipsnade a short time and were still getting used to farming. She'd been so busy during the day, working and trying to sneak food to Ben, by the end of the day she was exhausted; she hadn't thought about what would come next. Her eyes locked with Betsy's; it was just like the day they'd signed up for the land girls, the idea that they may be assigned to different farms was daunting. It increased the pressure to find Ben. How could Grace move on without finding Ben first?

Grace, Betsy, and Alice with the reins in her hands, squeezed together on the seat of the wagon as they left the stack with a full load of hay.

"I didn't think we'd be leaving Orari so soon," Alice remarked to the others.

"I've only just started getting letters from Roland and William," Betsy said. "How am I going to get them redirected?"

"I don't plan on going anywhere until we find Ben." Grace scanned under hedges and trees searching for the lost man.

"He may have been in the cow shed last night," Betsy said.

"What!" Grace snapped. "Why didn't you say?"

"I haven't had the chance. You keep biting my head off."

"Yes ... sorry." Grace apologised. "I'm just really worried about him. What if Duncan mistook him for a rabbit and accidentally shot him last night?"

"Yuck!" Alice said. "It's bad enough that Duncan shot the rabbits. I had to have two plates of porridge. I don't think I'll be able to eat rabbit stew for dinner."

"How do you know he was in the cowshed?" Grace wanted to bring the chatter back to Ben.

"It looked like one of the milk-can lids had been removed. I'm sure there were three full cans. One of the lids was on crooked and when I checked, the can wasn't full anymore."

"Dam," Grace cursed. "I thought I'd left him enough food."

"Well at least, wherever he is, we know he has eaten," Betsy replied.

Three sets of eyes scanned the paddocks as the wagon headed to the back of the farm. The sound of gunfire echoed across the land; rapid fire was punctuated with resounding blasts of canons. Every boom reverberated in Grace's chest, tightening the grasp her nerves had on her heart. She felt for Ben, imagined his terror. There was no wardrobe to conceal himself in, in the expanse of the farm. She wondered how many more days the army training exercise would continue and hoped that the troops would soon be gone.

"Stop!" Grace yelled. "Stop the wagon."

Alice pulled on the reins and Jess drew up. Grace had seen something under the macrocarpa trees and she ran over to get a better look. Several broken branches had been arranged in a pile, their brown needles forming a mat between the protruding roots of an old tree. Grace sighed with relief. Ben was alive, he must have used the needles as a bed. She scanned the area looking for blood and smiled when she saw no evidence that he'd been injured. Several feet away, Grace noticed the earth was blackened with ash, the remnants of a fire. She bent down and picked up a scrap of cloth. It was the distinctive khaki of Ben's uniform, singed at the edges but proof that he never wanted to return to the army. Grace stood and scuffed the area over with her gumboots, mixing the ashes with the earth, she destroyed the traces of his presence.

"He's been here," she said as she climbed back on the wagon. "He's alright."

"I wonder where he is then," Betsy said.

"He's probably hiding, if we keep talking, he might hear us and realise it is safe to come out."

The trio chatted away while they fed out the hay, first to the cows and then to the sheep. Grace was despondent by the time the wagon was empty. There were no further signs of Ben's presence.

When Moira arrived at Bill's farm, she found his car in the shed beside the house and his truck parked outside the back porch. The small porch enclosed two wooden doors painted in matching faded green. Moira assumed the one without a window would be the toilet so knocked politely on the other door. She waited a few seconds, listened for noises from inside but heard nothing. Moira walked back around to the window and peered in expecting to see Bill asleep in a chair. The glare of the sun reflected off the window and made it difficult to see anything. Moira wasn't going to let the opportunity pass so she returned to the back porch, gingerly turned the brass door handle and pushed gently on the door. It opened straight into the kitchen which was bathed in sunlight and warmth and beckoned her inside. She removed her gumboots and tiptoed across the linoleum. She was trespassing but curiosity got the better of her. The room wasn't untidy, it was lived in, there was a pile of old newspapers but they were neatly stacked on a chair in the corner. A dishrack on the bench was full of dishes, but they were clean and ready to be put away. Laundry was draped over a rack hung from the ceiling, drying in the warmth radiating from the coal range. A grey tabby cat slept on a cushion on the window seat. Moira moved quietly so she wouldn't wake the feline and give away her presence. She turned to leave but a mahogany sideboard crowded with photo frames drew her attention. Two rows of neatly ordered photographs spanned the top of the recently dusted sideboard. Each one held an image of a very attractive woman, sometimes with Bill, sometimes alone but always looking beautiful.

Moira's stomach churned. The woman must be Bill's wife. The prominently displayed portraits were evidence of his feelings for her. Moira had given herself to this man last night, their passion had been all consuming but what was she to him in the cold light of day? This morning Bill had scurried out the door, seemingly eager to be gone. Moira rung her hands together as her thoughts seesawed. Bill always left in a hurry, that was just his way. Then Moira remembered Bill giving flowers to someone in Geraldine. Perhaps Bill had a number of women on the go and she was just one of them. Did that matter? Moira straightened her back. She just wanted to have some fun and if fun was what she was having with Bill, then whatever else he was doing didn't matter. Moira left the house, closed the door behind her and kept telling herself that it didn't matter.

"You need to sit down, Grace," Betsy was sprawled on her bed writing letters and Grace's anxious pacing backwards and forwards across the bedroom was distracting.

"I'm just going over everything," Grace replied. She sat on the edge of her bed but jiggled her legs up and down.

"You look as if you want to go somewhere."

"Duncan said we've got to give the sheep another drenching before lambing. I haven't checked the woolshed. Have you?"

"I didn't, but one of the others might have," Betsy replied.

"I'd better go and have a look; in case we drench tomorrow." Grace stood back up, her hands on her hips and a deep frown furrowing her forehead. "I'd hate for Ben to get caught."

"It's dark outside."

"It'll be better dark, if I need to sneak him back here."

Before Betsy had a chance to reason with Grace that Ben would still be in the house if he'd wanted to be, she was gone out the door. Betsy shrugged and turned her mind back to her letter writing. One letter to Roland and one letter to William. She repeated the exact same news in each letter, relaying details about the weather, their jobs on the farm and the highlight of the week, their trip to the cinema. She wrote that the movies reminded her of them, she didn't elaborate how or why. She assuaged her guilt by not writing about her feelings for either of the men. When she'd filled two pages with her neatest handwriting, Betsy sat staring blankly at the drawn drapes, tapping the end of her pen on her chin, while she contemplated how to sign off. Eventually she settled for 'Yours, Betsy', deciding that it said as much or as little as she needed it to, and as the recipients wanted it to.

Grace pulled the collar of her jacket up under her chin, tucked her hair into a woollen hat and plunged her hands deep into her pockets as she set off on her search for Ben. It was not a good night to be out. Although it was theft, she hoped Ben had taken some more of Captain Boyle's clothes, a warm jacket or raincoat to protect him from the elements.

She made her way down through the garden, initially following the same path her and Ben had taken to the river but knowing the water would be freezing tonight she turned and headed towards the wool shed.

Empty of sheep the shed stood quietly, the odour of wool, lanoline, and dried excrement redolent of its purpose. The door handle creaked in her hand. If Ben was inside, it would have warned him to hide.

"Ben," she called quietly into the emptiness. "Ben," she repeated, an edge of desperation creeping into her voice.

From afar dogs barked into the night but the woolshed remained quiet. If Grace had listened to reason, she would have known Ben wasn't in the shed but she needed to be certain. She vaguely recalled where the light switch was, mounted on the wall along by the shearing platform. She also remembered the myriad of spiders that had claimed the wall as their own and spun an elaborate maze of cobwebs to trap the unsuspecting. Grace had no choice, she had to be brave, for Ben's sake. Gingerly she traced her fingers along the timber framing, skimming over the silken webs, trusting in the darkness she left the spiders undisturbed.

When her fingers found the switch, she let go the breath she'd been holding but sucked it in again as light flooded the shed. She blinked several times, adjusting her eyes to the brightness.

"Ben, it's only me, it's safe to come out."

Grace scanned the pens, peered down the shearing chutes and looked through the grating into the yards beneath the shed. She checked the corners of the woolshed where the light didn't reach. Even the rafters in case Ben had decided the timber framing would conceal him. He was nowhere to be found.

Eventually, Grace conceded Ben hadn't taken shelter in the woolshed. She turned the light switch off and headed out the door.

"What are you doing here?" Duncan's gruff voice pierced the night. He stood, gun in hand and dogs at his heel, his headlamp capturing her in its beam.

Grace jumped with fright. Stunned, her spine went rigid while her brain raced to find an answer to Duncan's question. An answer that would seem a viable explanation for her presence at the woolshed in the dark of night without giving away the real reason.

"Aah! I didn't see you."

"I saw lights on in the woolshed," Duncan said. "I came to investigate."

"Just me." Grace splayed her hands out, palms up, a look of innocence on her face.

"Well, I can see that. What I want to know is why?"

"I thought I'd lost something." Grace seized onto the almost truth. "I thought it might have been left at the woolshed." Duncan moved closer.

"It's not though." Grace stepped away from the shed. "It's not here. I'd best be heading back. Get an early night. I don't want to catch a chill. It's cold out tonight, isn't it?"

She saw Duncan roll his eyes and knew her jabbering had distracted him enough.

"You can take these then." Duncan had his night's catch of rabbits tied together by the feet and strung across his shoulder. He handed Grace the bundle. "Then I'll be able to keep going and get some more. The blighters are everywhere."

"Oh!" Grace cringed as she hooked her fingers under the blood-stained string and held the half dozen dead rabbits at arms-length. Blood seeped from their bullet wounds, staining the fur, tainting the innocence of their short white tails.

"Just put them in the washhouse tub. I'll deal with them when I get back."

"Okay." Grace had no choice.

Unable to continue holding the weight at arms-length, she lowered the bundle but that brought it and the pungency of death closer. She set off back the way she had come accepting the chore as punishment for her lying. It was better than revealing her involvement with Ben though. That would surely bring a much greater penalty, for them both.

Back at the farmhouse she did as instructed and left the rabbit carcasses in the tub. She washed the blood from her fingers, grateful that it wasn't Ben's. Grace hoped her actions wouldn't cause the very thing she was trying to prevent.

Betsy had switched her light off by the time Grace returned.

"What happened?" she whispered into the darkness.

"I couldn't find him," Grace replied despondently.

"You've looked everywhere, Grace," Betsy said. "Perhaps he has gone home. Where was he from?"

"I never got the chance to find out." Grace had to admit Ben hadn't revealed anything about himself. "If only, I hadn't gone to the movies, I could have spent the night with him."

"Grace, if you'd spent the night with Ben, you'd be no happier than I am. You would have given more only to lose more."

"I didn't mean to sleep with him." Grace heard herself say the words, but in her heart, she wasn't convinced they were entirely truthful. "I just meant to talk to him, to get to know more about him, to get him to agree to write and to find another place for him to go safely to."

"You'll just have to trust that he has found that safe place without you."

"But ... I wanted to help him."

"You did all you could," Betsy said. "You can't save everyone, Grace."

Grace lay down on her bed and stared unseeing into the darkness, hoping that exhaustion would soon take her into a deep sleep, otherwise she would spend the night thinking about Ben.

"We'll be moving on from here soon anyway," Betsy said.

If Betsy's words were meant to comfort Grace, they didn't. When, not if, she was moved onto another farm, then Ben would have no idea where she was. Perhaps he wanted it that way. Perhaps he hadn't cared at all. Perhaps Grace had imagined there was anything between them. Tears threatened. She blinked them away.

The rooster's early morning crow resounded through Grace's head as if the fowl was at her bedside. Her temples throbbed and her body ached. She tried to remember what they had been doing yesterday to make her muscles so sore. Feeding hay wasn't that strenuous, it can't have been that.

Inhaling through her nose wasn't possible. The cool morning air she sucked in hit the dryness in her throat and sent her into a coughing fit.

"I didn't think you should have gone out last night." Betsy was already up and dressed in her overalls ready for the day. "You've gone and got a chill now."

Betsy was right. Grace had all the symptoms of a cold but she wouldn't admit it was because she'd gone out last night. She'd caught it from Ben. Memories of their dance, their kiss, everything that he made her feel, that no one else had ever done before – if they were the price to pay for a cold, she'd do it all again. Despite how her body felt, Grace smiled.

"What are you smiling for?" Betsy asked.

"It's Ben's cold." Grace lay back on her bed and stared dreamily at the ceiling.

"Oh!" Betsy tutted. "You have got it bad."

"Yes." Whether Grace was talking about her cold or her love for Ben, it didn't matter the outcome was the same. It was likely to get worse before it got better.

Chapter Twenty-Six

Grace's cold was like the weather too. It got worse before it got better. An out of season dumping of snow arrived with a southerly wind that felt like Antarctica was their neighbour. Snow covered the paddocks, hid the animal's fodder beneath its frozen blanket and forced the land girls out into the weather to feed out the hay necessary to sustain the sheep and cattle.

The girls were kitted out in knitted hats, scarves, and gloves. Grace put a pair of woollen tights on under her overalls but still the cold air seeped through. Snowflakes fell in graceful swathes, landing on their oilskin jackets to vanish leaving only a chill.

"I always thought snow was beautiful." Grace's nose dripped. She'd given up trying to wipe it with her now sodden glove. "But I'd rather not be out in this."

Before this change in the weather, she'd held out hope of still finding Ben hiding somewhere on the farm. Now, if he was out in this storm overnight, he'd have died of hypothermia. Grace stopped looking for his face under the trees, in the hedgerows, behind the tufts of tussock dreading that if she did see it now, it would be attached to his corpse.

When they'd emptied the wagon of hay, they searched the paddocks for sheep stranded in the snow. The white wool was a camouflage in the snow-covered paddocks.

"Here's one," Alice yelled. "Come and help."

"It's well and truly buried," Grace said. "Lucky you spotted it."

"I saw the pink of its nose."

Alice didn't hesitate to dig her hands into the snow. She scooped it out from around the sheep, removing the weight that compressed its belly.

"You take the front," Grace said. "I'll grab the back."

With handfuls of wool, together they foisted the sheep from the frozen confines of a rut. It shook itself, bleated loudly and trotted towards the line of hay being enjoyed by the flock.

Grace hoped that Ben, like the sheep, had made it to somewhere safe. Perhaps he had chosen to go home to his family and the love for their kin would allow them to see the strength of his beliefs and overlook society's condemnation of those who chose not to fight. If only she'd discovered his last name, she could have made enquiries, looked on the electoral role and found an address to write to.

The realisation that he was finally lost to her was as bitter as the wind that burned her nose and cheeks and froze the ends of her fingers and toes. Grace had no choice but to concede that she could no longer help Ben. His fate was beyond her control. If she didn't shake herself out of her melancholy then it would be she that would need rescuing.

Several days passed before the snows melted and the pastures returned to an edible colour except for where the herds had sheltered against hedges. Those areas were now muddy quagmires, hooves having destroyed the grass, allowing the melting snows to drain into the soil.

Grace had to accept help from the other land girls. Alice got lemons from the orchard and brought hot lemon honey drinks to Grace morning and night. Betsy made a steam bath with eucalyptus oil and insisted Grace sit with a towel over her head and breathe in the vapours until her sinuses cleared. Even Moira offered some clean handkerchiefs when Grace's supply had been exhausted.

Captain Boyle's bedroom remained closed and unused and no further signs of Ben's presence were found out on the farm either. The army had moved away, each day their artillery fire quietened until finally the noise ceased, returning the countryside to its peaceful norm. That was, until Duncan decided the sheep needed a final drenching before lambing proper started. At the sheepyards, pens full of ewes baaed and bleated at the inconvenience of being removed from the pasture and jostled into crowded yards for another dip in the bluestone drench.

After a few failed attempts, Moira got the hang of using the shepherd's whistle again and had the dogs barking to her command. Grace and Betsy were back on the poles and Alice on the gate. They'd put half of the flock through by lunch time when Nel turned up with sandwiches, fruit juice and a thermos of hot tea. Drenching, the second time around, proved just as strenuous as the first and the land girls were grateful for the break, their arms and backs ached and their throats were parched.

"You'd better go and get that lamb, when you've finished eating," Duncan told Alice. "It can go out into the paddock with the sheep."

Alice stopped. She took small bites of her half-eaten egg sandwich and chewed slowly as if wanting to delay the inevitable as long as possible. Duncan was onto the last few mouthfuls of his cup of tea when Alice finally left the yards to go and fetch the lamb.

Lulu came running when she saw Alice approach the fence, expecting her to have a bottle of milk, she bleated with anticipation.

"Not this time," Alice opened the gate and picked the lamb up. "Sorry, Lulu," she said hugging the woollen bundle tightly. The lamb wriggled and almost escaped. "If I let you go, little one, it could be to an even worse fate."

Alice walked as slowly as she could back to the yards. With her back to Duncan, she kissed the top of the lamb's head and whispered her goodbye as she lowered Lulu into the pen. Alice took up her position at the gate without any of the enthusiasm she'd had before lunch.

"Oh, I forgot," Nel said as she packed up the lunch basket. "Good news, Betsy. Three letters arrived in the mail for you today."

"Three!" A smile lit up Betsy's face. "Who are they from?" she asked.

"One from William," Nel replied. "I can tell his writing. I think one is from Roland, but I don't recognise the handwriting on the other."

Grace caught Betsy's eye. Her smile had banished any hint of fatigue, now there was an eagerness to get the job done, to get back and read the news. Grace smiled too and with a fresh burst of energy, together she and Betsy pushed the sheep through the trough with vigour.

"How many letters is that?" Grace hoped her question didn't convey the pang of jealousy she felt.

"This will be the fourth from William." Betsy beamed.

If that was how a letter could make you feel, Grace wanted the other letter to be for her.

"And the third from Roland but I guess he is further away, closer to the fighting so won't be able to write as often."

"Any letter would be nice."

Betsy glanced around to check Duncan wasn't within earshot. "I'm sure you'll hear from him soon."

"Come on, you mongrels," Moira growled at the animals as she pushed them angrily from one pen to the next.

"Moira doesn't sound happy," Betsy said. "What's her problem?"

"She hasn't had a visit or a phone call from Bill since that night."

"What did she expect?" Betsy shook her head as if 'I told you so' was on the tip of her tongue. "I thought she just wanted a bit of fun. It certainly sounded like that's what she got."

"I think that's what she wants us to believe, but …"

"It's just a brave front," Betsy finished Grace's sentence.

"Yes, I think so."

"Well, we all have to do that," Betsy said. "Put on a face, fake it and carry on." Grace pushed an errant tendril of hair off her face with the back of her hand, careful that no bluestone could stain her.

"We do," she conceded as they pushed the last of the sheep through the drenching trough.

"Phew! Finished." Betsy leaned backwards to reverse the arch in her spine.

"Not yet," Alice yelled. "Here comes Lulu and the lambs."

Lulu emerged from the pen with the other lambs and ran down the race. Alice had no choice but to open the gate and set them free. Lulu, head down and rushing to join the rest in the freedom of the paddock, didn't give Alice a second look or a farewell baa. Alice swallowed hard.

"Bye, Lulu," she said.

"Animals will come and go," Duncan said. "You're just going to have to get used to it."

Grace heard Duncan's advice to Alice and thought it applied equally to humans. Ben had come and gone, and Grace was just going to have to get used to it.

Dinner wasn't quite ready when the land girls made it inside after the long and strenuous day. Duncan sat at the dinner table; the day's newspaper held open in front of him.

"Here are the letters, Betsy," Nel said as she handed over the three envelopes. "I'd love to hear William's news. If you don't mind."

Reading the letters in the privacy of her bedroom wasn't an option for Betsy tonight. She slipped a finger under the flap of the first envelope and pulled out William's letter. Nel smiled with anticipation, one eye on Betsy and one eye on the savoury mince simmering on the stove.

"We received our first gift boxes from the National Patriotic Fund Board.

Chocolate and cigarettes were eagerly accepted by everyone. Some more of Mother's baking would have been wonderful, but I will look forward to that when I return. I enjoyed the last of her biscuits last night."

Betsy stopped reading and looked up at Nel; the pair smiled happily before Betsy continued.

"We haven't received any mail but are told it will be awaiting our arrival in Bombay. I look forward to news from home. I'm also looking forward to being on dry land again. They take our letters for posting but we stay aboard. It will only be a short stopover for supplies before we are onto our final destination. Sleeping arrangements on the ship are rather cramped. The narrow bunks are two high and ten to a cabin and usually full of snoring soldiers. Our sergeant says we should be grateful; we will be sleeping in the trenches when we reach the front. Sorry, there isn't much news, each day just seems like the last. Goodbye for now, William."

A blush, coloured Betsy's cheeks as she carefully folded the letter and put it away for later. Grace imagined she kept a special something for herself. Next, Betsy opened the letter from Roland.

"Are you going to share Roland's news too?" Nel asked.

Betsy quickly scanned the letter, there was nothing personal, so she read aloud.

"We made it. It is wonderful to be ashore but the heat is stifling. Nothing like New

Zealand has ever had. It brings with it the flies. If we don't eat our rations fast enough, we have to share them with the parasites and their larvae. Last week the wind blew for three days, constant day and night. Fortunately, we had dug our trenches and were able to hunker down and escape the sting of the sand whistling overhead. We can hear the battle raging away, getting ever closer. Rumour has it we will be joining the front tomorrow. So, I write, on the eve of battle, filled with trepidation of what tomorrow will bring and praying that we will be triumphant in our endeavours and there will be many more tomorrows. Thinking of you, Roland x."

The kiss at the end of Roland's letter did nothing to console Betsy. Her bottom lip trembled as tears threatened.

Nel sniffed and cleared her throat.

"What's your other letter, dear?" Nel asked. "Perhaps, it has better news to cheer us up,"

"Well, I never," Duncan said from behind the newspaper, oblivious to the women's conversation. "Who would have thought?"

"Who would have thought what, Duncan?" Nel tipped the mince into a serving dish.

"Soldier Recaptured," he read from the headline.

Grace gasped and clutched her arms to her chest, an involuntary response she'd been unable to suppress. She breathed deeply to regain her composure.

"Where?" she asked quietly, silently hoping it wasn't at Orari, but knowing that it must be, or Duncan wouldn't have commented.

"After more than five days' liberty, the soldier who escaped from the southbound express near Orari, was arrested. When left alone for a few minutes, he had jumped from the train, which was stated to be travelling at forty miles an hour," Duncan read from the paper.

Grace wanted to ask if the article stated the soldier's name, but she already knew it was Ben and didn't want to give herself away.

"What do they do with escaped soldiers?" she asked, dreading to hear the answer.

Duncan lowered the newspaper. "In the last war, they shot some of them."

There was a collective gasp from the women.

"They wouldn't." Grace's eyes went wide with terror. "Would they?"

"I don't think they're doing that this war," Duncan continued. "He'll probably just be sent to prison. Army prison though, I don't think they are quite as comfortable as the prisons for the ordinary criminals."

Grace's shoulders slumped. She'd failed Ben, failed to keep him safe just as she had been unable to keep her brother from the clutches of the war. Two young men who wanted no part of the arguments of others in far-away countries; whose lives were now ruined. Grace hoped all of her brothers would return safe and that Ben would be eventually freed from prison but she doubted their lives would pick up from where they had been before the war broke out. As for her own relationship with Ben, if one ever existed, it was now over before it had a chance.

While everyone had been digesting the news of the captured soldier, Betsy quietly read the third letter. It was from Roland's parents.

Dear Betsy,

We are sorry our first letter to you is the bearer of bad news.

Betsy couldn't stop the tremble that shook her hands and the thin paper of the letter, clutched so tightly her knuckles had gone white. Her face too went white, the blood draining as she contemplated the news that was to follow.

We have received a telegram. Roland gave us your address and asked that we should let you know if anything should happen to him. We regret to advise that Roland has been recorded as missing in action. We are unable to elucidate further. We pray that it means what it says and no more, that he is missing and will be found alive and well. We will let you know if we hear any more.

Kindest Regards, Tom and Dell Flavell

Betsy let out an uncontrollable sob and sagged into the chair, the letter fell from her now limp hands and floated to the floor.

"What's the matter, dear?" Nel rushed to Betsy's side. "What's the matter?"

In a voice choked with tears, all Betsy could manage was "Roland."

Grace picked up the letter, scanned its contents and repeated the sad news. "Roland is missing in action," she said, coming to Betsy's other side. Grace pulled Betsy up into a comforting embrace, as much for herself as for Betsy. The pair wept uncontrollably onto each other's shoulders.

Nel wrapped her arms around them. The letter could so easily have been about William. Tired and emotional at the end of a long day, Alice and Moira joined the hug as well, each with their own reasons to feel sad.

Duncan coughed awkwardly and lifted the paper back up to resume reading.

The restless rustling of Duncan's newspaper eventually drew the women's attention, and they broke away from their consoling hug. Eyes, red and puffy were wiped on sleeves, hankies were retrieved from pockets to clear runny noses but cheeks remained blotchy.

"We'll be having that mince for breakfast if we don't get a move on," Duncan moaned.

The mince, abandoned on the bench by Nel, had cooled slightly by the time she carried it to the table. Duncan dished himself up a generous portion but the women had lost their appetites and only took a small amount, knowing that they would need sustenance for tomorrow. The mince was eaten in silence, each woman digesting their thoughts along with the meal. Nel's mince had a reputation for being delicious, but although she had added her usual diced onions and special combination of herbs, the meal tasted bland.

"Thank you, Nel," Betsy said quietly as she placed her empty plate on the bench. "I'll excuse myself and see you tomorrow."

"I'll be going too," Grace added, looking, and feeling just as forlorn. "Thank you, Nel."

Moira followed as well and Alice headed off to feed the lambs, leaving Duncan and Nel alone with half a dish of mince and a pile of dishes. Nel ignored the dishes and sat down across from Duncan.

"I think Betsy should stay on here at the end of the land girls' training," she told him.

"Pardon?" Duncan had trouble assimilating Nel's suggestion. "I thought it was Alice that you reckon we need to keep an eye on."

"Alice will be fine, as long as she's got some animals to take care of."

"She gets far too attached to them." Duncan shook his head. "Fancy naming a lamb."

"It's not a crime. We've all done it when we were kids."

"But she's not a kid."

"Anyway," Nel interrupted Duncan. "Betsy is our connection with William. I think she should stay here when the others move on," she explained as if it was plainly evident what should happen.

"The regional co-ordinator is finding farms for them all as we speak."

"You can apply for a helper." Nel had listened in on Duncan's recent meeting with the co-ordinator. "The co-ordinator has asked for your suggestions. Suggest that Betsy stay here."

"There are four more trainees coming," Duncan countered. "Four more women, as if I need any more. If Betsy stays, that'll be six women and me. That doesn't sound good whichever way I look at it."

"Betsy can help train them," Nel suggested.

"There are only three rooms at the big house," Duncan reasoned. "We can't let them use Captain Boyle's room."

"Betsy can move in here. We have two spare rooms."

Duncan gulped. "You've got that determined look on your face. I know what that means. Okay, I'll think about it, but you'll not railroad me, Nel."

"How much longer have the girls got with us?" she asked.

"Another couple of weeks," he replied. "Why is that?"

"You said before they came, that I needed to teach them about gardening. They've been so busy on the farm and the weather hasn't been the best, I haven't showed them anything. I'd better have them for a day in the garden."

"Yes," Duncan conceded. "That's true. They are meant to be trained in gardening too."

"What are they doing tomorrow?"

Duncan's mouth fell open and he shook his head.

"Tomorrow … umm … the rest of the cows are ready to be dried off." Duncan thought of all the reasons why tomorrow wasn't a good day. "The cowshed will need to be scrubbed, so … not tomorrow, sorry."

"The day after then," Nel declared resolutely, before getting up from the table to make a start on the dishes. "Best to do it while the weather holds."

"We've still got some more fencing to do. We need to get them up to scratch before lambing begins in earnest."

"Well, the end of the week then." Nel wasn't giving in.

The crockery chinked and the cutlery clanged as Nel busied herself at the sink, blindly going about the chores while her mind was racing with ideas, scheming, and planning to achieve what she wanted.

Chapter Twenty-Seven

"Isn't that Bill's car?" Grace asked Moira as they approached Captain Boyle's house.

"Mmm," Moira replied.

Bill was leaning against the car, dragging on his pipe, and blowing puffs of smoke into the night.

"I was hoping you would turn up soon," he said when he noticed the women. "It's getting a bit chilly out."

Moira took that as a hint that he wanted to come in and issued the invite. Grace and Betsy headed straight upstairs while Bill and Moira went to the sitting room.

"I've missed you so much," Bill said as he pulled Moira into an embrace.

"You have?" Moira tilted her head away from Bill so she could see his face, gauge whether he was lying or just buttering her up. "Where have you been for the last three days?"

"I'm sorry," Bill apologised. "I've just been so busy on the farm, with the snowstorm and everything. I haven't been able to get away."

He kissed her on the cheek and released her. Bill took Moira's hand and led her to the couch.

"It's quite good really," he said, smiling from ear to ear.

"It is?" Moira remained unconvinced.

"Well, I thought of a solution."

"A solution to what?" Moira frowned; she turned her head to await Bill's response.

"I can't manage all of the farm work at my place, by myself. It means I'm too busy to get to see you. So ...." He said excitedly as if a drum roll was preceding his announcement. "I thought I could apply for a land girl."

Moira's shoulders slumped.

"Why the long face?" Bill asked. "Don't you want to come and live with me?"

Moira swallowed and her eyes narrowed. "Me? Me, come and live with you?"

"Yes!" Bill answered, taking her hands in his. "I could apply to the Women's Land Army for help, Duncan could recommend that you would be good for the position, and you could come and live at my house without any questions being asked."

Moira looked around the room, anywhere but at Bill while she absorbed his plan.

"I don't think Duncan is likely to make that recommendation," she said. "I don't think he approves."

"I'll work on him, that is, if you are keen."

The room went silent except for the tick tock of the mantle clock.

"I can see you need time to think about it," Bill tempered his excitement.

Moira glanced at Bill, her face a myriad of the emotions racing about her head, none of which she could give voice to.

"I'd better go then." Bill stood up to leave. "Let you sleep on the idea. I'll come by tomorrow night and get your decision before I approach Duncan with the idea. Okay?"

Moira's lack of response had zapped Bill's enthusiasm and confidence. He retrieved his hat from the coat stand in the passage and nervously twirled its brim in his fingers.

"Okay?" Bill repeated nervously.

"Yes, Bill. I'll think about it. I'll let you know tomorrow."

Upstairs in the bedroom, Grace and Betsy huddled together in Betsy's single bed. They each drew warmth and comfort from the other but it wasn't enough to stem the flow of silent tears which dampened separate spots on the white pillowcase. Even from the other side of the world the war had brought them grief. Betsy, for the loss of Roland, although he may be still alive, he was still lost to her in the meantime and not knowing almost seemed worse.

Grace thought of Ben, she thought of Frankie, and all of the other unknown soldiers that had been forced into a war they wanted no part of. She had always thought life should be fair for everyone, but war didn't seem fair for anyone.

Grace and Betsy woke from separate beds with bleary eyes and aching bodies. Restless tossing and turning had forced Grace back to her own bed in the cold of the night. It made no difference though; sad thoughts still pervaded her mind wherever she lay. Her head pounded and she struggled to breathe through her nose. She hoped it was just the after effects of crying, and her cold hadn't returned.

Robotically they dressed in their farm clothes and headed out into the morning. Even a brilliant sunrise painting the snowy mountains a golden hue wasn't enough to lift their spirits. Alice and Moira joined them as they left the house. Four women transformed by a few months in the country.

Patch announced his arrival with a cold nose nudging Alice's hand.

"Good morning, Patch." Alice patted the dog's head and stroked his floppy ears. "Shall we go and get Jess and the cows?"

Patch barked in response, wagging his tail as they veered off to the horse paddock.

"Perhaps, Betsy, we should just befriend an animal," Grace suggested.

"It might be easier," Betsy replied. "Alice seems happy."

"But so is Moira." Grace looked over at the redheaded land girl who was smiling as if the world had just landed at her feet. "And I guarantee that won't be because of an animal. Come on, Moira, tell us what's got you looking so happy."

"You two," Moira said.

"What?" Grace looked askance at Moira. "You're happy because we're feeling miserable."

"No, that's not what I meant. Seeing you two with your bottom lips nearly dragging on the ground has made my mind up."

"About what?"

"That life is too short not to seize opportunities when they arise."

Grace looked at Betsy and voiced what they were both thinking.

"We thought you already believed that. What's happened now?"

"Bill has offered me a chance at happiness."

"He's proposed?"

"No!"

"How is he planning to make you happy, if he's not asking you to marry him?"

"I'm not like you, Betsy," Moira said. "A big white wedding has never been in my life plans. If what he intends doesn't lead to a proposal then I'm not going to fret about it."

Grace's thoughts went to Ben. She'd pictured them sitting on a veranda surrounded by children but had never imagined how they got there. She thought her parents would want their only daughter to have a big white wedding, a lavish affair with all of the family. That is, assuming the war was over, and rations of fabric and food no longer existed but family did, returned safely from the fighting. She sighed, there was no Ben so all of it was irrelevant.

"What is he proposing?" Betsy's eyebrows arched with curiosity.

"He wants me to move to his farm when we leave here."

Grace gulped. She tried to keep a straight face while she digested Moira's unexpected answer.

"I see," was all she said in response, unsure whether the offer was made as lovers or farm owner and land girl. "What are you thinking you'll do?"

"I wasn't sure." Moira stood; a deep frown furrowed her brow. She pushed her hands to the bottom of her overall pockets as if the answer was to be found in their depths. "I've always been one to have fun."

A little giggle escaped Grace as she heard Moira's understatement but when she saw Moira's serious face, she raised her hand over her mouth, pretended it was a cough and urged her to continue.

"Betsy's news ... the war ... Ben's capture ... life can change in an instant. I don't want to miss out on all it has to offer."

Grace looked over at Betsy.

"True," she replied, still not knowing just what sort of arrangement Bill was offering. "What animals does he have on his farm?"

"Cows," Moira said. "I know he's got cows. Hopefully no pigs. I've finally got rid of the smell of them from my clothes."

"I didn't think we got to choose where we went after this. I thought the powers that be, just assigned us somewhere." Grace hadn't given much thought to where she was going at the end of their training. She hoped that her and Betsy would be sent to the same place again.

"It's an opportunity to work alongside him."

"How?"

"As his land girl."

"Do you think Duncan will allow that?"

"Bill is going to ask Duncan to put in a recommendation."

"Oh," was all Grace could say. She wanted to add a wish for 'good luck' but she didn't want to dampen Moira's spirits as they went their separate ways, Grace to the pigsty and Betsy and Moira to the cowshed.

Duncan met Betsy and Moira at the shed.

"That snow has knocked these cows. We'll make this the final milking for them," he advised. "We'll scrub down the cowshed after breakfast."

The milking went without incident. The rhythm of the milking machines had its usual calming effect on the cows who stood chewing their cud but the even tempo of the pulsators did nothing to ease Betsy's sadness this morning.

"Goodbye, girl." She scratched the cow's neck and released it back into the race. Duncan watched, undetected from the door of the machine room.

"You have to admit," he muttered to himself. "She is good with the cows. If she is going to stay, then at least the cattle will be looked after."

He filled the hot water cylinder up so they'd have plenty of water for cleaning the shed and left the woman to it.

"What's taking you so long?" Moira asked. "I've milked three cows and you're just starting on your second."

"There's no hurry. I'm not rushing back to get the mail. I don't want another letter; they only bring bad news."

"William's don't," Moira said.

"Not yet." The contraction of Betsy's heart was echoed in her sigh. All were lost in the sounds of the shed.

Moira shook her head. "It's impossible to cheer you up at the moment but I would appreciate you going faster so that I can take the milk to the factory and see Bill."

"All right! All right!"

It was Nel who eagerly rushed to the mailbox when she heard the postie's van go down the road. She stretched the rubber band holding the folded newspaper and several letters until it flicked off the end of the bundle and flew into mid-air. Nel was too busy studying the handwriting on the envelopes, hoping to see William's familiar scrawl, to notice where the rubber band landed. Her shoulders slumped with disappointment; the mail only included bills. They weren't going to cheer anybody up.

She hurried back up the driveway and inside with another plan to raise morale - pancakes cooked on the griddle. Nel's pancakes, drizzled with honey or molasses, had a reputation for deliciousness. The kitchen clock's big hand was nearly vertical, everyone would be inside by eight, there was no time to dally. Nel stoked up the coal range, put the griddle on top and fetched her biggest mixing bowl from the cupboard. There was no need for measuring cups or scales, Nel knew just the right amount of dry ingredients to sieve and milk and eggs to whisk. When a dollop of butter on the griddle melted with the heat, Nel added spoons full of her smooth batter. She waited with a vigilant eye, flipping the pancakes when the tell-tale air bubbles popped. There was a stockpile of light and fluffy pancakes keeping warm between folded tea towels by the time everyone came in for breakfast.

"Quick, sit down," she said, carrying a plate of pancakes to the table. "Enjoy them while they are still warm."

Duncan chuckled at his wife. Right from when William was a child, she always made pancakes when he was sad.

It turned out that they were everyone's favourites. Nel had to set aside a couple for herself on the bench beside her or they would have been eaten too. No-one spoke as their cheeks bulged and their chins caught drizzles of sticky molasses.

"Thanks, Nel," Grace purred, rubbing her contented belly when she'd finished her fifth pancake. She felt more relaxed, not having to limit her own meals or to worry about sneaking food out to Ben.

"Yes, delicious, thank you," Betsy added with a smile.

Nel's plan had worked, pancakes had brought smiles to everyone's faces and she smiled back at them.

"Just as well we have a big job ahead of us," Duncan said. "Scrubbing down the cowshed will soon work off this breakfast."

Grace wasn't sure if Duncan intended to put a damper on the mood, or just bring the women back to reality, but he succeeded in doing both.

There was one last pancake on the plate, the perfect excuse that Grace needed to take longer than the others.

"Does anyone else want that last pancake?" she asked.

"I'll explode if I eat any more." Betsy blew her cheeks out.

"The rest of us will get going then." Duncan had finished his breakfast and was ready to leave.

Grace drizzled molasses over the pancake and sliced it into small pieces. While she ate as slow as she could she glanced around the kitchen while Nel busied herself at the sink. What she wanted was sitting in a pile beside Duncan's armchair – yesterday's newspaper lay neatly folded on the top of the stack.

"Is there something you were needing, dear?" Nel returned to the table to collect the last of the plates.

"Oh, umm ..." Grace nearly choked on pancake. "I just thought I'd read the paper while I finished my breakfast."

"Help yourself, dear, not much good news in there though."

Grace grabbed the paper and scanned its pages until she found the article about Ben. She hoped Duncan hadn't read it all, that there would be some more information about Ben, something that would allow her to contact him, to know that he was going to be okay.

"It's wash day," Nel said. "If you could rinse your plate when you've finished, I'll get started on my next chore."

"Certainly," Grace agreed.

There was no time to fully read the article now, Grace needed to get to the cowshed. She quickly devoured the rest of her pancake and when Nel left the room, carefully ripped the article from the newspaper, folded it and safely stowed it in her overalls pocket for later.

Grace helped Moira load the milk cans on the back of Duncan's truck.

"Do you want me to come with you to the factory?" she asked.

"No!" Moira bit, but then tempered her words. "No, thank you, I'll be fine. I'm going to call in on Bill on the way back from the factory to discuss his offer."

Grace nodded. The reason for going to the factory alone apparent, they rolled the last of the milk cans onto the truck.

"I'll see you when you get back then." Grace went back into the shed to help Betsy.

Jake and Bob saw Moira pull up in the truck and eagerly strode over to help.

"Well, look who we have here, Bob." Jake rolled his sleeves up and smiled at Moira as she got out of the truck. "Hello, Miss Moira, you're looking as gorgeous as ever this morning."

Moira giggled. At least if things didn't work out with Bill, she could come and find Jake for a fun time.

"Hi Jake. Hi Bob. The last of the milk, I'm afraid. The cows have been dried off."

"Oh, you're going to miss us aren't you," Jake joked. "Tell us your heart will be broken without our smiling faces to brighten your day."

Moira laughed again.

"Go on, admit it," Jake teased. "We can't take your milk until you admit you're going to be lost without us." He held onto the milk can on the back of the truck.

"Well, I won't be lost," Moira replied. "But I am going to miss your smiles."

Bob removed the last of the milk cans while Jake completed the docket. He jumped down off the platform and spun around in front of Moira, showing of his athletic prowess to hand her the docket. On the pretence of securely delivering the docket, Jake took both of Moira's hands in his and held on longer than necessary, before he lifted her hands to his mouth and kissed her knuckles.

"Until we meet again," Jake said in farewell.

"Bye." Moira climbed back into the truck, leaned out the window and added. "For now."

When Bill saw Duncan's truck come up the driveway, he put down the cup of tea he'd been enjoying, swallowed a mouthful of the moist fruit loaf Mrs Terrill had kindly made for him and ordered his thoughts.

"Here goes." He patted the cat on the head. "My chance to convince Duncan. I can't get this wrong."

He was at the back door before the knocking stopped.

"Good morning, Dun—" he said as he opened the door.

"Not Duncan, sorry, just me." Moira smiled nervously.

"Come in, come in." Bill stood back and enthusiastically ushered Moira inside. "Would you like a cup of tea? The pot is still warm. Here, have a seat. I'll just clear away the mess. There is some of Mrs Terrill's fruit cake too, if you would like," Bill jabbered away, as he pulled a chair out at the dining room table.

"Thanks." Moira took the proffered chair knowing, but unable to admit, that it would leave the sideboard full of photographs looking directly at her. "A cup of tea would be lovely."

In the kitchen, Bill took his best china cup and saucer from the cupboard and sliced a generous piece of loaf.

"Would you like butter on the loaf?" he called to Moira.

Moira sat, head down at the table, wringing her hands in her lap, trying to find the courage to confront the photos, to tell the dead woman that it was time for Bill to move on and that she was here to help him.

"That would be lovely, thanks." Moira looked directly towards the kitchen but her periphery vision defied her, it saw the sideboard. Out of the corner of her eye, Moira saw all of the sideboard, the polished dark timber was bare of the two rows of photos. All, but one, were gone. Her mouth gaped. Moira sat in stunned silence absorbing the significance of the change. Where had the photos gone? More importantly, why had the photos gone?

"Are you alright?" Bill asked, returning to the table with the tea and loaf. "You look like you've seen a ghost."

He followed Moira's line of sight.

"Oh, you have seen a ghost," he chuckled uncomfortably. "That's my wife. Well, she was my wife. She passed away. Six months and five days ago." Bill stopped his explanation and took a deep breath as tears threatened.

Moira looked from the sideboard to Bill and back to the sideboard. She couldn't admit that she knew there had been many more photos. She saw his emotion, knew that the feelings were still raw, and it reconfirmed her decision, life was too short not to make the most of it.

"I've decided I'd like to come and be your land girl." She let the words escape before she lost her bravado. "If you would like me to," she added, giving Bill an out.

"Oh, Moira, that's great news," Bill pulled out the seat opposite Moira's and sat facing her. He took her hands in his and the tension in his face and shoulders melted away. "That is such wonderful news."

Bill grinned from ear to ear, his eyes sparkled, his dimple dimpled. He released her hands, raised his own to cup her face and leaned in to kiss her but he was too close to the table. His elbow hit with a thump, the precious china cup rattled, tea spilled into the saucer and the moment was lost.

Chapter Twenty-Eight

The cowshed walls, posts, railings, and floor were brushed with boiling water until no traces of cows remained. The clean milk cans were scrubbed and left upside down to drain. The rubbers from the cups were removed, cleaned and sterilised in buckets of boiling water, then reassembled when the water had cooled sufficiently for them to be touched and Duncan had inspected them for cracks and perishing.

By the time Grace had a spare private moment to retrieve and read the newspaper article, her hands were wrinkled and red. She shook them, trying to get some blood to return to her fingertips. She reached into her overalls pocket, careful not to knock her knuckles which she'd gouged on the concrete floor. She'd dropped the scrubbing brush in a moment when her mind had drifted to thoughts of Ben in prison. It was another subtle message that Grace should forget about Ben but it was a message she wasn't willing to hear.

Water had splashed her overalls and seeped through to the paper. It threatened to tear as she cautiously unfolded the article. Grace digested every word, looking for clues to Ben's whereabouts, even his full name but there was nothing more than what Duncan had read out loud. The lack of information should have deterred Grace but it only strengthened her resolve to find out what had happened to Ben. She didn't know if he had anyone else to help him, it fell to her to do so. She wouldn't have it any other way.

"I think we're all finished." Betsy hung her apron on a hook in the machine room.

Grace jumped with fright. She hadn't heard Betsy's footsteps and quickly stuffed the newspaper article back in her pocket.

"Umm ... yes ... I think so," she mumbled.

"What was that?"

"What?" Grace's mouth fell open and her hand flew to her chest, feigning innocence. "Nothing."

"Grace, you're looking sheepish, and I caught you stuffing something into your pocket." Betsy held her hand out. "Now hand it over."

Grace knew Betsy's stance, the look on her face, she wasn't going to give in. Grace handed over the now damp, creased piece of newspaper.

"Oh, Grace." Betsy shook her head. "I thought you were all finished with this."

"I just wanted to check, see if Duncan hadn't read it all out."

Betsy scanned the article. "But he did, Grace. There is no more information about Ben here."

"I know."

"You are going to have to let him go." Betsy refolded the article and gave it back.

"I know," Grace said, hoping that Betsy would believe her even when she didn't believe herself.

Without the cows to milk, the days began later and were more relaxed. They'd spent several days fixing the fences on a large flat paddock which was ideal for lambing.

"Right, I'm off to move the sheep." Duncan downed the last mouthful of his second cup of tea. "I'll leave you ladies to it."

"What do you want us to do today?" Grace asked.

"Nel's in charge," Duncan nodded towards his wife. "She'll tell you what to do."

Nel in charge. Duncan letting any woman be in charge, it wasn't the done thing. Wide eyed, the land girls looked at Nel in stunned silence. What did she have planned for them?

Nel giggled. "Don't look so worried. We've just got to tend to the most important part of the farm. The garden."

The land girls laughed with relief. Gardening, that would be easy.

The familiar ring of the telephone interrupted the conversation.

"I'll get it, can't keep you ladies from your gardening." Duncan chuckled and headed to the phone.

"Hello, McKnight residence," he said into the receiver as he pulled the door closed behind him to shut out the chatter.

"Duncan. Ah, Duncan." Bill knew his neighbour's voice but anxious about the impending conversation he nervously repeated his name.

"Yes."

"It's Bill here."

"Yes, Bill, I recognised your voice." Duncan was impatient to get to the day's farm work. "Is this just a neighbourly chat or is there something I can do for you?"

"Umm, well, umm … I wanted to ask a favour."

"Yes …"

"Umm, well, you know the land girls are going to be reassigned soon."

"Yes, I had a meeting with the regional co-ordinator the other day."

"Oh, bugger," Bill cursed. "It's too late. I've missed the boat."

"Too late for what?"

"I want to apply for a land girl."

"Well, you need to phone the co-ordinator, not me."

"Not just any land girl." Bill's stomach gurgled noisily as its contents churned. "Moira," he blurted before his nerves thwarted him.

"Mmm," was the only reply Duncan gave.

Bill had no choice but to continue.

"I was wondering if you could put in a good word. You know, say that I was a responsible farmer and well able to provide good work and shelter for a land girl."

"There is no denying that. You are one of the better farmers on the road. It would be an ideal situation for a land girl but I'm not so sure it's ideal for Moira."

"Oh."

"She's a redhead, Bill. She's got a mind of her own."

"So, I've discovered. Do you think you could help though?" The silence at the end of the phone while Duncan pondered the pros and cons, did nothing to calm Bill's nerves.

"You'd better phone them," Duncan replied. "Put in an application. It may already be too late. I don't know."

"Oh ..." Bill would be gutted if he missed out and Moira was sent elsewhere.

"You'll have to list a referee. You can put my name if you like," Duncan offered. "It's the least I can do for a neighbour whose helped me out."

"It's a bit neglected I'm afraid." Nel stood, hands on hips, surveying the overgrown earth that should be her neatly organised garden. "We'll weed it first, then dig in some fertiliser before planting the winter vegetables. If you work in pairs, one with the fork to loosen the roots and the other to pull the weeds, we'll make sure we get all of the roots and the pesky weeds won't regrow."

As Nel expected, Grace and Betsy paired up. They had her garden wheelbarrow and she fetched another from the pigsty for Moira and Alice.

"I'll fork." Moira looked at her freshly manicured nails. "You can pull the weeds," she ordered Alice.

Alice shrugged. "If that's what you want."

"Where would you like to go when we finish here?" Grace wanted to get Betsy thinking about the future.

"Don't know, don't care." Betsy grabbed a stubborn weed with both hands and yanked with all the might she could muster. When it finally came unexpectedly free, she fell backwards, landing on her bottom in the dirt. She angrily tossed the weed at the wheelbarrow.

Grace reached out to help Betsy up. The gesture reminded Betsy that Grace was always there for her.

"Wherever I go, I hope it is with you." Betsy stood back up and wiped the dirt from her overalls.

"That would be good." Grace liked the idea too. "Perhaps there is a farm around here that needs two land girls. We could ask."

"No point asking." Betsy stabbed the fork into the ground. "I've asked every night for Roland to be brought home safe. Look how that turned out. Besides, they've probably already decided."

"Yes, you're right. I think we're supposed to get letters any day now."

Betsy cringed. "I don't know if I can cope with any more bad news."

"Where do you want to go, Alice?" Grace already knew where Moira wanted to go, but the quiet little Alice was an unknown.

Alice stood, stretched her back muscles which were protesting and pondered Grace's question.

"If I had my wish, it would be a farm with animals of every kind and humans only of the female kind. A place with a bedroom like mine, a tiny, safe haven, warm and comfortable, where I can escape to at the end of the day. But some male has probably already decided. I would like to stay here though, until Lizzy and Bella are weaned. They're still needing several feeds a day."

"I'm sure there will be lots more lambs needing your mothering, Alice."

"I'm going to go to Bill's," Moira boldly announced. "Well, I hope to."

With full wheelbarrows, Grace and Moira disappeared to dump their loads on the compost heap.

"Can you bring back a load of pig manure, please," Nel asked. "We'll dig it in to the ground."

"Great!" Moira groaned sarcastically. "I thought my days of dealing with the stench of pigs were over."

Nel waited until Grace and Moira were out of earshot then pretended there was a missed weed next to Betsy. Bending down beside her, Nel whispered.

"I've asked Duncan to make a request for you to stay here."

"You have?"

"Yes, he thinks it is a good idea," Nel extended the truth a little.

"He does?" Betsy grappled with the idea.

"You can help teach the next lot of trainees. Duncan says you are good with the cows."

Betsy stopped weeding.

"We'll be able to share William's news when he writes. And you'll be able to see him when he comes home. You can move into our house; we've got a spare room. I can make it nice for you."

Nel paused. She looked at Betsy, tried to read her face, see whether she'd said enough to convince her it was a good idea. She could see Grace and Moira walking across the lawn.

"We won't know until the letters arrive. Best, not say anything to anyone else until we know."

Betsy nodded in agreement. The letters. Life was dependent upon the letters again. If she received a letter saying she was staying at Whipsnade, that would mean she'd be separated from Grace.

"Is it confirmed that you are going to Bill's?" Grace asked Moira as they lugged the heavy wheelbarrows now full of pig manure back to the vegetable garden.

"Pardon?" Moira had turned her face away from Grace and the offensive aroma wafting from her wheelbarrow and hadn't heard the question.

Grace repeated her question.

"Nothing confirmed yet," Moira answered. "But we've agreed it's a great idea."

"That's good. I hope it works out for you," Grace said. "If we're all still around here, we could get together."

"Bill cares, you care." Moira smiled. "We could meet up when we get a day off," she suggested.

"You two look happy," Nel said as they arrived back at the garden. "If we dump one wheelbarrow on each side then we can rake it in."

"We just thought us girls could meet up, on our days off."

"That would be lovely for you."

They had to repeat the process three more times. Six more wheelbarrow loads of weeds dumped at the compost heap and six more loads of pig manure dug into the garden. By the last load, the vegetable garden was beginning to smell like the pigsty.

"I've got cabbage, cauliflower, broccoli and silver beet plants here." Nel stood over the wooden tray of tiny seedlings Duncan had bought when he was last in town. "We'll plant a row of each, about a foot between the rows and a bit less between each plant. We've got to give them room to grow. You do a row each and I'll fetch the hose so we can water them in."

By the time they had finished the garden had been transformed from an overgrown mass to a fertile oasis with four straight rows of baby plants soaking up the shower of water spurting from the hose.

"Well done." Nel clapped her hands. "Thank you, ladies. Fresh vegetables for everyone in a few months' time. Well, for whoever is here anyway."

Alice was out the back of the farm checking the sheep with Duncan when the letters finally arrived. Out in the wide expanse of the paddock, she was in a fluster, excited and amazed by the wonders of nature for one sheep to have produced four healthy little lambs.

"The sheep will need a hand to feed all of them," she said. "Won't she?"

"No, Alice." Duncan was firm. "Quadruplets are rare, but the ewe is capable of feeding all of them."

Two of the lambs huddled together for warmth while the other two, mouths latched onto a teat, bunted at the ewe's udder, and wiggled their tails in delight at the resulting milk flow.

"Right then." Duncan climbed back into the truck to hide his amusement at Alice's zest. "We'd best check the rest of the flock and get back for breakfast."

Alice reluctantly climbed back in the passenger side, straining her neck to glimpse out the back window and keep an eye on the lambs as Duncan drove off.

"I'd better feed Lizzy and Bella." Alice gasped. "I mean the lambs."

Duncan rolled his eyes at Alice's naming of the animals despite his warning not to. "They can wait, come in and have breakfast first."

The smell of bacon wafted through to the washhouse as Alice lathered her hands with the bar of Sunlight soap. Her tummy rumbled in response, confirming that the lambs could wait, she'd best feed herself first. She rinsed her hands, dried them on the towel which hung on a hook beside the back door and followed Duncan through into the kitchen.

Duncan stopped abruptly at the sight of three women crying. Alice, her thoughts a million miles away, didn't see Duncan stop and bumped into his back.

"Oops, sorry," she apologised.

"What's wrong?" Duncan asked, more gruffly than he needed.

"I wasn't concentrating, sorry, it was the smell of the bacon," Alice replied.

"Not you." Duncan moved to the side so Alice could see the others. "This lot. What's happened?" he directed his question to Nel.

Nel smiled. "Nothing."

"Nothing?" Duncan shook his head in frustration. "Then why on earth are you all crying?"

"The mail arrived." Nel took a handkerchief from her apron pocket and wiped her eyes.

"Another letter from the war office?" Duncan asked with trepidation.

"No, the placement officer. The girls have their next assignments."

Duncan waited for Nel to explain further but fat spitting in the frying pan drew her attention to the coal range.

"So, what have the powers-that-be decided, are you to be sent to the front?"

"No!" Betsy, Grace, and Moira groaned in unison.

"Well," Duncan reasoned. "No need for the tears then."

"I've been assigned to Bill's farm," Moira said as if that explained everything.

"Mmm, can't say I think that is a good idea but it's none of my business. You wanted to go there, and you are. So, I repeat, no need for tears."

"Mine are happy tears." Moira wiped her eyes with the back of her hand and smiled.

"And I'm to stay on here," Betsy added tentatively. She glanced at Nel but got no assurance from her back. "If that's okay."

"I repeat again, no need for tears."

Betsy wiped away the tears hoping that action alone, would appease Duncan.

"So, are you going somewhere horrible?" he asked Grace.

"Orari Estate?" Grace had no knowledge of the farm she'd been assigned to. All she knew was that her and Betsy were being separated. She'd convinced Betsy to join the land girls on the basis that they'd be together and now they were to be apart.

"Don't see the need to cry about that either." Duncan took his seat at the table and proceeded to fill his plate with scrambled eggs and bacon. "Great piece of land, wouldn't mind farming there myself."

"How far away is it?" Grace asked.

"You've probably been past it a few times," Duncan answered casually, oblivious of the importance of his answer to Grace. "The big dark red brick house back up on the main road. No shortage of money when they built that place. I don't know that there is any employee accommodation, so you'll probably be living in luxury."

Grace took Betsy's hands in hers. "We'll be able to visit one another then," she said, a smile creeping back onto her face.

Duncan shovelled a large fork full of toast, eggs and bacon into his mouth and observed the summersault the land girls' emotions had just done.

"And me too," Moira joined the pair.

"That'll be wonderful," Nel smiled.

Everything was going to work out for the land girls. Then Grace saw Alice, standing wide-eyed, her hands buried in her overall pockets.

"Alice, come, sit down, your envelope is on the table."

Alice slowly moved towards her usual seat at the dining table where the brown envelope that held her future within its folds was innocently reclined against the cup and saucer.

"Open it, Alice," Grace encouraged.

"Yes, come on, Alice," Betsy urged. "Let's see if you're close too."

With trembling fingers Alice picked at the sealed flap. The room was silent bar the rustling of the letter being withdrawn from the envelope and unfolded. Everyone waited with bated breath, watching Alice's eyes as they read from left to right, line by line. They looked for her reaction, a sign of happiness, a hint of sadness, something that would reveal whether the news was good or bad.

"Well?" Duncan prompted. "Why you women make a drama out of everything I'll never know."

"Geraldine Flax Mill." Alice's shoulders slumped.

"That's close," Duncan said. "Just a couple of miles from Geraldine. Frank Pratt from up by Orari Bridge converted some of his farm to growing flax, tempted by the six pounds per acre on offer, but Captain Boyle wasn't interested. Problem solved; you'll all be able to see each other. Now, you'd better get on with breakfast, there's still farm work to be done, you haven't left yet."

"But …" Alice's lip trembled as tears threatened. "Is it a factory or a farm?"

"A factory. Doing its bit for the war though, supplying linen flax to the British." Duncan stopped; his face screwed up as if he'd just swallowed something rotten. He put his knife and fork down and frowned at Alice. "Bloody hell," he cursed.

"Duncan!" Nel growled.

"Well, Nel, heaven forbid," Duncan shook his head in disbelief. "I've spent all my time training Alice and now she's being sent to work in a factory. Which woman decided that was good for anybody?"

Alice held her breath, it was caught in her throat, stuck on the word 'factory'. Grace saw Alice's fear, the trembling of her lips, the flitting of her eyes. It was like that first day she'd seen the petite woman when they were volunteering at the Christchurch Town Hall. Grace had wanted to rescue her then and felt the same now. Alice had wanted to go anywhere but where there were men. A factory is where men work.

Nel stood behind Alice and placed her comforting hands, on Alice's shoulders.

"I thought you were just a child when I first saw you in my vegetable garden, but you've got strength and determination. You've proven size isn't a limitation. It'll be alright, dear, just you wait and see."

Grace nodded in agreement. Alice would survive wherever she was. Just like the men at the front, Alice, Grace, Betsy, and Moira would all have to soldier on.

Alice grabbed a dry piece of toast. "I'll go and feed the lambs."

She was gone before anyone could protest or stop her.

"Where's the newspaper?" Duncan asked. He'd finished his breakfast and poured himself a cup of tea.

A small white envelope fell to the floor when Nel picked the paper up to pass it to Duncan.

"What's this?" Nel picked up the envelope. "More mail. Addressed to Grace. Just Grace. No surname." Nel looked at Grace. "A letter from someone who knows where you live but not your surname." She turned the letter over in her hands. "And has no return address. Do tell us more, Grace."

Grace coloured from head to toe. She took the proffered envelope knowing it could only be from Ben, knowing that it would be impossible for her to open it here.

"Thank you." She tried to sound calmer than what the thumping in her chest indicated. "I think I forgot to turn a tap off. I'd better go and check."

Like Alice before her, Grace was gone from the kitchen, out the back door before anyone could protest or stop her. She ran, and she didn't stop running until she reached the implement shed. She went back to where it had all begun. She sat down on the very sacks that had been Ben's bed when he'd first hidden on the farm.

With trembling fingers, she lifted the envelope to her nose and inhaled deeply, hoping to smell something of the man that had turned her life inside out and upside down. There was no distinct aroma, nothing that confirmed her hopes. She looked at the writing, wondered whether the large, evenly spaced letters were Ben's but his handwriting style was another in the long list of things, that Grace didn't know about him. She had no choice but to open the envelope.

Her shaking hands struggled to hold the envelope let alone allow her fingers to slip under the flap and open it. Grace closed her eyes and took several deep breaths to still herself before attempting again.

It contained a copy of the newspaper clipping that Grace already had. Where hers was torn, this one had been neatly cut with scissors. **SOLDIER RECAPTURED** stared at her in large bold type as if she needed reminding.

It was the normally blank area around the article that held what she wanted; tiny scrawl jammed in to fit as much as possible into the space available. Grace turned the paper around and around in her hands, trying to decipher where the message began and in which direction it flowed. Words leapt out at her. Grace. Kiss. Escape. Sorry. Goodbye.

Grace dropped the clipping into her lap and covered her face with her hands, while she rocked backwards and forwards. Ben had written to her. She hadn't imagined his feelings for her. She could still help him. Goodbye wasn't for ever it was just for now.

Acknowledgements

The 13 February 1941 edition of the Christchurch Press tells us of the generosity of Commander A D Boyle, who absent on active service, offers his farm as a training facility for the Women's War Service Auxiliary. That is the beginning of this Kiwi Land Girls series which seeks to honour the services of nearly 4,000 women who worked the land during World War II.

Dianne Bardsley interviewed 130 of those wonderful volunteers and captured their stories in **The Land Girls, In a Man's World, 1939-1946**. Those interviews and photographs of war time farming have been a constant source of inspiration for the experiences of my fictional characters.

In trying to capture the emotion of living during war, I also acknowledge the valuable stories, recollections and resources provided by:

- **The Girls They Left Behind** – Betsy Goldsmith & Beryl Sandford

- **Wartime Women, A Mass Observation Antholo**gy – Edited by Dorothy Sheridan

- **Good Luck to all the Lads, The**

Wartime Story of Brian Cox 1939-43 – Peter Cox

- **You'll Be Sorry! How World War II Changed Women's Lives** – Ann Howard.

When the research and the writing is complete there are so many people involved in bringing the story to life. To all my beta readers thank you for your honest feedback and support. To my Mum – thank you for your genuine delight in my writing – I know my writing apprenticeship is worthwhile when I can please an avid reader like you. A huge thank you to my fellow writers who retreat with me into the writing bubble and critique the work that flows in such inspirational company and surroundings.

To all the professionals involved in this process, my heartfelt thanks. Especially Kura Carpenter for her cover design and Annie Seaton for her editing skills.

Throughout this there is the darling man who leaves me in peace to write, edit and re-write. Thank you, Mike for your love and support.

And lastly, but of course not least, there is you the reader. Thank you for taking the time to read Wings of Grace. I hope you enjoyed the story of the Kiwi Land Girls.

To stay informed about the next book in the series – **Ally for Life** you can find updates through:

My Website - taniarobertsauthor.co.nz
Facebook – Tania Roberts Author

If you would like to read more about Grace, Alice, Betsy, and Moira, then look out for Book Two in the Kiwi Land Girl Series.

Ally for Life

The factory loomed ominously in front of Alice. She needed to conquer her fear that every dark place held a threat, but what would she find this time; another boss demanding more than she was prepared to give. You can do this she whispered to herself.

Gingerly, Alice wrapped her child-like fingers around the worn brass door handle, polished gold by all the hands that had gone before hers. It required all her strength to turn. She could hear the rumbling of the machines as she edged the door open. A wall of heat rushed to escape the confines of the factory into the cool morning air. It carried the oily stench of the equipment. Alice recoiled, the cloying combination of heat and odour stuck in her throat.

"Get a move on, there's work to be done," a baritone voice bellowed orders from the darkness. Alice couldn't see the man behind the command, didn't want to imagine his towering stature or what else he would demand of her. That which she hadn't been able to willingly give to any man. "Do I have to drag you in here?"

The early morning sun, rising at her back, cast a wedge of light across the factory's concrete floor, like an arrow pointing the way.   Alice had no choice but to follow its direction and step over the threshold of what was to be. She was only here because of men. Men on the other side of the world whose power struggle resulted in another global war. Men from the plains of Canterbury who'd enlisted, voluntarily or otherwise, and been taken from the land that was their lifeblood to fight a battle that wasn't theirs. And men much closer to home, that decided that she, after training in the basics of farming, should be assigned to a factory. Her resentment at men, for all of these reasons and more, was a load that sat heavy in the pit of her stomach like the bowels of this factory.

Alice tried to turn back; her attempts were futile. She felt constrained, unable to escape her fate. She wanted to run from her future, to return to Bella and

Lizzy, the lambs she'd been feeding. A movement to the left caught Alice's eye, she shrieked with fright. A beady-eyed rat stared defiantly at her before it scampered away behind the metal shroud of a machine, its tail leaving the only evidence of its presence, a slithery spoor through the flax dust on the floor. Alice's heartbeat thundered in her chest, echoed by the pounding of the machinery. A drumbeat, allegro in its tempo, sounded at her ear. It was so close, Alice was too frightened to look for its source, but the banging continued, increasing in volume and urgency.

"Alice! Alice!"

The female's voice was familiar. Alice found herself drawn to it, knowing that it would offer comfort. The call rang out again and she recognised it as Grace's voice but what was Grace doing at the factory? Hadn't she been assigned to Orari Estate?

"Alice! Open the door." Grace thumped her fist on the bedroom door.

"It's open," Alice replied in her semi-awake state. She'd just walked through the door, of course it was open.

Grace rattled the handle again. "No, you've locked it. I can see the key blocking the keyhole."

Alice stirred and opened her eyes to the familiar surrounds of the tiny bedroom that had been hers for the last three months. The sun shone through the lace curtains in the dormer window letting her know the day was ready for her. The patchwork quilt of her single bed, which she snuggled under on the cool autumn nights, was now as dishevelled as she felt, scrunched up and twisted around her legs.

"Just a minute," she called to Grace, unravelling herself from the bedding and rearranging her nightie to a respectable length. The wooden floorboards were cold to her bare feet as she tiptoed across to turn the key.

"Are you alright?" Grace rushed into the room and took Alice by the shoulders. "You screamed so loud. I thought someone must be attacking you."

"No."

Alice looked around the room, reassuring herself that there was no intruder. She realised, the thoughts of the factory that seemed so real and terrifying, must have been nothing more than a nightmare. Her body shuddered.

"It's alright." Grace wrapped her arms around Alice. "You're safe now."

The warmth of the blonde woman's embrace was like the heat beneath a mother bird incubating her eggs in a nest. Like a hatchling, Alice was going to have to break out of her shell. She felt safe but she couldn't stay there forever. Just as she had to when she signed up for the land girls, Alice was going to have to rise, to stand as tall as her petite frame would allow and face the world. She broke free from the hug.

"I'll be alright," she said as much to herself as to Grace.